UNSTABLE

Carrie King

Copyright © 2023 by Carrie King

All rights reserved. No part of this publication may be reproduced, distributed, or transmitted in any form or by any means, including photocopying, recording, or other electronic or mechanical methods, without the prior written permission of the publisher, except in the case of brief quotations embodied in critical reviews and certain other noncommercial uses permitted by copyright law.

To request permissions, contact the publisher at www.carriekking.com/contact

ISBN Hardcover: 979-8-9883003-0-4
ISBN Ebook: 979-8-9883003-1-1

First Edition: June 2023

Printed in the United States of America

Edited by Katie Baker and Arianna Bauer
Cover art by Emma McGoldrick

This is a work of fiction. Names, characters, places, and events are the product of the author's imagination and are used fictiously, and any resemblance to actual persons, living or dead, business establishments, events, or locations is entirely coincidental.

First Edition
14 13 12 11 10 / 10 9 8 7 6 5 4 3 2 1

Hillary, happy reading! :)

UNSTABLE

Carrie King

Carrie King

Happy reading,
William
:)

[signature]

For those who live vicariously through stories.

Chapter 1

For as long as I could remember, my mind had felt like a war zone, constantly stuck between what I wanted and what I was afraid of—usually, those were the same thing. As I scrubbed my hair and washed my freshman year of college down the drain, I was struck by the sense that this summer, and the fresh start that came with it, had the potential to put me in the path of everything I'd tried to avoid but secretly hoped for.

Leaving a trail of wet footprints behind me, I made my way from the bathroom down the hall to my new bedroom. The ivory walls and dark hardwood floor fit the coastal style my dad had chosen when remodeling the place. It felt sort of like a summer home meant to be occupied for three months out of the year by people escaping their city lives, only to be covered in bedsheets come October. For a moment, I let myself daydream of hours laying on the beach with a good book, taking long bike rides along the coast, or aimlessly browsing boutiques in this quaint seaside town—an escape from reality that would make this summer feel almost like the long vacation I yearned for.

I pushed the thought aside.

I made my way through a labyrinth of open suitcases scattered across the floor of my room to reach a box sitting in the corner. Sifting through a pile of half-folded items, I found my worn-out Cleveland Cavaliers T-shirt and a pair of faded denim shorts from the box labeled "Summer Clothes" and slipped them on. My familiar wardrobe felt out of place here. Most of my clothes had been waiting for me to arrive since December when they'd been shipped from Ohio. In the meantime, I'd been at school in Boston, only getting to Newport the night before. It felt like a time machine having access to these clothes again, even if it had only been a few months. It seemed as if everything had changed since then.

I stepped over an overflowing box of books on the way to my mirror—mostly romance novels. *Ironic.* I could never understand why I couldn't have a romantic moment of my own without an equal and opposite moment of pain recollecting it afterward.

I didn't want to end up like my parents. Their divorce was filed the minute I'd moved into my freshman dorm, and I only questioned why they hadn't split any sooner. My mom stayed in Painesville, Ohio, where I grew up, while my dad made the big move to the East Coast. I assumed this was to evade the memories of his failed marriage. My dad said he should have known it would be hell living in a town called Painesville. He'd only moved there to be closer to my mother. As soon as they were divorced, he'd traded the Great Lakes for the Ocean State, and I was glad at first. Initially, I figured it would be great to take weekend trips away from school to see the fall foliage in Rhode Island and to enjoy the beaches for a few weeks in the summer. That was before I knew that his decision to move would be part of the reason I wouldn't be returning to Ohio as often as I'd wanted to, or at all really.

My desk, pushed up against the wall opposite my bed, was empty apart from a single photo of the Boston skyline that I'd taken as a goodbye. It was pinned to a corkboard, surrounded by nothing else.

Lots of space to fill with new things.

I'd printed the lonely photograph the night before in hopes of finding a decent frame and adding some decoration to my walls. I'd only spent one night here so far, but I was eager to make it feel more like home… since technically, it was. It would take a bit longer to get used to that.

While staying with my dad, I was required to work two shifts a week at Briarman's Books, the relocated family business, and attend some occasional family dinners—which would be just the two of us now. Other than complying with my father's wishes, my goal for this much-needed summer break was simple. I was determined to find a way to stockpile some money before the impending tidal wave of responsibility that would be my sophomore year began. Tuition bills had been weighing on me ever since I'd gotten my first email from the Financial Aid Department, and the summer would be the perfect time to get ahead of the payment schedule, since I wouldn't have classes or homework eating up my spare time. My parents' divorce, however conveniently timed they thought it to be, really put a damper on the funds allocated for college—meaning I would have to find a way to make it work all on my own if I still wanted to attend my top school. My dad had always given me a decent wage at Briarman's, but I knew it would take more than that to even make a dent in what I already owed from my first year.

My hair was still wet as I headed downstairs. I grabbed my keys from a hook above the kitchen counter and made my way to the back door.

"I'm heading out," I shouted before closing the door behind me and turning the lock. I felt lighter than I had in weeks, finally letting the weight of finals fall off my back. The afternoon sun was high in the sky as

I slipped on my sunglasses and took a deep breath of sea air. Our backyard was charming, as was to be expected from a suburban beach house. I could hear birds chirping as they splashed around in the stone birdbath, and I could just make out the sound of waves crashing in the distance.

My first shift at the bookstore wasn't until tomorrow, so I had the whole day to get to know my surroundings a bit better and begin to acclimate. Maybe find a second job?

Desperate for some caffeine, I searched for the nearest coffee shop on my phone. Coastal Toast—it seemed like a good enough place to start. I typed the address into my GPS and noticed that the cafe was near the route my dad had driven me through downtown Newport on the way home the night before. Last night, the sunset had cast a golden glow on the waterfront and drenched the buildings and boats in orange light. I'd reached for my camera, wanting to capture it, but we were back on the side roads before I could get the exposure right to snap the picture. It could wait—I knew I'd have a chance to photograph everything here over the next few months.

After parking in front of the coffee shop, I slid a few coins into a meter and checked my bag to make sure I had remembered to bring my book.

The cafe was quaint, its wooden exterior weathered from years in the briny air, making it fit in well with the historic buildings surrounding it. A bell jingled as I opened the door, catching the attention of the barista who smiled in my direction. She sprang into action as the landline beside her started to ring, picked up the phone, and held the receiver to her ear.

"Thank you for calling Coastal Toast. Yes…today's special is strawberry and hazelnut toast on whole wheat. We're open until 3 pm today. Uh-huh…great, see you then." She set the phone down with a huff. "It's been ringing off the hook today."

Her blonde hair was pulled into a messy bun, and she wore silver rings and teal nail polish on her fingers. Definitely college-aged, like me. She smoothed out her apron and asked, "What can I get for you?"

I scanned the chalkboard menu behind her as if I was still deciding. "Could I have an iced cold brew with skim milk please…and one of today's special?"

"Name for your order?" she asked, holding a plastic cup and Sharpie at the ready.

"Charlotte," I replied, then shook my head. "Charlie."

The only person who called me by my full name was my mother—there was no use for that formality here. I watched as the barista crossed out what she had written and revised it.

"Charlie is much more fun," she said with a smile. "Your order will be out in just a sec."

I grabbed a seat by the window, surrounded by mismatched chairs and worn-out couches, and took a bite of my breakfast before rummaging in my bag for my book. This week's read was the Boston Public Library's copy of *Emma* by Jane Austen. The stamp on the inside front cover reminded me that it was due back at the library by tomorrow, not that I'd be back in Boston any time soon. I had a bad habit of keeping books long past their due date, sometimes never bringing them back at all. I wasn't proud of this character flaw of mine, but it couldn't be helped. I was much too forgetful for my own good.

My love for classic literature was the only resemblance between my mother and me that I still chose to acknowledge. I knew I had her brown hair and green eyes, but I tried each day to convince myself that we looked nothing alike. Sometimes, if I looked quickly, I would catch a glimpse of her in my reflection. I'd made a habit of avoiding mirrors.

I ran my fingers along the spine of the book—clothbound, my favorite—and my mind wandered back to the library in our Ohio house. My parents had always been avid readers—hence the bookstore—and even my name had been inspired by a fictional character from one of my mom's favorite stories. My mother always said she loved Charlotte Heywood because of her quick wit and curious nature, since women weren't supposed to be so outspoken in the Regency era. This character came from the very last thing Jane Austen had written, an unfinished novel called, *Sanditon*. Jane had died in the middle of writing it, and my mother said that since Charlotte's story would never have a conclusion, she thought I should carry on the name and give it a second chance. Of course, she had to choose the one story that didn't have a built-in happy ending to look forward to. *Thanks, Mom.*

I might have left my relationship with my mother in Ohio, but I refused to leave behind the stories I'd spent most of my life revering. It was my mission to make it through Austen's entire literary collection by the end of the summer, and so far, I was only two books in. I'd already requested that my dad keep the remaining books stocked at the store for when I needed them, so I was fully prepared.

I took another bite of toast, chewing as I got lost in the banter between Emma and Mr. Knightley, and when I reached for my coffee to take a sip, I missed my mouth and spilled it directly on the novel open in my lap. I jumped up and scrambled to grab a napkin from the dispenser across the room—admittedly taking way more than necessary—when I was distracted by a bulletin board mounted on the wall.

My eyes scanned the image of an ocean vista with a horse galloping down the eastern coastline. *Take a trail ride this summer at the most prestigious equestrian academy in Rhode Island*, it read.

Remembering what I was doing, I tore one of the pull tabs from the bottom of the poster to use as an impromptu bookmark and rushed back to where I had been sitting. After dabbing the mess until it looked more like an intentional tea stain than a spill, I saved my page and tucked the book away in my bag. Best not to tempt fate and ruin more pages of a book that wasn't even mine.

My car rumbled to a start and a light on my dashboard indicated that the gas tank was nearly empty. I'd deal with that later. My dad was always nagging me to sort out my issue with forgetfulness, saying I needed to start taking responsibility for things now that I was an adult. I tried to explain to him that when I turned eighteen last year, it hadn't magically made me more responsible, to which he'd rolled his eyes. That was his usual reaction these days, he didn't push things like he used to. It was as though he had accepted the fact that I'd grown up and was allowed to make my own decisions. I was still his daughter, but things were different now.

I was living under my dad's roof for the summer, but in some ways I already felt like I was out on my own. Everything else I had, I had to pay for. I could tell my dad felt guilty for not having much to contribute to my tuition anymore. He tended to avoid eye contact whenever I brought up my looming bills. His obvious remorse made it a slightly easier pill to swallow as the statements piled up.

"I'm home," I yelled as I closed the door behind me. I'd spent the rest of my afternoon on the job hunt.

"How are you liking the town?" my dad asked from his favorite chair in the living room. It was the one piece of furniture he'd gotten in the divorce—my mom had good lawyers.

I leaned against the doorframe. "The lighting was gorgeous today."

My dad closed the book in his lap and smiled at me. "Make any friends?"

"Not quite," I said, turning to walk upstairs.

I hadn't had any luck finding another place to work yet, it seemed everyone was already fully staffed for the season. Restaurants, retailers, even ice cream shops were turning me away. I gave up after the seventh rejection and decided I could figure it out another day.

Note to self: *next year, apply for summer jobs in March.*

Chapter 2

I was sitting at the kitchen table the next morning, skimming the newspaper left behind by my dad when my phone buzzed. I ignored it at first, trying to focus on the article I was reading about the local art gallery scene while munching on a spoonful of Cheerios. My dad wouldn't keep anything other than his non-dairy milk options in the house, so I was stuck with the bland taste of almond milk with my breakfast. He was newly vegan, which I liked to refer to as his recently-divorced life crisis.

I still felt groggy from all my 4 am study sessions the week prior, which was why I'd struggled to get out of bed before noon. I folded the newspaper and pushed it to the side in defeat, unable to shake the foggy feeling in my brain. My shift at the bookstore started in an hour, so I'd have more time to read then, if it wasn't too busy.

As I took one last bite, my phone buzzed again. I placed the now-empty bowl in the sink and pulled my phone out of my back pocket.

Missed call from Mom.

My stomach lurched. I hadn't heard from her in months—not since Christmas break.

What could she possibly have to say to me?

I deleted the notification and slid my phone back into my pocket, closing my eyes and pushing out a slow breath.

Forget about it. Don't let it ruin your day.

***

I felt like I was back in Ohio when I stepped into the Newport location of Briarman's Books for the first time. The nautical decor and smell of freshly printed pages was reminiscent of the old place, but the space was unfamiliar and new. I found it funny that my dad thought he needed to set a condition for me to work here. Didn't he know I'd hang out here for free?

Briarman's Books had been my dad's pride and joy for the last four years since he'd finally taken the plunge and leased a storefront in Ohio. He had worked in publishing ever since graduating college but always dreamt of slowing down and opening up a small bookshop where he could call the shots. The place in Painesville had been a safe haven for me in high school. I'd spent hours after school curled up in the corner reading any dystopian romance novel I could get my hands on.

It felt sort of peaceful being surrounded by the books I'd poured myself into over the years, almost like catching up with old friends. Unlike the main characters from my favorite genre, I hadn't had much luck with romance in real life. I loved to use the excuse that I was born in the wrong time period—preferring stolen glances in ballrooms to hook-ups in the backseat of a car—but in fairness, I hadn't let anyone get close enough to have an opinion on the subject.

Since I'd already read most of them, my dad put me in charge of organizing the young adult books on the back wall of the store. After careful consideration of whether to display *Twilight* or *The Hunger Games* on the most prominent shelf, I emptied the rest of the YA boxes and settled into the seat behind the register.

My station was in the very back corner of the store, far away from possible interruptions and providing the perfect place to get some reading done during a shift. I reached into my bag for my planner to double-check my schedule for the week and drew a slash through the current date: May 28th. All but three squares were blank for the entire month ahead—my only commitments being my bookstore shifts and a dinner with my dad to celebrate my homecoming. Maybe once I got a second job, my schedule would look a bit less pathetic.

I returned to *Emma* in an effort to pass the time, and since I only had a few chapters left, I'd already grabbed *Northanger Abbey* from the classics section and set it aside. It was next on the list. As I opened the page where I'd left off, a slip of paper fell into my lap, the tab from the poster advertising horseback riding.

My overactive imagination took over for a moment as I envisioned an idyllic summer at a horse barn by the ocean, dune grass swaying in the breeze, me laughing as I raced down the beach on some handsome man's horse…it sounded like something I would read about. Only in reality, I was definitely afraid of putting my life in the hands of an animal and there were no handsome men in my orbit to speak of.

Then it hit me. Barns are busy places with lots of people riding and working. I thought back to every western romance I'd read about the poor stable hand finding love in between schlepping bales of hay and mucking stalls. *I could be a stable hand, right?* I spontaneously decided it couldn't hurt to call and find out. Before I had time to change my mind, I dialed the number from my makeshift bookmark and shuffled into the supply closet for some privacy.

"Hello, Seahorse Stables. What can I do for you?"

"Hi, my name is Charlotte...Briarman." I didn't know why I kept introducing myself with that name. I cleared my throat and continued, "I saw your poster in the Coastal Toast Cafe about trail rides?"

"Yes, great. We're so happy to see that the advertisement seems to be bringing in some new people this year. What level were you thinking? We have private and group trail rides..."

"Oh...I'm a novice," I said, not trying to give any false expectations, regardless of how desperate I was, "but I'm actually calling about something else."

"Oh?"

"I just moved here a few days ago for the summer, and I'm looking for a job. Are you hiring by any chance?" I held my breath.

"Oh. Well, I'm not really the person to talk to about that. Could you hold on for just a minute? I'll go ask our barn manager." Her hand muffled the receiver as she shouted, "Ebony!"

A few moments later, a new voice came through the phone. "Hello? Are you still there?"

"Still here," I said, twisting a piece of my ponytail between my fingers.

"Hi, Charlotte. So, I'm told you're looking for work here at Seahorse."

I began aimlessly pacing in the closet. "Yes, I was wondering if you have any positions available for the summer."

"What is your experience with horses like?"

"None as of yet—but I'm a fast learner," I said.

"Hmm. We're fully staffed at the moment with stable hands, and I'm not sure what else we could have you do with such limited experience."

My heart sank as the equestrian daydream started to dissolve in my mind.

"Oh," was all I could muster in response. After a moment, I continued,

"Sorry to bother you then…I thought you guys might be busy this time of year."

I heard papers rustling in the background like she was checking just to be sure.

"You know what, we do have a few more boarders coming in this week for the summer…" Ebony trailed off.

Hope fluttered in my chest.

"Are you opposed to mucking out stalls?" she asked with a hint of sarcasm in her voice—a test.

"I'm open to anything," I said too quickly. I couldn't believe I might've pulled this off. "I'm a fast learner." *I said that already.*

"Well, I appreciate your zest, Charlotte, and we could definitely use some more girls working around here. There are a few new horses moving in tonight—the summer cottage crowd, if you know what I mean. Would you be open to stopping by tomorrow to see how things go?"

"Absolutely. Yes, definitely." I nodded my head as if she could see my enthusiasm over the phone.

"Great, we'll see you at 7 am. Ask for me when you get in. And just so you know, we require all of our barn staff to know the basics of riding, so if this is a good fit, we will have to get you started on some beginner lessons right away."

I tried to pretend that didn't scare me.

"Thank you so much, I'm looking forward to it," I said, then hung up the phone in disbelief.

Chapter 3

At 6 o'clock the next morning, an unusually early alarm buzzed in my ear, and I turned over to squint at my phone. I'd once thought waking up for a 9 am class was difficult, but this was on another level. I was desperately fighting the urge to sink back into the mountain of pillows on my bed and fall back asleep when my second alarm sounded at 6:02.

I groaned, rolled onto the floor to jolt myself awake, and reached for the phone on my nightstand. In the dim light, I found my way to the bureau across the room and got dressed in some leggings and a t-shirt, pulling on a pair of navy-blue rain boots for the finishing touch.

As I examined myself in my full-length mirror, I realized that transforming into a refined equestrian overnight wouldn't be possible for me and made a mental note to stop by the sporting goods store on the way home. Maybe I could find something that might resemble proper riding attire so I could try to blend in.

My dad was already sitting at the bay window with a glass of lemon water and the morning newspaper by the time I reached the kitchen.

"You're up early," I muttered as I made a beeline to the coffee pot, my eyes still puffy from my incomplete night's rest and my hair in a messy ponytail.

"No earlier than usual, you're just finally here to witness it," my dad teased, barely glancing up from the article occupying his attention. I was glad that he wasn't in the mood to converse at this ungodly hour. I watched him discreetly as I reached for a mug. He looked relaxed and comfortable for the first time since I could remember. Maybe even happy.

My coffee was already brewing in the pot I'd bought for the house since I'd set the timer the night before in preparation for my first day. My sleep schedule would eventually adjust, but this first week of sunrise alarms was bound to make me feel a bit jet lagged. Decaf was definitely not an option.

I poured my dark roast into the "Proud Dad of a BU Student" to-go mug my dad had bought during my freshman move-in and grabbed a granola bar from the lazy Susan below. Slinging my bag over my shoulder, I dragged my feet towards the door.

"Keys, Charlotte," my dad said without looking up. I was too predictable. I trudged back to the kitchen, grabbed my keys off the hook, and finally ran to my car. Another five minutes, and I'd be late on my first day—not the kind of first impression I wanted to make.

I typed the address of Seahorse Stables into my phone's GPS and pulled out of the driveway into our nautical, small-town neighborhood. We lived about a three-minute drive from the beach—close enough to walk or bike there in the summer but far enough to avoid waterfront pricing. I sped off down the winding backroads of my new town with the sunroof open and fresh air rustling my hair. As I drove past sunlit trees and ocean views, I thought to myself, *I could be happy here, too.*

I took the last left on my GPS, and my breath caught in my throat.

The sprawling property before me was all green fields and white picket fences lined closely by elm trees. I stopped my car in front of the stone entrance and a buzzing noise signaled that I was allowed in.

When I stepped out of the car, I was greeted by the smell of hay and fresh-cut grass. The stables stood tall before me with white wooden panels and black shutters on each window. I wandered towards the barn, looking around for anyone who might notice how out of place I was, and took a cautious step through the huge sliding doors.

The shade of the stables was a welcome contrast to the morning sunshine. Once my eyes adjusted, it was as if I had entered another world—one where I was completely unfamiliar with the rules. Surrounding me were rows of endless stalls, with horses poking their heads into the aisle and men schlepping hay bales and pushing wheelbarrows every which way. I squeezed my eyes tight for a moment and forced my feet to take me further down the aisle.

Everywhere I looked was foreign to me. The ceilings, walls, and stalls had the same white paneling as the barn's exterior, while the detailing and gates were polished black metal. The cobblestone floor was in pristine condition, and it gave me a feeling that I'd be spending a lot of time sweeping this summer.

At the end of the first aisle, a chestnut horse stuck its head out of its stall and let out a loud whinny. I flinched and scanned my surroundings for a reaction from anyone, but no one else seemed to notice. Since the horse was the only one to notice *me* so far, I walked over to say hello.

As I moved closer, the horse brought its face down to meet me, gently nudging my shoulder as if to say hi. I scratched its nose, suddenly feeling a little bit less alone in here, and took a baby carrot from the bag my dad had given me to feed to the horse. My dad had done some research the night before and told me that fresh produce was the fastest way to any horse's heart. It seemed to be working as my new friend devoured the carrot in a few happy bites.

"Good girl," I said, smiling as the horse nuzzled my arm again. My fingers traced the nameplate welded into the stall door. "Lightning."

"What do you think you're doing?" an angry voice said in my direction. I spun around and met the glare of a young man. His dark eyes, brimming with disapproval, matched his dark hair and black riding attire. It was as if he'd stepped out of an equestrian catalog or a J.Crew advertisement.

"Sorry...I'm new here. I'm supposed to be looking for Ebony?" I said as he stepped closer. His brown hair was tousled, probably by the helmet in his hands, and he peered down at me in a way that said my answer was insufficient.

"Another seasonal stable hand, I assume," he said, circling me like a shark. "Maybe you should stick to mucking the stalls instead of loitering around my horse."

He stopped to rub the nose of his pet, and it struck me how he could be so tender with an animal while simultaneously so blatantly harsh with me.

"I'm...sorry," I said again—mostly to myself that time—because before I could get the words out, the stranger had already unlatched the stall door, stepped inside, and started grooming his horse.

I decided that was my cue to leave and turned away from him, but as I walked down the aisle, I glanced back every few steps to see if he might look up from grooming and rethink his decision to yell at the ignorant new girl today. He did not.

Who knew feeding a carrot to a horse could be such a crime?

A girl, who looked to be about my age, was leaning against a gate and watching me retreat from a few stalls down. She shared the same preppy aesthetic as the rest of the barn and was undeniably pretty. Her black hair was swept into a sleek ponytail as she unclipped her helmet and hooked it on the stall door. She made deliberate eye contact with me, and a smirk played on the edges of her glossy pink lips—seemingly amused by the tongue-lashing I'd just endured.

Before I could get caught up in comparing myself, a woman appeared at the top of the aisle and called my name. She was dressed in a pair of nice denim jeans and a navy windbreaker over a white polo shirt, and her eyes immediately landed on me.

"You must be Charlotte." She took a hand from her jacket pocket and reached out to shake mine. "I'm Ebony, we talked on the phone."

"So nice to meet you." I forced a smile. "I was just trying to find you."

"Likewise." She smiled back at me and turned to walk towards the office. Assuming that she wanted me to follow, I picked up the pace and trailed a bit too eagerly behind her. "It's going to be great having a few extra hands around here, especially this time of year. We just had a few new horses added to our boarding roster, so there's always a stall to be mucked or a horse to be turned out."

Breathe, Charlie.

"So, here's how this is going to go," Ebony said, glancing in my direction every so often as we speed-walked through the barn, "if things go well with your training, we will have you work Monday through Friday, starting promptly at 7 am to assist with the morning chores and afternoon turnout. We'd like to have you eventually help exercise the horses, so you will need to take at least one riding lesson each week with one of our trainers, which can be scheduled at the main office. Our trainers are exceptional, so I'm sure you'll catch on quickly."

I swallowed and tried not to think about it.

"In here," she gestured toward a door labeled *Tack Room*, "you will have an assigned locker to store your riding gear. You can rent what you need for free from our tack shop on the grounds and keep it in here for the season. Larry knows you're coming, so just pick up the gear when you get a chance. He'll also fill you in on what you should wear when riding and working."

I nodded as Ebony ran through the terms of my employment, trying my best to keep track of everything she was saying.

"So, Charlotte—Charlie?" She looked at me for approval. "You said you've never ridden before, right?"

I wished I could say that I had experience as I was surrounded by people who had likely been riding since birth, but the truth was, I'd never even stepped in a barn before this one.

"I've never been on a horse in my life," I said finally. I was pretty sure I didn't really need to know how to ride to be able to muck out some stalls. "But I'm open to trying it."

Ebony stopped in front of her office and turned to me again. Her dark skin contrasted with her pearly smile. "I'm happy to hear that, Charlie. Now, let's get your training started."

***

I collapsed onto my bedroom floor and let out a sigh, grateful for the chill of the hardwood beneath me. Today had already been exhausting, and it was only two in the afternoon. Normally, I would've barely been awake at this point, but those days were behind me.

I had spent the rest of the morning learning all I needed to know about being a stable hand—from feeding to mucking to grooming and everything in between. Now that I had a general grasp of what my responsibilities would be, I could finally allow myself to picture my summer for real. Yes, barn chores would be hard work, but they were nothing I couldn't handle. And there had been something kind of nice about that morning—the fresh air, the sea breeze, or maybe just the newness of it all.

I wanted so desperately to pull myself onto my bed and take an afternoon nap, but I could smell the hay stuck in my hair and the shavings from the stalls sticking to my sweaty clothes. I ruled against falling asleep on the floor and instead, dragged myself into the bathroom to take a cold shower.

As the water washed my day down the drain, I filed away the memories of my morning, pausing at one of the guy who'd yelled at me for feeding his horse. There was absolutely no way to deny that he was beautiful to look at, even as his scowling face flashed in my mind. The reader in me played with the idea of this being the start of an enemies-to-lovers trope come to life—Lizzy hated Darcy at the beginning of *Pride and Prejudice*, and look how that turned out—but the realist in me forced away the daydream. I knew I only fantasized about things that could never come to pass. Real romantic options only made my stomach hurt.

Chapter 4

The temperature was unusually high for a town by the sea in the first week of June. As I drove to the stables for my morning shift, the thermostat on my dashboard had reached eighty degrees—at 7 am. At least the tack room had a breeze drifting in through the window. There was no air conditioning at the stables, except in the office, but the tack room provided some relief compared to the rest of the barn.

After a few days of training, I felt *almost* confident enough to handle my daily assignments without asking permission before doing things. This morning, I chose to tackle the tack room first, since it was in obvious disarray. I was determined to get everything polished and organized before my first riding lesson.

As I sat on the thankfully cool concrete floor and pulled loose hair from the grooming kits, I heard footsteps coming down the aisle just outside. A moment later, the rude stranger who owned Lightning strolled in, pulling on a riding jacket and cuffing his sleeves. I'd somehow managed to avoid him ever since our anti-meet-cute last week, mostly by running the other way whenever I saw him, but there was no way of hiding now. Our eyes met for a split second before he went about his business with no other acknowledgment of my presence. I took a pained breath, suddenly feeling a bit suffocated as I tried to focus on my task. Even with the makeshift riding pants I'd purchased a few days prior, I was still covered in dust and horsehair while he towered over me in his custom, hemmed training attire—a navy polo under his jacket and khaki riding pants. I tried to force my eyes away from him, but this proved to be difficult, maybe due to the fact that he was gorgeous and annoyingly tall and didn't give a shit about me. I clung to that last point, trying hard not to romanticize this asshole.

Before the silence became too loud, another person walked into the room. I remembered this boy, Nils, from my second day at the stables.

"James," Nils said, slapping his friend on the shoulder. *So, that's his name.* James turned around and smiled—something I wasn't aware he was capable of. "How's the summer been treating you, man?"

"It's been alright." James's tone was relaxed, and his deep voice was almost soothing, nothing like our first interaction. "I haven't seen you around here in ages."

"I just got back from school last week," Nils said. "Two years down, two to go." He was equally adorned in expensive riding clothes, tapping the breast of his shirt where his university's chest was embroidered.

"How's vet school going? I heard the exams are brutal," James said as he rolled up a navy polo wrap that matched his shirt and tossed it back onto the shelf. Something in the way he spoke told me he was all too aware that I was listening to his every word.

Like I have a choice.

"Nothing I can't handle," Nils replied with a grin. "Are you taking Lightning out on the trails?"

"I'm about to hit the beach off the northern trail. You in?"

"Sure, why not? I've been dying to get out of the barn today." Nils laughed. "I'll get Copper tacked up."

As Nils turned to leave, he noticed me sitting on the floor, and like any properly socialized person would, he smiled at me.

"Almost didn't see you down there," Nils said. "How's your second week treating you?"

"Not too bad so far." I smiled back at him and glanced at James to see if he'd noticed his friend's acknowledgment of me. He'd already returned his attention to gathering tack.

"Glad to hear it," Nils said as he walked out the door. "See you around, Charlie."

I tried returning to my task, but my eyes drifted back to James. I watched as he reached for an English saddle hanging on the top rack. His arms flexed under the weight of the tack, and his polo shirt lifted, exposing sun-kissed skin and lean muscles I hadn't noticed before.

James turned and caught my eyes on him, which seemed to be the remedy for my staring problem. I immediately shifted my gaze to the floor and silently wished to be invisible, cringing as he walked away without so much as a word. I refused to be bothered by this jerk, no matter what he looked like. Even the most beautiful people had an ugly side, and I'd already become acquainted with his.

I finished organizing the grooming gear and swept up the mess I'd left on the floor, making sure everything was in its place again. My first riding lesson was in an hour—this was not the time for distractions.

During my first week at the stables, I'd been fitted for a helmet and boots and assigned a riding instructor named Jeff. He'd assured me during our introductory meeting that I was in good hands and promised that he would only put me on horses that I could handle. His warm smile made me *almost* believe him as I tried not to engage with the voice in my head telling me I couldn't handle any of the horses.

On that same day last week, Ebony had taken it upon herself to teach me how to lunge a horse. She told me to groom a quarter horse named Claudia and meet her in the indoor round pen. After taking a second to remember how to properly halter the horse, I made my way to a large, circular room with sand footing on the far side of the barn.

When I stepped inside, the overhead lights were still off and sunlight streamed through the dusty windows, illuminating the debris that hung in the air. By some miracle, the room had managed to stay ten degrees cooler than the rest of the stables—the gray sand that covered the floor seemed to insulate the chill—and it made me want to stretch out my arms and breathe it in.

Having heard me come in, Ebony gestured for me to meet her in the center of the ring. In her hands was a long black whip which she carefully unwound as I led Claudia forward.

"Have you ever seen someone lunge a horse before?" she asked.

I shook my head and tried to hide my uncertainty. I didn't have a clue what lunging even meant.

"Well then," she said, "I'll show you how it's done."

She gestured to the space beside her. "You can remove the lead rope from Claudia's halter and stand here."

I did as I was told, unhooking the rope from the horse's headcollar and standing back. Ebony made a clicking noise with her tongue to get Claudia moving.

I watched in awe as the horse followed the whip dragging in the sand and began to trot. Ebony snapped the whip against the ground and the horse responded by moving faster into a canter. A small cloud of dust flew behind the animal, hitting the light beams, and my hands itched for my camera. Claudia made strides around and around the ring, following Ebony's lead without restraint.

"You're going to want to warm her up with a trot for five minutes, then canter for about five more minutes on each side," Ebony instructed.

My head was starting to feel dizzy from following Claudia's path with my eyes, spinning round and round in the center of the room.

"It's important to continue exercising these horses, even when it isn't competition season," Ebony said, keeping her eyes on the horse still galloping around us. "They need to stay in shape, just like people do when we go to the gym."

As she said this, Claudia broke from her path and started bucking towards the center of the ring. I looked over my shoulder, and the horse seemed to be making her way directly towards me, faster than I could have anticipated. For such well-trained creatures, their mood swings were jarring.

All I could do was stumble backward, my hands stinging as they caught me in the sand.

"Whoa...whoa...." Ebony said as she moved in front of me and stretched her arms wide. This seemed to calm Claudia down. Ebony reached for the lead rope sitting in the sand and hooked it back onto the horse's halter before turning to me.

"Claudia can be a bit naughty sometimes, but we still love her." She turned back to the now docile horse and kissed her on the nose.

Once the initial shock had worn off, I'd felt sort of stupid for being afraid. Everything had seemed so out of control only seconds before. I only hoped my reaction didn't make Ebony think twice about hiring me—I was just beginning to like it here.

Today, however, I needed to keep my doubts at bay and focus on staying calm in the face of uncertainty. Once Patterson, the red and white Paint horse booked for my first lesson, was properly tacked up with an English saddle, I met Jeff outside by the back paddocks. My pounding heartbeat challenged the sound of Patterson's hooves clip-clopping against the cobblestones as we walked through the barn. Jeff was waiting on a set of bleachers as we stepped into the sunshine.

"How are we feeling today, Charlie? Ready? Excited?" Jeff shouted from a few yards away. He was practically vibrating with energy, and it was only making me more nervous. I took a deep breath. *If he was enthusiastic about this, why shouldn't I be?*

"Patty will be perfect for your first ride," Jeff continued as I got closer, rubbing the horse's nose. "He is basically a big ol' grandpa, so don't worry about him taking off on you or anything like that."

I tried to bring myself to smile. I had made it this far, I couldn't back out now. Jeff reached out and lightly jostled my shoulders to rid me of some obvious tension.

"Shake it out, girl," he said, shimmying a bit himself, making me laugh. "Horses are very empathetic. The easiest way to be safe while riding is to keep yourself calm. Patterson can hear your heartbeat from up to four feet away, so relax and don't forget to breathe."

I nodded, trying to remember everything he was saying as my brain went into information overload. Jeff gave me a look of mock bravery that made me laugh again. *He's good at this.*

"Let's do this," I said finally.

Jeff pivoted and led Patterson towards the mounting block, gesturing for me to step up. Holding on for dear life, I slid my leg over the saddle and took a seat. It felt higher up there than I'd imagined it would. Jeff lent a hand as I got my toes in the stirrups and showed me the proper positioning.

This isn't too bad...

We started off by walking around the arena, and Jeff said I should try getting used to balancing as the horse's weight shifted back and forth. It wasn't so scary with him guiding me. For a moment, my fear subsided, and I let myself take in the scenery and try to enjoy it.

Out of the corner of my eye, I spotted a tall silhouette standing at the edge of the barn. After squinting for a moment, I knew exactly who was watching me. James's judgmental stare was barely visible through the glaring sunshine—or maybe I'd just imagined it. I knew what he must've been thinking, his harsh voice echoing in my mind.

The new girl is so inexperienced that she has to be led around the arena like a toddler at a birthday party. At least she's decided to wear proper riding pants today.

My skin prickled. I didn't want to care about his opinion of me.

Suddenly, I was feeling less comforted by the fact that I had been put on a thirty-year-old horse and more embarrassed by it. Jeff led me on another trip around the arena, and by the time I looked back at the barn, the doorway was empty, and James had disappeared into the shade.

✳✳✳

My dad was focused on his menu as I drummed my fingers on the dinner table between us. I'd already chosen my meal for the evening, but this process usually took longer for him. I gave him an extra minute to check the dietary symbols.

My phone buzzed against the white tablecloth, but I reached for it before he could see who was calling. I already knew who it would be. I declined the call from my mother and slipped my phone into my bag on the floor.

"Who's calling you?" my dad asked, glancing at me over his reading glasses.

"No one important," I said.

He lowered his menu and met my eyes. "Is it her again?"

I paused for a moment. "Yup."

"You don't want to answer it?"

"I have nothing to say to her."

"Maybe she has something to say to you," he said. "Perhaps an apology?"

"It doesn't really matter what she has to say since I've already chosen to move on from all of it." I spat my words, taking out my frustration on him. It was an accident, and I immediately recoiled at the sound of my voice. Quieter, I added, "I don't want to talk about her."

"Fair enough," my dad said. "I'm ready to order if you are."

Our meals arrived twenty minutes later with steam rising from the plates, and we engaged in our usual dinner chatter. It had always been easy for me to talk to my dad, almost as friends.

"Did you have any issues getting the hang of things at the store yesterday?" my dad asked. "Should I add anything else to the order sheet for next month?"

"As long as we have all of Jane Austen's books in stock, I'm all set," I said between bites of my burger.

"Oh yes, how could I forget about your marathon? That shouldn't be an issue."

"Good." I nodded.

"And what about the house?" he said. "Do you need anything else to get you settled in? Anything for your room?"

"Everything's great, really." I looked up at him. "I love my room."

"Good. But if you think of anything, just let me know." He wanted me to be happy here, like he was.

The restaurant turned out to be a nice choice. I could tell Dad was happy with his corn chowder and beet salad, and I was pleased with the view. My seat overlooked Newport Harbor with a bridge crossing over the water to Jamestown, which my dad informed me was very scenic. It was close but just out of reach without paying a toll. I ignored the irony there.

A few sailboats were docked only ten feet from the open window and a gust of sea air blew past us. I reached for my camera in my bag, adjusted the exposure, and snapped a picture.

"I like it here," I heard myself say.

"Good," my dad responded, and I knew he was holding back a smile.

The sun had fully set by the time I reached the door to my bedroom. I was full from the burger and fries I'd just consumed and haphazardly stripped myself of my dressy attire, replacing my sundress and cardigan with soft cotton pajama shorts and a Boston University T-shirt.

I found my laptop under the covers of my bed, took the memory card out of my camera, and slipped it into my adapter, waiting for it to pop up on my screen.

I'd always loved collecting photographs. There was something so bittersweet about capturing a moment in time, yet never truly being able to revisit it. I scrolled to the bottom of the photo import and double-clicked on the image from the restaurant, sending it straight to the printer on my desk. The machine churned out my newest photo and spit it out onto the drying rack.

I'd always kept my photo journal on my nightstand. I liked to have it on hand, sometimes just to flip through to entertain myself, other times to calm me down, and often to distract me from the present moment. It was comforting to look at the past and realize that my worries from those times were long gone—but then, so were the good memories. Everything was fleeting, but at least I could keep something of the good parts with me, cutting them out and pasting them to these pages where nothing could touch them.

I got up from my bed to grab the now-cooled picture from the printer tray, and, on a fresh page of my journal, I taped down the edges and labeled it *Clarke Cooke House with Dad*. My first Newport memory.

Chapter 5

One of the girls who boarded at Seahorse Stables was scheduled for an afternoon lesson, so I was assigned the task of grooming and tacking up her horse, Dandelion, in preparation. The horse was dusted with shavings when I found him in his stall, likely from rolling around during the night, so I carefully brought him into the aisle and hooked him up to the nearest cross ties. Halfway through using a curry brush to get the dirt from underneath Dandelion's golden coat, the owner appeared behind me.

"I grabbed my tack already," she said, lugging an English saddle and bridle, with the reins dragging behind her. I looked up to greet her.

"Charlie?" She looked at me with wide eyes.

"Um…yes?"

"I'm Gwen, from Coastal Toast?" She watched as I put the pieces together. "I didn't know you worked at Seahorse, otherwise I totally would have given you the 'friends and fam' discount the other day at the cafe." She smiled and outstretched her free hand to shake mine. Her blond hair was pulled into a loose ponytail with fringe framing her face. "It's nice to *officially* meet you."

"I just started last week," I replied, shaking her hand. "So, you're Dandelion's owner?" I patted the horse's neck. Gwen dropped her saddle on the nearest tack box and wrapped her arms around Dandelion's neck in a gentle squeeze.

"Isn't he the sweetest? Never bucks or bites. He's the best horse in the barn—but don't tell Zuri I said so," she said with a smirk.

"I heard that!" Another girl came around the corner with a gray and white horse on a pastel pink lead rope and matching halter. "Sophie would beg to differ." Her brown hair was tied up in double braids, and she wore a pink polo shirt—matching her tack—with white riding pants, and polished black boots. Zuri hooked her horse to another set of cross ties before joining us.

"Charlie, this is Zuri," Gwen said, glancing between the two of us. I shook Zuri's outstretched hand as she smiled warmly. *Everyone's so formal around here.*

"I haven't seen you around before," Zuri said. "Are you new to Newport?"

"I'm new to Rhode Island," I responded. "My dad just moved here last fall, and I live with him now when I'm not at school."

"Where are you from originally?" Gwen asked.

"Ohio," I said. "I live in Boston most of the year now, for school." It felt weird to say it out loud. I was so used to Ohio being my only home.

"Which school?" Zuri asked.

"Boston University?" I said it like a question. It had already been a year, but it still felt like it wasn't really mine, like one missing tuition payment could take it away.

I finished grooming Dandelion with a soft brush to get her coat nice and shiny and reached for some fly spray. Gwen lifted her saddle over her head and secured it onto the lavender-colored saddle pad resting on her horse's back.

"We go to Providence College," Gwen said, "but I've always wanted to live in Boston someday, near Newbury Street or something. You'll have to tell us all about it."

"And we'll tell you all there is to know about Newport," Zuri said. "There's always some sort of drama going on around here, especially at Seahorse."

"Who's dating who…" Gwen said.

"Who *wants* to be dating who," Zuri added with a laugh. "What's the deal with the *very* attractive vet assistant, fresh from veterinary college."

"There's always something to talk about," Gwen finished.

I swallowed. I'd rather fly under the radar this summer. It would be easier that way when I'd eventually have to leave at the end of the season. Still, I forced a smile of interest. My mother often told me I had a tendency to act cold and unfeeling around strangers—I tried my best to not show it.

"There has to be something in the sea air that makes the people of Newport extra salty," Gwen teased, poking Zuri's shoulder on the last two words.

"Especially you know who…" Zuri said under her breath.

I looked at them expectantly—admittedly, a small part of me was intrigued.

"Jenna," Zuri said in a whisper. "You may have seen her around a bit by now since you've been here a week. About my height? Great hair? Judgmental smirk?"

I knew exactly who she was talking about.

"Yeah…she's not the nicest person you'll ever meet," Gwen said. "She can be a bit intense."

"But the guys love that about her." Zuri rolled her eyes. "She's kind of a hot commodity around here. She can cast quite a spell on people when she wants to. Her boyfriend's a few years older, in his last year of college, I think. Apparently, they got together over the spring at a riding camp in Switzerland, so they're doing the whole long-distance thing. It was all anyone could talk about for a while."

"It hit James pretty hard," Gwen said.

That got my attention.

"Jenna and James had a whole on-again-off-again thing going on for a few years before that. He was apparently crushed when she broke it off this last time. I felt kinda bad for him, she was a good distraction," Gwen said, glancing at Zuri.

"Speaking of which, are you seeing anyone?" Zuri asked me, a devilish look on her face.

"Um—" I looked from Zuri to Gwen. "Not at present."

Zuri turned to Gwen. "Maybe we could set her up with Ren?"

The prospect of this made my palms begin to sweat. I didn't need to start something just for it to come to a screeching halt come September. With such a short window of time for me here, it wasn't like anything serious could happen. I twisted the ring on my index finger until I realized I was doing it, then crossed my arms over my chest. Maybe they weren't thinking it would be that serious. Why did I always have to overcomplicate things? I could actually *try* to have some fun this summer.

I took a breath. "Who's Ren?"

"He's the stable's vet assistant. His mom's the veterinarian for the whole town," Gwen said.

Zuri's eyes scanned the aisle we were standing in as she said, "We'll find someone for you before the summer's over, don't you worry."

"I wouldn't get your hopes up," I said. They didn't know me well enough to know that their efforts would be fruitless. I wasn't planning on turning this summer into a Hallmark movie come to life. Trying to be sociable, I asked, "What about you both? I'm sure you've got tons of guys on your rosters."

Gwen cleared her throat, suppressing a laugh. She shrugged at me before changing the subject.

"I'm gonna take him out." Gwen gestured to her horse, then looked at Zuri. "I'll wait for you at the trail entrance." Zuri was still brushing Sophie's mane and spritzing her with fly spray.

Gwen handed me her reins for a moment and pulled a stray piece of hay out of Zuri's braids. Zuri laughed, dusting off her otherwise immaculate shirt. Then, Gwen looked both ways, checking for onlookers, before pulling Zuri close and kissing her.

"See you out there," Gwen said with a spark in her eyes. She turned back to me, winked, then strolled away with Dandelion in tow.

I was not expecting that.

"Gwen's the best," Zuri sighed, entranced by the afterglow of her girlfriend's presence.

I smiled at her. I admired people who were happily in love. It sort of felt like looking at art in a museum. I could observe it from a distance, but it would never be mine.

"I should get back to work, but it was really nice meeting you," I said before walking off to find another chore to do.

I was wandering into an open stall to check the water buckets when I accidentally ran into something—someone—kneeling on the ground next to a horse lying down on the fresh shavings.

"Sorry," I said. "I didn't see you over the stall guard."

"All good, I'm almost done here anyways." The stranger looked up at me with sparkling eyes that swept over me and a warm smile on his face.

He was dressed in baby blue scrubs and holding a stethoscope to the horse's stomach. I noticed that this was the horse from my lunging practice with Ebony last week.

"Did something happen to Claudia?" I asked, taking note of her tired appearance. "Is she okay?" *Could I have caused this somehow?*

"She's perfectly healthy, just due for her yearly checkup," he said, obviously amused by my misplaced concern. He focused on the sounds from the horse's stomach for one second more before hanging his stethoscope around his neck and looking up at me again. "You must be Charlie."

"I am." *How does he know that?* "And you must be—"

"Ren." He stood up, dusted the shavings off his knees, and extended his hand to shake mine. *Again, with the formalities.* He was taller than me, enough that I had to tilt my chin up to meet his eyes.

"We routinely check for warning signs of common diseases, just to be proactive. This one has a history of colic, so I try to be extra diligent." As if she could tell that we were talking about her, Claudia popped up on her feet in one swift motion.

"Colic?" I asked.

"It's the most common cause of death for horses. Claud's case was mild because we caught it early, but not all horses are so lucky."

"Wow," I said. "What do you look for?"

"Mostly, the horse isn't eating or they start pawing at the ground. In more severe cases, they will even kick their stomach from the pain.

It's pretty brutal. But as long as you catch it early it doesn't have to end badly," he said. "Claud's owner knew the signs, so she didn't waste any time and called us right away. She kept her walking until my mom arrived. Probably saved her life."

I tried to make a mental note, filing this information away in the now overflowing folder of horse facts in my brain. I needed to carry a composition book around here just to keep track of everything.

Ren turned back to Claudia who was bobbing her head in his direction, probably looking for a treat for good behavior.

"This one's a champ," he said, taking a carrot out of his back pocket. He easily snapped it in three and fed the first two pieces from his open palm.

"You wanna try?" he asked, looking at me.

"Sure." I stepped forward as Ren took my hand in his and tucked my thumb underneath my fingers.

"Like this," he said. It felt strangely intimate, being so close to someone I'd only just met, but not entirely in a bad way. His fingers were warm and calloused, and I could just barely smell mint on his breath. He dropped the third piece of carrot into the center of my palm, and I moved my hand closer to Claudia's nose until she brushed her whiskers against my skin and took the vegetable, munching loudly.

"That kinda tickles," I said, glancing at Ren, but when I met his eyes, I noticed how attentively he was watching me. My stomach tightened, and I felt sort of overwhelmed by his gaze—feeling a bit like a slide under a microscope.

Don't look so closely, I thought to myself, *unless you like disappointment.*

I needed to get Ren's eyes off me, so I turned back to where Claudia was searching my hand for more treats.

"Ouch," I said, pulling my hand away.

Ren's face turned white as he reached for my palm. "Are you okay?"

"I'm messing with you," I said, stifling a laugh as he accounted for each of my fingers. My heart rate slowed. "You're so gullible."

Ren exhaled and pushed his fingers through his thick black hair. "Well, you're trouble."

I shrugged as Ren gave Claudia one last pat on the neck before leading us out of the stall and sliding the door closed behind us.

"If you ever need an extra set of hands, I'm around the barn all the time, and I'd really like to learn more about all this," I said as we walked down the aisle.

"Do we have another future vet on our hands?" Ren said, looking genuinely intrigued.

"Definitely not," I said. "I'm just interested."

"Well, I might just take you up on that, Charlie." Ren's smile reached his dark brown eyes as they met mine. He turned to walk toward the office, stealing one more glance at me when he thought I wasn't looking.

"I'll see you around," he said, and a part of me was actually looking forward to it.

Chapter 6

My arms ached under the weight of two half-empty water buckets as I carried them outside behind the barn. I was getting stronger every day I worked at Seahorse Stables, but I still didn't have the stamina to rival my peers who had all been training for the past decade. Water splashed against my shins as I poured the leftover contents onto the grass. Zuri and Gwen followed close behind me into the sunshine, carrying their buckets without much effort.

"That should be all of them," I said with a huff, overturning one of the now-empty buckets and collapsing into a seat.

"Zuri, can you grab the soap?" Gwen said. "I'll get the hose." She could probably tell I needed a minute to catch my breath.

My friends rounded the corner of the barn with supplies in hand, and we spent the next hour filling each bucket with sudsy water and scrubbing until our hands got pruney. Finally, we rinsed the last of the buckets and collectively let out a sigh of relief. With dozens of horses in the barn, this was no small task. It probably would've taken me all day if Zuri hadn't offered her and Gwen's help when she saw me struggling that morning.

The heat picked up as the afternoon dragged on, and I could feel sweat dripping down my neck as I collected the clean buckets to return them to their stalls. When I reached for the last bucket, I spotted a massive spider crawling on the handle. I jumped back and cupped my hand over my mouth to stifle my scream. Out of instinct, Gwen pointed the hose at the bucket, spraying it down until the stream ricocheted directly in my face.

"Gwen!" I screamed, but laughter took over before I could fully get her name out. Her eyes were bright as she gave me a mischievous grin and sprayed the hose at me again—this time on purpose.

"Oops!" Gwen said, unable to contain her bubbling laughter.

"You shouldn't have done that!" I grabbed one of the buckets still brimming with clean water and hurled the contents at her. Gwen dodged the attack and dropped the hose, running to Zuri for backup. I bolted toward the hose and held it up to protect myself.

"Oh no, you didn't!" Zuri yelled, grabbing Gwen's hand in solidarity. It was two against one, but they didn't have the water source. They each took a bucket, counted to three, and charged at me from opposite directions, but as I turned to defend myself, I heard the sound of hooves approaching us.

It was already too late by the time I saw James riding Lightning around the corner, directly in the line of fire. The spray from the hose caught his chestnut horse off guard, and suddenly, she was kicking her front legs up in the air. Lightning reared up so high that I was surprised to see James still holding on. His hands gripped the reins, knuckles turning white, but his face remained calm until his horse returned to the ground. Then all hell broke loose.

James dismounted from his horse in one swift motion and landed firmly on the ground. I would have found it graceful—comparing it to my sad attempts at hopping down from the saddle—if I wasn't so preoccupied with what he would do next. It only took him three strides to reach me before he grabbed the hose out of my hands and pinched it to stop the water from flowing into the dirt. I knew he was looking at me, but I couldn't meet his eyes. For once, I deserved his hostility, which only doubled the pit in my stomach.

"Do you have any idea how bad it could have been if it had been *anyone* else coming around that corner?" He wasn't yelling, but James's icy tone affected me more than any shouting might have. I forced myself to look at him, and his eyes burned into mine, making me long for the days when he had ignored me completely.

"If it had been any of our trail horses coming through here, someone could have easily been thrown," he continued, shaking his head at my ignorance.

I wracked my brain for something to say but kept coming up blank, probably because he was right. James reached for my wrist and placed the hose back in my hand. I felt my skin heat up where he touched me, rough and agitated. Without another word, James grabbed Lightning's reins and strode into the barn.

I was frozen. I just stood there, stunned, as Zuri and Gwen turned to look at me with wide eyes. They rushed over to me, each taking one of my arms.

"Don't worry about James," Gwen said. "He's always so serious."

"I'm sure he'll forget about it by tomorrow," Zuri added. "It could've happened to anyone."

"Yeah, but it happened to me," I muttered, swimming in self-loathing. *And why did it have to happen in front of him?*

With the last two water buckets in hand, I made my way over to the stall I'd been avoiding in the first aisle. I lowered the buckets on the cobblestone floor, careful not to make a sound, and knocked softly on Lightning's stall door.

James was standing inside, meticulously grooming his horse. He glanced over at me before returning his attention to brushing a spot on Lightning's back—at least he wasn't blatantly ignoring me anymore.

"I'm just bringing back Lightning's buckets," I said, breaking the silence. "I'm Charlie by the way. I don't think we've been properly introduced." I paused for a moment to see if James dared to overexert himself with a response, but he seemed content ignoring me. I put the buckets back on their hooks and pulled the string that hung from the ceiling. Fresh water began to flow from the overhead pipes and filled them up.

I studied James's side profile as I waited for the water to reach capacity, not concerned that he might bother to look up and see me staring. His eyes were glued to the same spot he'd been brushing since I'd arrived, even though it was definitely well-groomed by now. The muscles in his jaw were tense—like he was biting the inside of his cheeks to keep from speaking.

I watched as he fidgeted with the brush in his hands, almost dropping it. This wasn't comfortable for him at all, I had been mistaken. Maybe meanness didn't come as naturally to James as it had seemed. For a moment, we stood there in silence, both pretending to be occupied by our respective chores. Once the buckets were full, I released the lever, took a breath, and turned to him.

"I'm really sorry about spooking your horse," I said almost in a whisper. I paused for a second, but still, there was no response. The masochist in me kept speaking. "I'll be more careful around here from now on."

Another beat of silence. Then to my surprise, James turned to look at me.

"I don't have time for your childish antics, Charlie," James said, making my name sound like an insult.

Ouch.

He stared directly into my eyes while speaking, then went back to grooming, as if to dismiss me. I complied and walked away, mostly because I didn't have a suitable response. All I wanted to do was hide in a corner somewhere with a good book and forget about this.

As I stepped out of Lightning's stall, I noticed Jenna was watching me from the doorway. Her usual mocking smile was twisted into a pout, and her eyes drifted from my face to my shoes as I walked past, presumably judging everything about me. I was starting to understand the way Gwen and Zuri felt about her.

After enduring the rest of the afternoon trying to avoid further embarrassment, I was desperate to get home and distract myself from my lingering self-pity. I grabbed the bag of sour candy that I'd hidden in the cupboard and a bag of popcorn and made my way upstairs. Since I'd finally finished reading *Emma*, I pulled out my laptop and rented the 1996 film online before climbing into bed and hiding under a pile of blankets. It must've been at least eight or nine years since the last time I'd watched this adaptation—it wasn't one of my favorites. I pressed play and was immediately drawn in by the chatter between Emma and Mr. Knightly and the frivolousness of balls and picnics, which was my usual remedy for social afflictions. Although this viewing experience had all the proper ingredients to make it enjoyable, I still felt a pit in my stomach.

Further into the movie, a scene began to play where all the characters go on a picnic in the countryside. As they sat under umbrellas, surrounded by red, blooming flowers in a sunny field, a memory of my own unearthed itself from the depths of my mind.

I remembered my mom and me recreating this classic picnic after watching the film so many years ago. We'd explored the wooded paths behind our neighborhood until we found a similar spot on a sunny hillside, laughing as we shook out old quilts to sit on and adjusted the bonnets we had bought for the occasion. As we spread clotted cream on our scones and drank iced tea, my mom had turned to look at me—she had a softness in her eyes back then. She'd reached out her silk-sleeved arm and brushed my cheek with her thumb, the breeze rustling my hair as she smiled at me.

"I'm so proud of how you're turning out," she'd said, her voice as gentle as the wind that caressed me.

I must've been barely twelve at the time, but I couldn't think of anything better than an *Emma*-themed picnic with my mom. Even if we didn't have the company of the grumpy Mr. Knightley or the charming Emma Woodhouse, it had still been perfect.

Things hadn't been like that between my mom and me for a long time. I used to admire her. Her job always impressed me. I loved interior design and the way not an inch of our house was left without her artful touch. She was bold and commanded attention with every room she entered. I wanted to be like that.

Once high school came around, my parents started sleeping in separate rooms. They hadn't thought I'd noticed, but I had. *Of course, I had.* My mother had started to change. Her warmth began to fade into something cold and unfamiliar. It had started slowly, with her canceling our plans to hang out with her friends from work, or no longer making time for movie nights or shopping trips with me. I'd convinced myself that this neglect wasn't personal since it was directly correlated with her crumbling relationship with my dad, and that had made it hurt a little less. I was a constant reminder of her attachment to him, and I guessed that made her feel stuck.

By the time I'd turned fifteen years old, my loving mother was entirely unrecognizable to me. Suddenly, my daily actions were bombs waiting to go off. My bad days were no longer something we could talk through. I no longer received a gentle touch on my shoulder and reassurance that everything would be okay by tomorrow. To her, my sadness became weakness and desperation. My anger became threatening and problematic. My fear became cold resentment. The wrong facial expression would cause her to ignore me for a week, or worse, she would come into my room and lecture me about how I needed to be better. There was no comfort anymore, only eggshells to walk on. And I couldn't figure out how to be perfect as the foundation of my life creaked under every step I took, and my home that had once provided warmth and safety had begun to feel rickety and unreliable—like it might collapse around me at any moment. I could never be exactly what she wanted me to be. I was a lost cause.

I couldn't figure out how she had managed to change so much, so fast when I'd thought for sure I knew her better than anyone.

In December, I'd gone home to Painesville for winter break. Fresh off my first semester of Boston life, I'd been counting down the days until I could cozy up in my childhood bedroom with some tea and a good book. For weeks, I'd looked forward to seeing my high school friends and revisiting my normal life. I even thought the distance might've given my mother a chance to miss me.

In the days leading up to Christmas, my mother had been acting surprisingly cheerful. I'd assumed she was relieved from the divorce being finalized the month before, or the holiday spirit was getting to her. Even though this behavior was now rare for her, I still clung to the good moments, hoping that things might be permanently back to normal somehow.

On December 26th, I'd gone downstairs for a late breakfast and found her in the kitchen cooking up a storm. I couldn't remember the last time we'd had a meal together, just the two of us. I'd tried to enjoy it, breathing in the scent of fresh muffins and bacon, still wearing my flannel pajamas. But something had felt off. She was being too polite, too nice, and I wasn't used to accepting that kind of attention from her anymore.

"Something smells good," I had said as I yawned and rubbed the sleep from my eyes. The morning sun had shone through the curtains over the kitchen sink, and holiday nostalgia hung in the air. My guard had lowered.

"I hope you're hungry," my mom had said with all the charm of a mother in a 1950s sitcom.

She'd fixed both of us breakfast plates and placed them on the table. I remember thinking how nice that was. She'd gone back into the fridge to get a bottle of maple syrup before taking a seat across from me.

My mom and I had a perfectly pleasant conversation as I drenched my pancakes in syrup and she carefully buttered her muffin and dropped a cube of sugar in her coffee. She'd seemed interested in my life for once. Afterall, I was her eighteen-year-old daughter, going to a great college in a great city, making good grades. She'd updated my education status on her Facebook profile a few days prior—*she was very proud.* She'd asked me how my classes were going, and if I was making friends. She'd even asked about my love life, which we never used to talk about. Our relationship had declined before I was of the normal dating age, so it had felt sort of strange discussing it with her. But it had felt good to confide in her. I'd wanted her to know me again. I'd wanted her to want to know me again.

Later that night, she'd gone out for drinks with some of her friends, and I'd stayed home, trying to sort out some things for the new year. January was right around the corner, and I'd had a gnawing feeling in my stomach telling me to finish up my financial aid forms for my sophomore year. The application for student loans was due at the end of the spring semester and I'd known if I pushed it off, it could easily slip through the cracks of my busy schedule during the semester. I'd decided I would cross it off my To-Do list before classes even started.

I'd made my way downstairs and into my mom's office to get the necessary documents together, but when I'd opened the top drawer of her antique desk where my tax info had been kept ever since I filed after my first job, the papers were missing—or at least moved somewhere else. I rummaged through the drawers below, flipping through piles of paper and searching for anything resembling the forms I'd needed.

Finally, at the bottom of the bottom drawer, I'd found an envelope and quickly pulled out the contents to check for the elusive paperwork. My eyes had scanned the pages, trying to make sense of the words. It had taken me a minute to fully comprehend what I had discovered. There had been no address, only my mother's name written in my grandmother's handwriting—I knew it well from years of receiving letters of my own. My mom and her mother had made a tradition of communicating this way, even using red sealing wax and vintage stamps like the olden times.

Laura,

Your sister visited me this week and mentioned that Charlotte has been accepted to Boston University. There's nothing quite as exciting as moving away and starting a new adventure, and I don't wish for anything *to burden her during this time. I've been putting some money aside for a few years now for this very purpose since she has always made me very proud to be her grandmother. I was able to save $20,000 from one of my real estate investments, so I will deposit it into your account next week. I hope that it will take some of the stress of loans off her, so she can focus on her studies. Please give her my love.*

Sincerely,
Mom

I'd stood there in disbelief. My grandmother had suddenly passed away in May, a few months before I'd left for Boston. She'd lived in Florida, so we only saw her on holidays. She hadn't been particularly tech-savvy either—hence the letter writing. That meant…I hadn't seen her between the time she'd written this and the time of her death. So where had the money gone? Why hadn't my mom mentioned this to me?

Later that night, my mom had tiptoed through the house, tipsily trying not to wake me. I had still been sitting in the yellow chair in her office when she stumbled down the hall.

"Mom?" I'd called out.

I'd watched through the doorway as she flinched and caught her breath.

"My god, Charlotte, you scared me." She'd reached down to take off her heels and held them by the stems in one hand as she walked into the office. "What are you doing in here so late?"

I'd looked up at her, studying her expression for any hint of guilt that I might've missed before. Her eyes had traveled from my face to the envelope in my lap.

"What are you doing?" she'd repeated, sobering.

"Just sorting out my finances for the fall semester." I'd spoken with intentional coldness, but she had made me this way. I'd stared at her, waiting for an explanation.

"Go to bed, we can work on it tomorrow."

"Mom," I'd said, keeping my voice steady, even though I could feel my hands shaking, "why didn't you tell me about this?"

I'd held up the letter. She'd turned away from me, and in some way, that was all I'd needed to know. But I'd wanted to hear her say it.

"Where is it, Mom?"

She'd reluctantly looked back at me, her cheeks still flushed from the wine and dancing, or maybe from shame.

"Do you know how much good divorce lawyers cost?" she'd said.

"You didn't…"

"Your father wanted us to sell the house, and I couldn't. I just couldn't do that, sweetie. We would've had to start over, and we wouldn't have a home anymore. Not like this one." Her eyes had welled up with suppressed guilt, as if tears could make me ignore this indiscretion of hers. As if I could just act like it never happened.

"What about me? You *know* what that kind of money would have done for my future. That money was *mine*." I'd looked down at the documents for reassurance. It was all there in black ink, proving me right.

"It's done, Charlotte. The money is gone." Her face, wet with tears from just a minute prior, had turned stone cold. "Go to bed."

At that moment, I'd realized the money wasn't the only thing that was gone. My trust in her, the small amount that had survived our tumultuous relationship, had vanished into thin air, and there was no way to ever get either of them back. I couldn't tell what cut deeper, the fact that I was $20,000 further in debt than I should've been, or the fact that, even for a brief moment, I'd thought my mom had actually cared about me again.

But it had all been an act. And I'd been stupid for falling for it.

By the next morning, I'd packed up most of my stuff to ship off to my dad's unfinished house in Newport. My dad had just made the big move to Rhode Island and was busy with home renovations and finding a location for his store. It had felt weird not spending time with him on Christmas, other than a quick phone call. It had felt strange that he wasn't living in our house anymore. Even though he'd turned in his keys while I was away at school, clues of his time spent there had lingered. His favorite salad dressing still sat on a shelf in our fridge, half empty. His socks still infiltrated the laundry room and ended up in my basket somehow. But he was nowhere to be found. It had occurred to me then that my disappearance would likely have the same effect on the place, but I couldn't stand to be under the same roof as my mother for one more minute. I'd cut my winter break short and gotten on the earliest flight to Boston, desperate to get away from the house that had cost me so much.

Suddenly, the access I'd always had to my hometown had been revoked, and my place there, my past life, had been erased. Even my friends from high school had seemed to lose interest in keeping in touch once they'd found out I wouldn't be around anymore. I was in a self-inflicted state of exile, but it didn't really feel like my choice.

My mother had never called, never texted. It was as if she had nothing to say to me, and I guessed maybe she didn't—until now.

I felt a single tear roll down my cheek as the picnic scene came to an end. I quickly wiped it away and continued watching the film until the credits began to roll.

Chapter 7

A bell jingled to signal my arrival as I opened the door to Coastal Toast and took my usual seat by the window. The noise caught Gwen's eye from behind the counter, and she gave me a quick salute before turning back to the customer in front of her. While waiting, I made progress on my next Austen novel. *Northanger Abbey* was proving to be a fun read, perfect for getting my mind off things.

Before I knew it, Gwen was taking a seat across from me with her lunch in hand. She placed an iced coffee on the small table between us and gestured for me to take it.

"Thanks," I said, taking a sip of the cold brew she knew I liked.

"I have fifteen minutes," Gwen said as she tore the wrapper off her sandwich.

"No toast today?"

"I've had enough toast to last a lifetime," she said, taking a large bite. "So...how have you been since *the incident*?"

I shrugged. "I'm slowly recovering from the embarrassment."

"It's too bad," Gwen said, resting her chin in her hand.

I gave her a puzzled look.

"If you and James weren't always butting heads, he could totally be your barn boyfriend," she explained.

I practically spit out my coffee. "Yeah, I really like guys who are unnecessarily rude to me all the time. That's definitely my type," I said, as if a part of me hadn't considered that every day since I'd met him.

"You've got to admit, he was sort of justified for that last argument," Gwen said with a suppressed grin.

"I am painfully aware of that, but thank you for the reminder," I said, only half-joking. "But seriously, what's the deal with him anyway? I don't think I've ever seen him smile, let alone have a pleasant interaction with anyone, other than Nils."

I tried to hide the blatant curiosity in my voice, not wanting Gwen to get any more ideas, but I was desperate for more information. James was an enigma that nagged at my thoughts, and even though I knew it was against my better judgment, I needed to know more about him.

"He's not bad once you get to know him. Maybe because I knew him before…" Her voice trailed off.

"Before what?" I looked at her expectantly.

Gwen's voice lowered, and her expression shifted to something more solemn than I was used to seeing on her face.

"James was happier when we were younger. We actually did all our pony camps together, and he competed on the Seahorse team in high school with Zuri and me up until he committed to his college's program.

"He's always kinda kept to himself, but in school, he was quite the catch. He had this quiet demeanor about him that no one could crack, always listening but not often contributing to the conversations around him. The girls in our grade were crazy about him, always trying to capture his attention. He was mysterious—even I had a crush on him for a bit, before Zuri and I got together, of course."

Gwen seemed far away as she recounted these old memories.

"We used to have team dinners at his house. His mom always made the best chicken parm and mashed potatoes, and we'd eat until we were stuffed. Afterward, we'd have a giant bonfire in their backyard with s'mores for dessert. It was tradition.

"Mrs. Everton was a champion Hunter Jumper back in the day. She made it on the US Equestrian team and everything. She even bred Lightning from her own prize-winning horse, so James could be a champion, too."

I listened carefully to Gwen's every word, wanting to understand. I'd had no idea James's mom was so accomplished. I imagined the weight that must put on his shoulders—having more support but fewer excuses to fail.

"A few months before starting at Brown, James's mom was in an accident on one of the trails past the beach. Her horse must've gotten spooked or something, no one really knows exactly what happened. She didn't come home one afternoon, and nobody knew where she was. They tracked her phone and found her that evening in the woods, lying on the ground. Her horse was grazing nearby. She was already gone."

"Oh my god," I heard myself say. My breath caught in my throat.

"After she passed, James was never really the same. He didn't talk much before, but after the accident, he was practically mute, barely even looking at anyone anymore. He moved into a dorm in Providence, so we barely saw him at the stables, except for the summers when he would come home and stay with his dad. We all felt horrible, but we didn't really know what to do. He started getting irritated with newcomers at the barn—like they had no clue the dangers they were getting themselves into or something. I think he didn't want to see anyone else getting hurt. I thought for sure he'd never ride again after what happened, but he just couldn't leave Lightning behind. It wasn't what his mom would've wanted."

"I can't even imagine…" I trailed off, unable to find the words.

"We all hoped he would bounce back, but it's been four years. He talks to Nils, then he had that thing with Jenna, but otherwise, none of us really hang out anymore. Jenna made it easy for James to be miserable, she accepted it with him, maybe even encouraged it. When he was a dick, she gave it right back—she's always liked the moody types. I guess he sort of hid himself away in her and just embraced the darkness."

I blinked in disbelief as Gwen finished the story. The pain he must have felt, losing someone that close to him, was unthinkable—and to continue riding. I felt the puzzle pieces start to click into place. *Of course*, he was overprotective with Lightning, that was probably one of the strongest connections he had left to his mom. And *of course*, he was upset when I spooked his horse the other day. It was all so much deeper than it had originally seemed.

I picked at a thread on my sleeve, unsure of what to say.

"Anyway," Gwen said weakly, trying to change the subject, "how are your lessons going so far? Are we gaining a new team member by the end of the summer?"

"I wouldn't get your hopes up," I said. "I should probably learn to trot first."

"I'm just impressed that you haven't fallen off yet. All the newbies do at some point."

I looked at her with wide eyes.

"It's basically a rite of passage. Consider it horse hazing," she said.

"Is this a barn or a frat house?" I said, squeezing my eyes shut at the prospect of plummeting to the ground from a horse's back, but that only made the image more vivid.

"I'm telling you, it's inevitable," Gwen said. "What do you think helmets are for?"

I shook my head. "I have no intention of falling anytime soon," I said, as if by sheer force of will, I could make it true.

"Whatever you say..." Gwen took another bite, shoving what was left of her sandwich into her mouth.

"So," I said, attempting to get my mind off riding, "what've you been up to this weekend?"

Gwen gulped her iced latte before answering. "Can't complain. Dandelion and I did some training this morning. He clears the three-foot jump almost every time now." She smiled to herself.

"That's great," I said, taking a sip of my coffee.

"And Zuri's stayed over last night, which was fun," she continued, glancing up at me.

"You're lucky your parents are so cool about that," I said. "I'm not sure my dad would like someone I was dating to stay over." I cringed at the potential implications over the breakfast table.

Gwen stared into her latte "Yeah, well...they aren't actually that cool about stuff like that."

"What do you mean?"

"They don't actually know that we're together...I haven't even told them I'm into guys *and* girls yet..." she trailed off again, her face turning a light shade of pink. "I'm still figuring out what to say...how to explain it to them. They aren't the most open-minded people on Earth, if you know what I mean."

I knew what she meant.

"You seem so *out* at the stables," I said. "How have they not found out yet?"

"No one from the barn would ever have a reason to bring it up to them, or at least they haven't so far. It's not like I post about Zuri and me online or anything."

I nodded.

"You can always talk to me about this kind of stuff, you know that, right?" I said, meeting her gaze. "Even if you just need to vent or something."

This was really starting to feel like an actual friendship.

Gwen nodded and smiled, but the usual glimmer in her eyes seemed to be missing.

***

The bookstore was relatively quiet when I arrived, especially for a Sunday afternoon. I sat at the register, mesmerized by the slow drip of condensation on my melting iced coffee and the quiet tick of the wall clock across from my desk. As I took another sip, I heard the door open.

I flipped *Northanger Abbey* over, laying it face down to save my place, and got up from my chair. I hadn't made much progress with reading today anyway. My mind was preoccupied, pondering new information about a *certain someone*. I wandered toward the front of the store and peeked around the shelves to check if the customer needed any assistance.

Through a partially empty bookshelf, I could see a person browsing the historical fiction section along the front wall. Just as I stepped around the aisle to speak to them, I realized it was James.

Of course, it was.

He had his back to me and a pencil behind his ear as he perused the selection.

I held my breath and slowly backed away until I was out of sight. With only my eyes visible through the stacks, I peered between two cookbooks and watched as James read the inside covers of a few novels. He was hunched over slightly and ran his fingers along the spines of each book, looking for something.

He seemed more relaxed than I'd ever seen him, more approachable. He was wearing a navy long-sleeved button-up with thin white stripes woven vertically, and the top three buttons lay undone against his chest. His white denim pants were cuffed at the ankles, revealing a pair of weathered boat shoes.

Taking a deep—but silent—breath, I tried to convince myself that James was less intimidating in this environment. I owned this store, well, my dad did—but still. This was my place, not his.

He'd probably leave without buying anything anyway. That was what most people did when wandering into the new local bookstore. They usually left with a nice, *"Great stuff you've got here, we'll be back,"* never to be seen again.

I bet he doesn't even read.

I tiptoed back to my seat behind the register and held my book high enough to cover my face, lowering my seat for additional concealment.

As I flipped the page to start chapter sixteen, I heard someone clear their throat in front of me. I lowered the book to my eye level, and all my hopes of avoiding another unfortunate interaction left me.

James tossed a book on the counter before looking up at my face. As I watched him realize that it was, in fact, *me* staring back at him, I sensed a slight shift in his otherwise relaxed demeanor. His muscles tightened almost imperceptibly, like a wall had gone up just beneath his skin.

"Hi," I said. I closed my book and placed it on the desk next to me, still using the same tab from the poster as a bookmark.

"Hey." His tone was rigid and forced.

"I hope you found everything okay," I said, snapping into work mode.

"Yup."

The quiet beep of the scanner was all that challenged the silence between us. I would have found it uncomfortable if I didn't notice James biting the inside his cheek again and thrumming his fingers on his thigh. He was uneasy, which conveniently made me less so.

"I didn't know you worked here." He stole a glance at what I'd been reading.

"My dad owns the place."

I could feel myself quickly running out of small talk. I reached for the novel he chose and flipped it over.

"*Anna Karenina*?" I said, intrigued.

"Yup," James said again. This conversation was lasting longer than necessary, and he didn't seem to want it extending any further.

"Are you reading this for school or something?" I asked, glancing up at him as I tore his receipt from the printer and placed it inside the front cover.

"I graduated in May."

I felt my cheeks warm. Gwen did mention that earlier—I should've remembered.

"I like Tolstoy," he added.

"Gotta love the classics," I said, forcing a laugh.

James stood there for a moment, seeming to contemplate whether or not a response was necessary. He met my eyes for a second, and I could've sworn a smile pulled at the corners of his lips.

"Some people like reading from authors other than Austen, but to each their own I guess," he said.

Has he been watching me on my breaks at the barn?

James's eyes drifted to my book again and then back to me, but I didn't dare let my gaze waver from his face, unwilling to let him think he could affect me with his petty jabs—even though I'd technically started it.

I cleared my throat and said, "I've already read *Anna Karenina*. Twice, actually. And some of us prefer the female perspective, something you obviously wouldn't understand."

I rolled my eyes as I turned my attention back to the computer to exit out of the transaction. In my peripheral, I watched as James reached into his shoulder bag, pulled out a book of his own and placed it in front of me.

"Edith Wharton was female, was she not?" James said with the *slightest* hint of sarcasm. A copy of *The Age of Innocence* stared me in the face, and I felt my insides twist.

"Touché," was all I could muster in response. I slipped his new book into a brown paper bag and pushed it across the counter toward him. James collected his belongings and glanced at my nametag before turning to leave.

"See you around, Charlotte," he said over his shoulder as he made his way toward the exit.

"It's Charlie!" I called after him, but my words were overshadowed by the sound of the door as it swung closed, leaving me alone once again.

Chapter 8

A crack of thunder rumbled in the distance as I rode Patterson around the outdoor arena, warning of a storm quickly approaching. Jeff was on the ground, shouting directions at me to keep my heels down and loosen my grip on the reins.

"You're giving him mixed signals with your positioning," Jeff yelled. He studied my form from the center of the arena with his hands on his hips.

"Sorry!" I called back, trying to focus. The second I'd fix my feet in the stirrups, I would mess up the reins, or my posture, or my eye line.

Watch where you're going, not the horse.

"Okay, now bring him to a trot, no posting yet. I just want you to get used to how it feels. Keep your eyes up and try to stay balanced. Your legs and core should be engaged, but not tense."

Try really hard, but make it look effortless. This whole sport felt like a contradiction.

Patterson quickened his footing as I dug my heels into his sides, bouncing me up and down in what seemed to me like a random rhythm. I felt myself slipping to the left on the saddle and Gwen's warning echoed in my thoughts.

Everybody falls.

Well, not me, I decided. At least not today.

My form might not have won at the Grand Prix, but it was enough to satisfy Jeff's expectations for the lesson. After a few successful loops around the arena, he told me to hop off, and we walked back to the barn together as the clouds continued to roll in.

The cool air felt good in my lungs as I lunged Copper around the indoor round pen that afternoon. After putting Patterson away, I'd found a note on Copper's stall requesting I give him some decent exercise in preparation for some local shows coming up. Nils couldn't make it to the barn that day, so I took it upon myself to help him out. He was always nice to me—it was the least I could do.

The lunge ring was quickly becoming my favorite hiding place at the stables. It was sort of liberating being in there all alone. I felt myself getting dizzy as Copper circled around me again and again. I still couldn't believe I had the authority to do any of this. It seemed like Ebony trusted me more than I trusted myself.

"Whoa," I said, bringing the horse to a halt. I turned my back to grab the lead rope that I'd tossed in the sand. Copper met me in the center of the space, nudging me with his nose, and I reached into my pocket and fed him a mint to show my appreciation for his good behavior.

Other than a few minor slip-ups, Copper had been relatively tame today, which made my life a lot easier. As I clipped the lead rope onto Copper's halter, I noticed the door sliding opening and a pair of boots stepping inside.

"Is that all you've got?" Ren walked towards me with a grin on his face. His pale blue scrubs contrasted with his olive complexion, and his eyes lit up the way they usually did when he looked at me. "Copper looks like he's barely broken a sweat."

I knew he didn't mean it as anything more than playful banter, but to me, it felt like criticism—cold and prickly under my skin.

I swallowed, trying to come up with an excuse for my inadequacy besides the obvious—that I had no business being here at all. Maybe I wasn't pushing Copper hard enough? It was difficult for me to lunge horses by myself. I never really knew if I was doing everything perfectly, and I couldn't shake the fear that I could easily get hurt.

"I'm just switching directions," I lied, dropping the lead rope behind me and hoping Ren wouldn't notice. I gave the horse a quick pat on the neck and stuffed the empty mint wrapper in my back pocket. "Copper will be fully exercised by the time I'm through with him. Don't you worry." I punctuated my words for emphasis.

"Let's see what he can do," Ren said, standing next to me now in the center of the ring. As much as being scrutinized by Ren intimidated me, I also felt my shoulders relax and my reflexes slow with the realization that he could save me if things went horribly wrong.

I'd always been most afraid of dangers I couldn't see coming, like the ones that lingered just beneath the surface of this place, invisible yet ever present. The barn was peaceful most of the time, bucolic even—something I might envision behind heavy eyelids to help me get to sleep at night—but things were never as harmless as they seemed.

It reminded me of how I'd felt the week before when I'd swum in the ocean for the first time. As much as I'd tried to enjoy it, with each breaststroke and each kick of my legs, I was hyper-aware of what could be lurking just below my feet.

Everything here was calm on the surface too, with the impeccable stables and expensive clothes. But one false step, and it could all go wrong in the blink of an eye—James's mom was the perfect example of that. When I looked back at Ren, though, he didn't seem to be concerned at all, just waiting patiently for me to show him what I was made of.

I quickly got Copper up to a canter, working him a bit harder this time, admittedly to impress Ren. The horse kept trying to slow to a trot, but I followed closely to keep him in line.

"Not too shabby for the new girl," Ren said as I circled him. He wore a warm and inviting smile, the very antithesis of James. I felt a sense of good faith when Ren spoke to me, like he saw some hidden, untapped potential in me that I couldn't see myself. I wanted to believe him and enjoy the attention, but like so many other outwardly pleasant aspects of my life, it just gave me a pit in my stomach. I didn't know anything about him, not really. He, too, was good on the surface, but I still wasn't sure what hid beneath the waves. And he didn't know me well enough to know how he really felt either. I knew I'd shatter his rose-colored view of me sooner or later.

I brought Copper back down to a trot, mostly because I was tiring myself out trying to keep up, and turned back to Ren.

"Maybe I'm not hopeless after all," I said. A sarcastic joke for him or a genuine revelation for me, I wasn't sure what I'd meant it as.

"I'm impressed," Ren said, grinning at me.

"I like to think I catch on quickly," I smiled back at him before getting the horse to change directions, "once I put my mind to things."

"And what do you usually put your mind to? Other than being an expert equestrian, I mean." Ren's blatant curiosity was disarming. I felt his eyes on me with every step I took.

"I've noticed you read a lot…" he added, his voice trailing off, as if to let me finish the sentence. I hadn't realized so many people were keeping tabs on me here. Hopefully, Ren didn't have the same aversion to my love of Jane Austen as James.

"I do like to read," I said. "And I like to take photos...and I have a passion for switching college majors one too many times."

Ren raised an eyebrow at that. "Which one did you eventually land on?"

"Perpetually undecided, at least during freshman year. None of the courses really stood out to me, and my academic advisor got sick of me changing my mind all the time." I glanced at him again. "I'm sure I'll figure something out by the time my gen eds are done."

"You said you take pictures...so why not study photography?"

"Ha—I wish," I said flatly. "It's more of a hobby for me, just for fun and for my photo journal. I'm not like...a professional."

"Isn't that what school is for? To educate yourself and get better at what you're passionate about?"

"Not so much in the arts." I shrugged. I knew there was a certain amount of natural talent required that I didn't have. I could never find any solid proof that the lens through which I viewed the world was anything outside of the ordinary. It was something I'd accepted a while ago, and it felt almost self-indulgent to think otherwise.

"Art is subjective," Ren said. "I wouldn't sell myself short, if I were you."

The look in his eyes told me that he was being sincere, and his encouragement made my cheeks flush and my pulse speed up—or maybe it was the exercise.

What does he know anyway? He's never even seen my photos.

There was a firm knock on the door signaling that my time in here was almost up. The room had been booked at noon for a private training session since it had started raining outside. I checked my phone. 11:59 am.

Someone's punctual.

"We'll be out in a minute," I called towards the door as I slowed Copper to a walk to cool him down, but there was no response, only impatient silence. I secured the lead rope onto Copper's halter, forfeiting my final minute, and gave it a tug to guide the horse toward the exit. Ren followed closely as I slid open the door to reveal James leaning on the stall across the aisle. Somehow, he still looked rigid that way—statuesque—as if he was trying to act casual but was all too aware that I was watching, scanning him for cracks that could reveal something.

I averted my eyes, remembering the bookstore incident. Interactions between us only seemed to result in embarrassment and regret on my part, two things I would rather avoid that afternoon. I was getting tired of cringing every time he crossed my mind.

"How's it going, James," Ren said, breaking the tension between us that was likely felt mostly by me.

"Hey," James said coolly, his gaze switching between us as he led Lightning into the arena. I heard the door slide shut as we walked away toward Copper's stall. Ren looked at me as if I'd made a face.

"You okay?" he asked.

"Uh-huh."

Ren shot me another look, not believing me.

"Did I miss something?" he said.

I blinked at him and did my best to reverse the expression James had brought out in me, but Ren was determined to get an answer.

"Okay, fine," I said. "I just don't think James likes me very much."

"What?" Ren's eyes narrowed. "Why would you think that?"

"It's my own fault," I said, forcing a laugh. "I seem to have developed a talent for doing all the wrong things whenever he's around."

"He doesn't dislike you, Charlie," Ren said, his tone blunt.

I walked Copper into his stall and unhooked the halter from behind his ears. Stepping back into the aisle, I carefully latched the door and hung the halter on its hook, then turned back to Ren.

"How would you know?" I said.

He gave me a sideways glance. "I can just tell."

"Well, I assure you, you're wrong, even though I wish you weren't."

"You wish I weren't?" Ren's signature smile seemed strained.

"It would make my life a lot easier not having to worry about messing up around him all the time."

"Oh." Ren's face softened. "He's not that bad once you get to know him."

I sighed. "So I've been told."

As I turned into my dad's driveway after my shift, my phone buzzed in the cupholder beside me.

Call from Mom.

I hit decline without hesitation and left my phone behind in the car as I went inside to make a late lunch.

Chapter 9

Mucking out thirty stalls is a lot of work for a team of two stable hands, yet somehow, I was given the inconceivable task of doing it all by myself for the day. Apparently, half the staff had decided to take a vacation in the same week, leaving me to pick up the slack. I told myself I could handle it as I walked away from Ebony's office, muckrake in hand. I was getting stronger every day, so it wouldn't be impossible, it just wasn't going to be fun.

I grabbed a wheelbarrow from out back and dragged it toward the first stall on the first aisle. Taking a deep breath—but not too deep, because the smell of soiled shavings lingered nearby—I began mucking with as much positivity as I could muster.

By the time I got to the tenth stall, I desperately wanted to give up. I could feel beads of sweat dripping down my back under my T-shirt and pieces of hair sticking to my neck. I filled the wheelbarrow to the brim for the fourth time and steered it back towards the muck heap to dispose of its contents, and as I rounded the corner of the second aisle, I saw Zuri grooming Sophie in her stall. She waved at me as if nothing appeared to be wrong.

Maybe I don't look quite as disgusting as I feel? One could dream.

I pushed the wheelbarrow over the threshold of the barn with all my strength and stepped outside into the misty morning air. It was cooler outside, even as the sun broke through the clouds, and I took a millisecond to savor it before continuing on. I reached the muck heap, pushed the wheelbarrow up the ramp, and flung it over and into the pile—it was a lot heavier than it looked. As I pulled the now-empty wheelbarrow back towards me with the last shred of energy I had, it got stuck in the pile and pulled me, arms first, into the muck heap.

I caught myself palms first in the scratchy, squishy pile and internally screamed in disgust. Although the pile was made up of mostly lightly soiled shavings and hay, I could still smell the horse manure beneath me. I pushed myself off the heap as fast as humanly possible and brushed off some of the germy debris that was now clinging to my sweaty clothes and skin. The all-too-familiar stench of horse urine was inescapable as I tried for a second time to force the wheelbarrow back to a horizontal position. I pulled it again with everything I had, but overestimated this time, instead falling backward into the dirt. I felt tears of frustration welling in my eyes, but I forced them away.

What kind of stable hand can't even handle the muckheap?

To make matters worse, I had an audience. At that very inopportune moment, someone emerged from the path that came from the beach— that someone being James. He walked toward the men's locker room, and suddenly, the world around me seemed to shift into slow motion.

He was barefoot, with one hand holding a pair of boat shoes and the other tousling his dark, wet hair. He wore a pair of forest green swim trunks that cut off at the center of his unmistakably strong thighs—

probably from riding all the time. Every day was leg day for equestrians. My legs had felt like noodles after my first few lessons.

As James got closer, I could see saltwater dripping down his face and bare chest. His naturally fair skin was lightly kissed by the sun, leaving him even more radiant than usual.

I pictured it then, what it might be like bobbing up and down in the waves next to James, tasting salt on my lips and staring into his brown eyes, made golden from the light reflecting off the water and onto the solid planes of his face. I couldn't tell if I was jealous that he got to spend his morning that way or upset that I wasn't there to witness it. Instead, I was here, mucking out endless stalls and looking positively green with envy—or from exposure to the foul smell that now surrounded me. Whatever the feeling was, it quickly shifted to shame as I remembered the literal shit on my clothes. Yet again, I was all too aware of my inferiority here, comforted only by the fact that it definitely couldn't get much worse.

At first, James didn't seem to notice me sitting disheveled on the ground, covered in horse waste and day-old hay, but just as I thought I was out of the woods, I saw him crack a smile. He stifled a laugh, trying to cover it up by clearing his throat, and strolled into the locker room without a word.

Since I was unable to bury my head in my dirty hands, I got up and sprinted to my car to grab a change of clothes. I quickly rinsed off in the girl's locker room and tried my best to scrub the image of James looking like a Greek god from my memory before returning to work.

***

I clutched my shopping list in one hand and a to-go coffee mug in the other as I walked into Newport Grocery that afternoon. My dad had texted me earlier, saying that he wanted to make a tofu stir fry for family dinner tonight and asked me to pick up the ingredients. I went straight from the barn.

I took a gulp of what was left of my morning coffee, willing myself to stay alert, and as I made my way down the fake-meat aisle in search of my dad's tofu preference, I heard a familiar voice.

"Charlie?" I looked up to find Ren holding a jar of kimchi and looking back at me from the other end of the aisle.

"Hi," I said, trying to snap out of my mental fog. "What are you doing here?"

"Uh…buying groceries?" He gestured to his basket with the usual kindness in his eyes. "What else is there to do in a grocery store?"

"Sorry…I'm super out of it today. I just mucked out the whole barn all by myself," I said, pressing my fingers to my temple. "I'm surprised I even remember how to walk at this point."

"Look at you, settling nicely into the equestrian community." Ren chuckled as he stepped toward me. "Everyone's gotta pay their dues, it's just part of the sport."

"You should try telling that to our boarders," I said.

"Their dues happen to be paid in the form of money," Ren teased.

"How could I forget." I gave him a look that said, *woe is me.*

Ren's eyes drifted across my face. "You have a little something…" He gestured to my cheek.

I brought my hand to my face, feeling it flush. A grin tugged at the corners of Ren's lips as I tried to brush off whatever was there. No luck, he only grinned more.

"Allow me," he said, stepping closer. His thumb carefully grazed my skin, and he was close enough that I could feel his breath against my cheek.

There was something different about him today, maybe because he'd traded in his scrubs for a button-down flannel and jeans. I studied his face up close—his tan skin, the faint shadow from neglecting to shave that morning, the small scar just under his chin—I wondered how he'd gotten it.

"There," he said. "Much better."

I stood there, locked into his eyes for a moment too long before shifting my gaze to anything else.

"I can see why you make a great vet," I said, stepping back a bit.

I risked another glance at him, and Ren looked intrigued.

"You have an excellent bedside manner," I finished.

"I'm *technically* not a vet yet, but I appreciate the compliment," he replied with a smile that told me he was glad I'd said it anyway.

Ren turned away from me as a woman steered a cart into our aisle. Her eyes lit up at the sight of us.

"Who might this be?" she said with a playful smile.

"Mom, this is Charlie." He tilted his head in my direction. "She's the new stable hand at Seahorse."

"Oh! How wonderful, it's nice to meet you, Charlie. My son did mention some new faces at the barn," she said, turning to Ren before adding, "but you didn't tell me how pretty she is."

Ren's cheeks flushed in response, but he didn't contradict her.

His mom continued, "I've been so busy with farm calls that I haven't had the chance to come by Seahorse yet this summer. I'm Dr. Aki by the way, but you can call me Hana."

We talked for a minute about the current state of the barn's overall health, which horses were behaving better than others, how Hana's practice was doing, and what they were shopping for. Apparently, they also needed ingredients for their weekly family dinner tonight—they hadn't missed a week since Ren had moved out the year before. Hana looked remarkably well, especially having a son in his early twenties—her hair was slicked back into a low bun and a pair of sunglasses sat on the top of her head. After a few minutes, we ran out of small talk.

"It's nice to see a young woman like yourself pulling her weight at the barn," Hana said. "You're going to give the guys a run for their money."

"I don't know about that," I replied, "but thanks."

"Always humble, this one," Ren said.

"Maybe I'm just a realist," I replied before I realized how harsh it sounded. Hana laughed it off as if I'd been joking.

"Well, if there's ever an issue at the barn, even if you just need help with stalls or anything, you should give me a call," Ren said, and I could tell he meant it.

"That would actually be great," I said, letting myself smile at him.

"Here." He glanced at my pockets. "Let me give you my number."

I fished my phone out of my bag and handed it to him, all too aware of his mom's watchful eye as he typed his number. It felt almost old-fashioned being chaperoned like this—as if we needed to be properly introduced to each other's families before any serious connections could be formed.

"It was great to meet you," I said to Hana as Ren handed my phone back.

"Hope to see you again soon," she replied with a small wave as I turned down the next aisle to find the registers.

By the time I got home, my dad had started cooking some rice for the stir fry and was humming along to *Cello Suite No.1* playing from the kitchen radio. He gave me a one-armed hug when I walked in and took the grocery bags from my hands.

"Don't get too close," I warned him. "I smell gross."

"What happened to you?" he said with a laugh, getting a good look at me. I slumped onto a stool at the counter and put my head down.

"You don't want to know," I said, my voice muffled in my arms.

My dad didn't dwell on the subject, instead, he began unpacking the groceries. "Did you at least have a nice day?" he asked.

I had to admit, the hours of painstaking barn chores were surprisingly no longer top of mind.

"I did," I answered, my thoughts wandering back to the grocery store. I could almost feel warmth where Ren's hand had been.

"Just promise me you're being careful at the barn," my dad said—interrupting my daydream. "Make sure you wear a helmet whenever you ride."

"I will, I promise," I said, feeling almost guilty for making him worry.

"Why don't you go take a shower, and I'll handle the cooking," my dad said as he drained the tofu. I nodded, grateful to be excused as I made my way upstairs.

My thoughts began to swirl as the warm water washed away the evidence of my day, my mind switching in and out of focus as the afternoon came at me in flashes. Hana's knowing smile as she watched her son flirt with me. The golden flecks in Ren's eyes—only noticeable up close. The stinging of my palms and the scrapes on my knees as I fell into the dirt. The saltwater dripping in slow motion from James's skin. I remembered the heat in my cheeks and my clenched fists, but it was quickly overshadowed by the memory of that cheeky smirk on James's face—which he'd so poorly attempted to conceal—when he saw me lying there.

Just the thought of it thrilled me.

***

I had come to learn that the town of Newport was effortlessly charming on summer evenings. Zuri, Gwen, and I walked down one of the wharves that lined the harbor, passing ice cream shops and overpriced boutiques inside perfectly weathered buildings. We sat on the edge of the dock with a bag of blueberry scones and a tray of iced tea before distributing the goods between us.

Gwen took a huge bite of her scone as soon as she got her hands on the bag, and a smile spread across her face as she passed the rest to Zuri.

"These are, hands down, the best scones in all of Rhode Island," Gwen informed me, "and trust me, we've tried them all."

Zuri laughed. "Tea and scones is a bit of a weekly tradition for us." She reached out and squeezed Gwen's hand.

"And now it's a tradition for you too," Gwen added as Zuri handed me the bag.

My heart swelled in my chest. I liked having close friends here, I only hoped I wasn't intruding too much on their time together.

"Well, I'm honored," I said, breaking off a small piece of my scone and popping it in my mouth.

"So, Charles—can I call you Charles?" Gwen asked. I nodded. "Please explain your text from last night. What does '*Northanger Abbey* mud scene/veterinarian/tofu aisle' imply? Is that some kind of secret code we aren't aware of? And please tell me Ren is involved."

"I told you she would fall for Ren this summer," Zuri said as she took a sip of iced tea. She turned to me. "That *is* what's happening, right?"

"Not exactly," I said, then cracked a smile. "But yes, Ren was involved."

"I knew it!" Gwen said, jumping up and pointing at me as Zuri laughed. Very theatrical, these two. "Tell us everything."

Trying to explain the grocery store encounter without blushing proved to be more of a challenge than I'd anticipated. I didn't want to encourage Zuri and Gwen's overactive imaginations, so I told them the whole story in exact detail, trying to make it sound as practical as possible. They screamed excitedly as I reached the part where he'd offered me his number.

"He just felt bad for me after mucking all the stalls," I said, knowing it wasn't the full truth. "And shouldn't all barn staff members have the vet assistant's number in case of emergencies anyway?"

"Charlie, please stop fooling yourself," Zuri said. "It's *so* obvious that he's interested in you."

I knew this, I did. I knew what flirtation looked like. I'd longed for it ever since reading my first romance novel. But I couldn't accept it.

"I knew you'd end up with one of the older guys," Gwen added. "Girls who live in cities always give off a more mature vibe."

"I spent the first eighteen years of my life in Painesville, Ohio," I said, laughing now because they were both ridiculous and I was starting to love them for it. "And what do you mean older? Isn't Ren like twenty-two?"

"Twenty-three," they said in unison. I couldn't help but be amused by their enthusiasm. Then something stopped me. Something I remembered seeing in Ren's eyes as he'd stood so close to me. It had been fragile, that moment. His expression had been soft. I didn't like that. I could hurt him now. I could see it all over his face.

I needed to change the subject, so I pulled my camera out of my bag.

"The light is perfect right now," I said, snapping a few candids of the two of them eating their scones and sipping their tea through paper straws. The Newport crowd was apparently very into sustainability.

Another reason why Dad must love it here.

Through the viewfinder, I could see my surroundings from a new perspective. Zuri's face was glowing in the golden light—and surely from being so close to Gwen. The two of them looked so relaxed, so comfortable. It was peaceful between them.

I felt an ache in my chest as I watched the sunlight reflect off the water and dance over my friends' faces like firelight. It dawned on me then, that even my parents had once had moments like these, where everything had seemed so perfect. So *right*.

Gwen and Zuri made love look easy—but I knew better.

Chapter 10

I'd always thought that Mane and Tail shampoo was just an interesting branding method, but it turned out, it was actually meant for horses. As I stood in the wash bay with Roxie, a 12-year-old prize-winning Thoroughbred, I lathered up her mane and breathed in the familiar scent of the soap.

"There she is." I heard Hana's voice as she stepped onto the padded floor. I forced a smile, not because I didn't like her, but because I never really knew how to act around other people's moms. I did my best not to spray her with the shower hose as I rinsed Roxie off.

When I'd arrived at the barn that morning, I'd noticed that Ren's mom was in Ebony's office. She'd looked at me with a glimmer in her eyes as I'd passed by the doorway, like she knew something that I had yet to discover. I was sure she was just keeping an eye on me since, apparently, I was developing a friendship with her son.

"Dr. Aki—hi," I said, my sudsy hands reaching for the spigot to turn off the water.

"I'm glad to see you keeping yourself busy around here. Ebony was just telling me about your progress with riding." She was wearing light-wash jeans and a bright white windbreaker, seamlessly blending the equestrian and sailing styles that I was beginning to notice were popular in this town. "She says you're a natural."

"I assure you, she's exaggerating. I'm barely trotting," I said, twisting a ring back and forth on my damp index finger.

Hana nodded, her expression suggesting that she thought I was being modest—I wasn't.

"I'll have to tell Ren to give you a few pointers," she said. "He's always been an excellent rider, never much for competing though. I think it took the fun out of it for him. Still, I'm sure he would love to help *you*."

"I'll be sure to ask him when I see him," I said, reaching for a bottle of conditioner.

"He's around here somewhere," she said, glancing up and down the aisle. "Maybe you two will run into each other sooner than you think."

She winked at me so subtly that I almost convinced myself I'd imagined it, then said, "Alright, I've got to get back to the clinic. It was good to see you again, Charlie."

With that, she walked away, and I felt a strain in my cheeks as I turned off my smile. I was beginning to feel a bit like a zoo animal in this place.

After giving Roxie a thorough rinse, I grabbed a brush from the rack and began detangling the horse's dark hair. Other than a few flinches, Roxie lived up to her good reputation. I finished the process by squeegeeing the excess water off her back and spritzing her with fly spray.

"Good girl." I patted the horse's neck and unlatched the crossties that were holding her in place. Her ears twitched as I reattached the lead rope to her halter. "C'mon." I clicked my tongue to get her moving.

I walked Roxie back to her stall, her feet clip-clopping against the cobblestones, and led her through the open door. Usually, horses turned around instinctively, making it easy for me to take off their halter and exit the stall. This time was different.

When I reached the back of the stall, Roxie put up a small fight, distracted by a bit of hay in the corner. After tugging her a few times, I gave up, unhooked the leap rope, and unlatched her halter. As I slid it off her nose, the halter slipped from my hands and into the shavings below. I reached down to pick it up, and by the time I was upright, Roxy had noticed the wide-open stall door and was trotting away towards the front of the barn.

With the halter and rope still in hand, I took off after her, hoping no one would notice my mistake—but mostly hoping I didn't just accidentally let one of our best horses loose. I should've never left the stall door open, but I didn't have time to dwell on it. My chest tightened as I saw her pass the threshold of the barn, moving quickly towards the tall grass in the front fields.

Of course, she headed for the grass. Horses were always thinking about their next meal.

Panting now, I stopped at the edge of the barn and looked around. One side of the field had a white fence, the other was open to the road. Out of the corner of my eye, I could see Jenna leaning against her car door in the parking lot, watching the chaos unravel. She laughed to herself and just shook her head, making no effort to help me.

Without much time to consider my options, I took off running and tried to ignore the voice in my head telling me how stupid I looked.

"Charlie? What are you doing?" I heard Ren shout from behind me. I turned to look at him, unable to hide the panic on my face, before continuing after the runaway horse. I heard the sound of his footsteps as he chased after me into the grass.

As Roxie broke into a canter, I broke into a sweat. Ren quickly passed me, his height working in his favor. He got to the edge of the road, blocking it off as best he could with his arms outstretched. I followed his lead and covered the gap as we cornered Roxie into the fence. As if fueled by the excitement of temporary freedom, Roxie was more energetic than ever. She tried dodging us, whinnying and running back and forth as we closed in on her.

Finally, I got close enough to slip the halter back on the horse's nose and pulled it over her ears. She stamped her hooves a few times before eventually giving in to my control once again.

Ren's chest glistened with sweat as he stepped towards me, his sage button-down shirt coming undone.

"What happened?" he said, letting out a breath that made his shoulders relax.

"I left the stall door open by mistake," I admitted between breaths, my chest heavy from the exercise. "So stupid."

My own negative assessment of my actions seemed to make obsolete the speech Ren was likely about to give me on the importance of barn safety. His slightly furrowed brow and tight lips morphed into a smirk.

"Well, this better have taught you not to do that again," he teased, shaking his head.

"I'll be more careful, I promise," I said as I rested my free hand on my knee and looked back at the barn. We'd run pretty far.

Ren eyed my grass-stained pants and sweaty face and took a step toward me.

"You've developed quite a talent for becoming absolutely *filthy* every time I see you," he said, grinning still. "Is that a new goal of yours?"

"You wish," I said, tossing my head back in a laugh, adrenaline still rushing through me.

I pulled a piece of grass from my hair and tossed it at Ren in retaliation. He swatted it away before reaching down to grab one end of the lead rope in my hands. He pulled me closer with the other end still in my grasp, looking for something behind the smile on my face, something that matched what I saw behind his. I dug my nails into the rope, feeling it fraying beneath my fingers. Ren was like a ray of light—next to him, I felt like a dark storm.

"We better get back," I said, my chest still rising and falling as I tried to slow my breathing. I dropped the rope and stepped back.

"I'll race you," Ren said.

In a split second, he launched himself from the ground onto the horse's back. He was *strong*. I took note of the defined veins on his arms as his fingers gripped the lead rope and the broadness of his shoulders in that shirt. Ren grinned, catching my eyes all over him, before digging his heels into Roxie's sides and cantering toward the barn, leaving only a small cloud of dirt in his wake.

"Hey!" I shouted after him, but he was long gone, laughing as he got farther away. It was so easy for him to be charming when he wanted to. It gave me a prickly feeling in my stomach. The more time I spent here, the more I could feel my tight grip on control loosening. I shook my head, trying not to think about it, and took off running.

Chapter 11

A breeze blew through the open barn doors, cooling me off as I finished the evening chores. My dad had had a dental appointment that morning and had needed me to cover for him at the bookstore, so Ebony had let me switch my barn shift to the evening to accommodate him.

It was so much quieter at this time of day—barely anyone was around as I did the final sweep through the aisles, ridding the cobblestones of any stray hay or shavings that had accumulated during the afternoon feed. The sun was just starting to set, and light filtered through the dusty windows of each stall, casting a soft glow. This was the prettiest time of day here, I decided. Again, my palms itched for my camera.

There was something therapeutic about sweeping the barn. No matter what happened each day or how many messes were made, everything was reset by the next morning like it never happened.

Nils seemed to be the only person left at the stables aside from myself. From down the aisle, I watched him put Copper in his stall, latch the door, and walk toward me on his way to the parking lot.

"Working late today, huh?" Nils said, passing by me.

"Yeah, I've got the evening shift," I replied. Small talk had never been my forte.

"You're riding too, right?" he asked.

"A few lessons a week."

"Good," he said. "We could use someone like you on the team. Most of these people have never mucked a stall in their life."

"So I've been told," I said.

Nils gave me a look that said, *I've been there,* as he walked off.

I pushed a small pile of dirt and dust toward the end of the first aisle, and as I got closer, I noticed Lightning's head wasn't poking out of the last stall like it usually was.

Maybe she's sleeping?

I'd learned the hard way last week that horses often lay down at night when they sleep. I'd accidentally woken one up and nearly got stepped on.

I slid open the stall door and pushed a few stray pieces of hay inside, making sure to leave nothing on the cobblestones. The stall was surprisingly clean for this time of day—turn-in must have been hours ago—and Lightning was standing towards the back of her stall, facing away from me. This standoffish behavior wasn't like her. I stepped closer and gave her a scratch under her mane.

Instead of nuzzling my arm or perking up her ears like she usually would, Lightning began to paw at the ground, still not acknowledging me. I checked her grain bowl, and it was full to the brim, practically untouched. For a horse who could eat an entire bale of hay in one day if allowed, this was concerning.

I stood next to her for a minute, trying to cheer her up with a molasses treat from my pocket, when it hit me. I thought back to the day I'd met

Ren—when he'd told me about the disease that kills horses without much warning. He'd told me about the symptoms.

Not eating, pawing the ground…

I broke into a cold sweat—I wasn't qualified to handle this—and wracked my brain for what to do.

Make sure to keep the horse moving. That was all I could remember.

I scrambled for the halter and lead rope that hung on the stall door, slipped it over Lightning's nose—despite my shaking hands—and hooked the strap behind her ears. Clicking my tongue, I gave her a small tug to get moving into the aisle. With my free hand, I pulled out my phone and searched for Ren's number, trying my best to steady my breathing as I dialed.

He picked up on the third ring.

"Hey, Charlie," Ren answered. I could hear a smile in his voice. I did my best to gather my thoughts as my mind raced.

"Hi, um, I'm at the barn right now, and I was cleaning up when I noticed Lightning acting weird. I know I'm not an expert or anything, but the symptoms seem to line up with that disease you told me about…colic? I have her walking now, but I think you might want to come by to make sure she's okay," I said, speaking much too quickly. My heart pounded as I dragged the reluctant horse down the second aisle.

I glanced back as Lightning lifted one of her legs and kicked herself in the stomach.

"She just kicked herself, Ren," I added, panic rising in my throat. "I don't really know what to do here…I'm worried about her."

"It's a good thing you called," Ren said, his tone turning deadly serious. "I'm on my way."

He hung up before I could say anything else. I took a deep breath, relieved to have done something right, but when I looked back at Lightning, she looked even more miserable. I hoped that Ren would get there sooner rather than later.

Barely ten minutes had passed when Ren rushed into the barn with a duffle bag in hand. He sprinted to meet me in the center of the aisle, but his eyes were fixed only on the horse.

"Any changes?" he asked as he started his examination.

"Nothing new since I called."

"I'll take it from here," he said, to my relief, as he grabbed the lead rope from my hands. "Can you give James a call? He'll want to be here. His number should be in the address book in the office."

I sprinted to the office and frantically pulled open the drawers of Ebony's desk in search of the book.

This horse can't die. Not James's mom's horse. Not on my watch.

I found his number on the second page and dialed. The phone only rang once before going to voicemail. He must've declined the call.

I'd forgotten that James didn't have my number. He probably just assumed I was some telemarketer from Ohio. I wasted no time, dialing again in hopes that he'd get a clue.

"Hello?" he answered finally.

"Hi, James—"

"Who is this?"

"It's Charlie."

"Charlie who?"

"From the barn." I ignored the jab in my stomach. *Now isn't the time.*

"How did you get this number?"

"That's not important," I said. "Lightning is sick. I think you should—"

"What? What happened?"

"I don't know for sure, but I think she's colicing. Ren's here now, so—"

The line went dead before I could finish speaking.

"James is on his way," I said, sprinting back to Ren's side. He was checking Lightning's gums when I arrived.

"I'm going to need you to assist me with the rest of the examination, can you handle that?" Ren asked, still not looking at me. He turned to grab something from his bag.

"Whatever you need," I said, rolling up my sleeves. Ren handed me the lead rope.

"Don't let her move," he said, and I nodded.

Ren pulled a needle out of the duffle bag. His skillful hands surveyed Lightning's stomach before puncturing the skin. I almost turned away, not wanting to watch as he began to check Lightning's abdomen, but I didn't want Ren to think he couldn't count on me.

"No fluid, so luckily, it's not peritonitis. I think she has a case of gas colic, so it's good that you kept her walking." Ren rummaged through his bag, muttering under his breath. "Banamine—that's what we'll need to give her to stop the pain."

Lightning squirmed in an attempt to get free, but I only gripped the lead rope tighter and used my free hand to rub her nose. Ren administered the painkiller with a syringe, and we waited for it to take effect as we walked her up and down the aisle.

We both kept our eyes glued to Lightning, searching for any sign that she was going to be okay. Each tick of the clock on the wall seemed further apart until finally, Ren spoke.

"It looks like the meds have kicked in, which is a good sign."

"Does that mean she's out of the woods?" I asked.

"Not yet, but it's promising. We might need to administer some mineral oil through a stomach tube in case there's an impaction...I should call my mom for a second opinion," Ren said, stepping back and exhaling some of the tension from his chest. He looked relieved, which I took as a good sign. I watched closely as he dialed his mom's number. He was only a few years older than me, young enough to still have some boyish qualities. It was strange to see him acting so grown up.

"I'll be right back. Do your best to keep Lightning moving," Ren said as he turned towards the door and held his phone to his ear. "Mom, are you there?"

As Ren stepped outside for some privacy, James stepped into the stables. He found me in the second aisle, and I stopped walking so he could check on his horse. James's eyes were glazed over and there was a subtle sheen of sweat on his brow as he carefully brushed through Lightning's forelock with his fingers and looked for any signs of discomfort.

I wasn't used to seeing James like this. His shirt buttons were misaligned, and his hands were shaking. I felt the urge to reach for him, but I stopped myself. That was probably the last thing he wanted—it could actually make things worse.

"Ren says Lightning is on the mend, he just wants to monitor her to be sure," I said in an attempt to alleviate the terror in his eyes. "She responded pretty quickly to the pain meds, so things are looking up."

James took a step back and rubbed his neck, his breathing returning to a normal pace. He nodded.

The stillness of the barn was louder now that it was just the two of us. I was suddenly aware of every creek of the woodwork, every chirp of the crickets, and every shallow breath I took.

"Did she look scared?" James said after a moment. He looked at me for the first time since he'd arrived, sending goosebumps down my arms.

"She was in some pain, but it didn't last too long," I assured him, seeing concern wash over his face. James was always in control, but now he was unraveling before me—it felt like something I shouldn't be allowed to see. Maybe it was the horse's connection with his mom or the fear of losing something he loved again, but this seemed to have opened something up in him, something he usually kept locked away.

"It'll be okay," I said with no way of truly knowing. James's eyes were so sad and scared, and I couldn't stop myself. Against my better judgment, I reached my hand out to comfort him, but James grabbed my wrist before I could touch him.

"How would you know?" he muttered, giving my hand back with the unspoken condition that I would keep far away from him.

"I…I'm sorry…I didn't mean—" I managed to say before Ren interrupted us.

"I just got off the phone with my mom," Ren said as he jogged toward us. "She agreed with everything I said, we need to keep her moving until she is eating normally and try to get her to drink some water. My mom will be here soon to check on her, but someone is going to have to stay here overnight."

"Of course, I'll stay with Lightning," James said. He reached out to shake Ren's hand. "Thank you for coming in so late."

"You should be grateful to this one," Ren said, nudging my arm. "She's the one who called me. Charlie kept Lightning walking until I got here. If she hadn't noticed Lightning's symptoms, I don't know what would've happened."

Ren gave my shoulder a quick squeeze, but I was still staring at James. I watched as he lifted his eyes to look at me.

"Thank you," he said, not breaking eye contact so I knew he meant it.

Ren looked from James to me. His soft smile seemed forced now, but before he could say anything more, his phone rang.

"I should take this," Ren said as he reached for the lead rope in my hands. "I'll walk Lightning around the stables, you two should take a breather." He stepped back into the night air, leaving James and me alone again.

We stood there without speaking. I stared at my shoes and twisted the Ohio-shaped charm on my necklace until it dug into my fingertips. When I got the courage to look up, I saw James staring back at me. His eyes took stock of my face, my hair, my neck. I watched as he rediscovered the girl who he'd been ignoring for weeks.

"I owe you an apology," he said, his gravelly voice breaking the deafening silence. "I may have misjudged you."

I blinked at him, stunned.

"My temper can sometimes get the best of me, but that's no excuse for my behavior," he continued. "I have a hard time with new people…I'm sorry if I made you feel…unwelcome."

Each word came out like pulled teeth, and although his exterior was still rigid and cold, I could sense him thawing from within. Somewhere in there, was an undetected warmth that I had yet to encounter until this very moment.

"It's okay," I whispered, wanting to add, *I think I might've misjudged you, too.*

✳✳✳

Sleep was an impossible task as I pulled the blankets over my fatigued body and tried to lull myself into unconsciousness. I may have been exhausted physically, but my mind had never felt more awake. James's face flashed behind my closed eyelids, pain displayed on every feature, on the surface for all to see—or in this case, just me. Everything about him felt new to me now.

I replayed the whole night in my head, remembering the strained smile on Ren's face as he'd watched James thank me—jealousy didn't suit him. Ren's attention towards me had not gone unnoticed, but did he really think James would ever pay that kind of attention to me? Other than showing gratitude for me saving his horse, James couldn't stand to be near me.

After a moment, it dawned on me. Ren hadn't been upset by the fondness in James's eyes while looking at me, but the fondness in mine looking back.

Chapter 12

I was eager to get back to work as I drove to the stables Monday morning, feeling energized by my weekend away. I hadn't done much—other than working my shift at the store—and I'd been distracted for most of it anyway, still ruminating over everything that had happened on Friday night. The bookstore shift had dragged as I'd tried to make progress reading *Northanger Abbey*. Each page felt just out of focus, leaving me rereading the same paragraph on a loop until I eventually gave up.

This morning couldn't come soon enough, and when I'd rolled over in bed an hour before my alarm, I'd decided I couldn't wait any longer. I'd texted Gwen and Zuri, suggesting a sunrise beach ride, and they'd quickly agreed to accompany me. Even after a few weeks of lessons, I still didn't quite feel safe on my own yet.

Still a bit groggy from my restless night's sleep, I took my time grooming and tacking up Caramel, a sandy-colored lesson horse. I saddled her up and hopped on without using the block, putting my developing strength to good use.

I'd noticed that my barn chores were starting to take effect on my body. At the beginning of the summer, I could barely lift a bag of shavings and drag it from the supply room to the stalls. Now, I could carry a full bag without breaking a sweat, which sped up stall duty a lot. I could see the difference too—my arms and stomach looked leaner, my shoulders were definitely more toned—and my tight riding clothes highlighted these changes even more.

The horses seemed unphased by the time of day as we rode quietly to the beach, letting the briny air wake us up. Zuri and Gwen rode side by side a few feet in front of me, and Caramel blindly followed their horses' lead. Trail riding had become more meditative than it was stimulating as I got more comfortable with it. My mind wandered freely in the open air, and the slow swaying of the horse's back felt like being rocked back to sleep.

The sun was just peeking out over the horizon as we reached the shore. The clouds were painted a soft pink color, and the sky faded to orange as it dipped toward the ocean.

I took a luxurious breath and closed my eyes. Here, I could zoom out on my life—the resurgence of my otherwise careless mother, the seemingly insignificant interpersonal moments that haunted my thoughts, the ever-growing debt that weighed heavily on my mind, the general instability of everything I'd once believed in. Here, I could imagine all my problems were like the tiny grains of sand on this beach, just insignificant specks of earth, and for a moment I could almost forget that they even existed at all.

I wanted to bottle up this moment for safekeeping to have when I was back in Boston come September, so I took out my phone and snapped a picture. It wasn't quite the same, but it was better than nothing.

The stables were alive and bustling with activity by the time we got back. The three of us dismounted in the yard and walked our horses into the barn.

"We should do this again before the summer ends," Zuri said, giving Sophie a carrot from her pocket.

"Definitely," Gwen said. "I almost forgot how beautiful the sunrise is on Second Beach."

I smiled at them as we stepped into the first aisle. "It might actually be worth getting up so early."

James stepped out of the first stall with a lead rope in his grasp, probably taking Lightning for a walk around the grounds since she'd been feeling better. Ren had been texting me updates on Lightning's recovery all weekend as his mom monitored the horse's symptoms. Once Lightning was acting normally and eating again without showing signs of pain, she was finally deemed to be out of the woods. According to Hana, we caught the colic early enough to prevent it from causing any long-term effects. With some rest, Lightning would be good as new.

As James approached the three of us, I expected a return to his usual chilly disregard of my existence, or maybe a glance in our direction to avoid a collision, but—against all odds—James slowed his purposeful strides as he passed me by.

"Hey," he said, singling me out amongst my friends. My heart nearly jumped out of my chest.

"Hey," I responded, mimicking his nonchalant tone to the best of my ability. As I met his eyes for a moment, I noticed that they held something entirely new today.

Respect, perhaps?

Then, just as quickly, we went on our separate ways.

The interaction was incredibly small, yet profound somehow—at least to me. The contrast between his usual treatment of me and this tiny acknowledgment of my presence was not lost on Gwen or Zuri, who were now staring at me with wide eyes.

"What was that about?" Zuri said, poking my arm with her finger.

I shrugged, remembering that I still hadn't filled them in about what had happened Friday night—I was still deciphering it myself.

"Charles? Why does James suddenly not hate you anymore?" Gwen blinked at me. She always needed to be the first to know the latest barn gossip. "Please spill immediately."

"It's a long story," I said, giving Caramel a scratch on her nose.

"We've got time," Zuri replied, leaning against the nearest stall and crossing her arms.

I looked around to make sure all those involved were safely out of earshot before leaning closer to my friends and lowering my voice to a near whisper.

"During my chores the other night, on Friday, Lightning was acting weird. I thought she might be colicing, so I called Ren to make sure everything was okay," I said.

"Okay, Charlie, the horse expert," Gwen said with a smirk.

"It turns out Lightning really wasn't okay," I continued. "When James showed up, Ren told him I'd probably saved his horse's life. Lightning is doing fine now; she seems to be recovering nicely.

"So, you're telling me that you managed to be alone, after hours, in the barn with not only the hot vet…but also James?" Gwen exclaimed as quietly as she could manage.

"Ren's a vet *assistant*, but yes," I said, still a bit surprised by it all myself. Nothing like this ever happened to me in Ohio.

"Semantics, Charles," Gwen said.

"So, you admit that Ren is hot?" Zuri teased.

I rolled my eyes.

"Let's not skip over the fact that you totally saved James's horse," Gwen said, beaming. "You're a hero, Charles!"

"It was a one-time thing," I assured them. "I was just in the right place at the right time."

"And you were the right person who knew exactly the right thing to do," Gwen said. "Don't sell yourself short—and I can't believe you didn't tell us right when it happened. I propose dinner at my place tonight, so we can properly catch up on everything. I want a full recap, reenactment style, with *every dirty detail*." She grinned at me before walking Dandelion into his stall.

As I finished up my afternoon chores, I heard the clip-clopping of hooves against cobblestones and looked up to see James riding Copper into the barn, fresh off a trail. He must've been exercising Nil's horse for him and taking the opportunity to keep training while Lightning was in recovery.

James dismounted, unclipped his helmet—freeing his dark wavy hair—and walked towards Copper's stall where Jenna was waiting. The crease in his brow told me he hadn't been expecting company.

I could feel my usually fixed moral compass move slightly off-kilter as I slipped into a nearby stall and quieted my breathing. It was wrong to listen in on people's conversations—a total invasion of privacy—I knew that, but I couldn't help myself. I could never help myself around James lately.

"Jenna?" James's tired voice said her name like a question.

"I heard about Lightning," she said.

I strained my eyes, peeking over the stall gate until I had a clear enough view of the two of them. Jenna reached out to touch James's arm, and he let her.

I wonder what that's like.

She rubbed her thumb up and down his bicep in small strokes like it was something she'd done a million times. James watched carefully as she did this, something hopeful playing on his features. My stomach twisted.

"It was a close call," James said.

"Well, Lightning's special. I wouldn't dream of her getting taken down by a little colic," Jenna said wryly.

This made James soften. He gave her a small smile.

"Okay, well, I just wanted to make sure you were okay," Jenna finished. She turned to walk away.

"Jenna?" James said.

"Yeah?" She readily pivoted to face him again—like she knew he'd stop her—and her expression was a caricature of empathy.

James took a breath and let it go, like it had been the first one he'd taken in a while. Had he been holding his breath for her this whole time?

"Thanks," he said. Something in his eyes told me he'd been waiting for this interaction for a while.

"Anytime," Jenna said as she stepped back into the aisle and walked away.

After work, I stopped at home for a change of clothes, then drove to Gwen's. I rang the doorbell and waited as the sound of footsteps running downstairs and a dog barking escaped from inside.

"Coming!" I heard Gwen shout through the door. She swung it open, wearing her usual cafe getup, and held back the tiny furball attempting to tackle me.

"Zuri's almost here," Gwen said as I followed her through the mudroom and the double living room. Every inch of the house was spotless—even the air smelled of citrus and fresh laundry. When we reached the kitchen, Gwen propped herself up on the white granite countertop and reached for a jar of peanut butter, eating from it with a spoon.

"I brought some extra pastries home from work, if you want some," she said, gesturing towards the fridge. "The cafe wasn't super busy today, so there's a bunch of scones left. Feel free to help yourself."

"Thanks," I said as I opened the door to the fridge. "I'm starving after lunging Claudia today. I swear it ends up being more of a workout for me than for her."

"Still having trouble keeping her moving in the right direction?" Gwen asked.

"Uh-huh, and I've gotten way too comfortable jumping in front of her. One day, she's going to knock me over."

Gwen laughed and jumped down from the counter at the sound of the doorbell, but before she could make it out of the room, Zuri walked in carrying two large pizza boxes.

"Your mom let me in," Zuri said, placing the boxes on the counter before giving Gwen a hug that was much more reserved than usual. "So, what are we talking about?"

"Charles was just telling me about one of her near run-ins with death at the barn," Gwen said, waving her hand as if it was nothing out of the ordinary.

"Just another day at Seahorse then?" Zuri said. I forced a laugh, but I didn't love that she wasn't entirely joking.

"Ladies, what could possibly be so funny?" A woman walked into the kitchen. "Are we talking about boys?"

Zuri shot Gwen a look—a millisecond of discomfort—before they went back to smiling.

"Always," Gwen said. "There's been a lot of drama at the barn since *someone* showed up this summer. Mom, this is Charles, the new stable hand I told you about."

"It's nice to meet you, sweetie." Gwen's mom gave me a welcoming smile as she helped herself to a slice of pizza. "You can call me Pam."

I nodded at her and smiled.

"Charlie has not one, but *two* boys chasing after her already," Zuri added.

"That is so not true…" I said, feeling my face heating up. My friends really loved to exaggerate.

"Good for you," Pam said, raising an eyebrow at me. "At least someone in this house is putting herself out there. Maybe you could try rubbing off on these too while you're at it."

Zuri, Gwen, and I shared another moment of uncomfortable eye contact.

"What?" Pam said. "Dating is an important social skill. I'm just looking out for you girls."

"And one day, I'm sure Zuri and I will both find someone, and when we do, we will tell you all about it. But for now, I choose to focus on Charles and live vicariously through her."

"Okay…well, you better keep me posted if anything changes. I want to be the first to know," Pam said, pointing at her daughter and chuckling as she turned to leave. *Like mother, like daughter.* "Enjoy your dinner, girls."

Usually, I would rather avoid this kind of speculation about my romantic pursuits—or lack thereof—but I knew that at this particular moment, I was being used as a scapegoat. And I couldn't blame Gwen for shifting the conversation to me when she couldn't talk about her own dating prospect, who just so happened to be sitting next to her eating a slice of pepperoni.

These types of conversations had been few and far between with my mother. Even under these circumstances, it was sort of nice to see that Gwen's mom cared so much, but it also reminded me of something I'd been missing out on without even realizing it.

Chapter 13

I'd stupidly left my window open before going to sleep, so it was brutally hot in my room when I woke up the next morning. The weather report threatened a week-long heat wave, and I was not looking forward to it. I surveyed the clothing options in my clean laundry bin and decided on a light blue top and some black athletic shorts so I wouldn't be dying in the sun when I picked the paddocks. I pulled the shirt over my head, and by the time I realized how cropped it was, I was too lazy to change.

My dad was already at the bookstore taking care of an early delivery by the time I went downstairs for breakfast, so I had the house to myself. I poured some iced coffee into a to-go cup, slipped on my mucking boots, and ran out the door with a granola bar between my teeth.

I was starting to enjoy this routine—being outside first thing in the morning, getting active. It was refreshing. After pulling into the barn parking lot, I stepped onto the yard and took a deep breath of salty, hay-scented air, letting the warmth of the sun wash over my skin.

When I walked into the barn, I noticed one of the older barn hands—in his late twenties if I were to guess—looking at me. His eyes lingered a bit longer than usual before he returned to distributing the morning hay. I looked down and rolled my eyes.

Guys are so predictable.

I stepped into Dandelion's stall and was glad to find Gwen inside, grooming her Palomino. She looked over at me as I re-hooked the stall guard and reached for a curry comb to help.

"Charles?" She raised an eyebrow at me.

"What?"

"Look at *you*," she said, stepping away from her horse. "You look hot."

"No, I don't."

"Someone's been hitting the gym," she teased.

"Or just mucking stalls all day."

"Whatever," Gwen said, accepting defeat. "Cute outfit though."

"Thanks." I shrugged, feeling my palms starting to sweat. "It's a million degrees out today, I just wanted to be comfortable."

"If you say so," Gwen practically sang her words as she returned her attention to brushing Dandelion's white mane.

"I have to go pick the paddocks," I said—a convenient excuse. "I just came in to ask if you wanted to go on a trail ride later. I think Caramel is free after a lesson at two, so I'll probably take her after that."

"I have training with my dad this afternoon for the Dad Derby, but I think I can make time for it after," Gwen said. "Meet me in the yard at quarter past?"

"Perfect," I said, stepping under the stall guard. I turned back to her. "Dad Derby?"

"It's a competition for all the riding team members' dads." Her eyes lit up. "My dad wins every year."

I should've guessed.

There were way too many events around here for me to keep up with all of them.

I prayed for a breeze as I dragged a wheelbarrow towards the back paddocks, feeling sweat dripping down my back. One by one, I picked each paddock until they were spotless, just how Ebony liked them. As I pushed the now-full wheelbarrow across the yard and towards the muck heap, I noticed Nils and James in one of the outdoor arenas. They were setting up strange-looking poles with rings on the tops of them. Both of them had what appeared to be a toy sword hanging from their belt loops, and they were laughing as they mounted their horses.

It was weird to see James laugh. And smile. It confused me.

I forced myself to look down and keep walking.

"Charlie!" Nils shouted.

I squinted against the rays of sunlight as I looked up at him. "Yeah?" I shouted back.

He gestured for me to come over to them, and I obliged, assuming one of their horses must've had an accident or something and they needed someone to pick it up before they pissed Ebony off by mucking up the arena.

"Have you played any mounted games before?" Nils asked.

James stayed silent, his eyes anywhere but on me.

I shook my head.

"James and I are about to battle it out in a round of sword races, and we need a referee. You in?"

I looked from Nils to James, unsure how I could be qualified to ref a game I'd never seen, let alone played. I would've assumed James was much too serious for games anyway.

What had he said once about childish antics…?

I shrugged. "Sure, why not."

Nils grinned. He quickly explained the rules and demonstrated what the game would look like. Each rider would canter along their own set of poles, parallel to their opponent with a sword outstretched, as if they were on a battlefield. The objective was to get as many rings on their sword as possible and cross the finish line first. Drop a ring, and the rider would be disqualified. It seemed easy enough to judge.

"We'll do three rounds in total, best two out of three wins," Nils explained as he led his horse to the starting point. He turned to James on the other side of the arena. "You ready to lose?"

James had a devilish look in his eyes as he said, "You wish."

Then they were off on their first race, swords at the ready as they dug their heels in and cantered towards the finish line. Dust clouded behind them as they sped along the poles, gathering the rings on their swords. James clearly won the round, crossing the line they'd drawn in the sand a good three seconds before his friend. I had to give it to him.

"One point, James," I said, letting my eyes meet his for only a moment. They glowed with the thrill of victory.

Nils nodded and patted his horse's back. "Again," he said, already halfway back to the starting point. This time, James was still faster, but he lost a ring on the third pole, giving Nils the win.

"Damn," James said under his breath as he pulled back on the reins. Nils followed with a smile on his face.

"One point, Nils," I said, brightening.

"Woohoo!" I heard someone yell. I turned around to see a bit of a crowd forming. Jenna was on the far side of the fence, eyeing James, and Gwen was right behind me.

"The boys love their mounted games," Gwen said, laughing and shaking her head. "Who's winning?"

"It's a tie," I said. "Next point wins."

I turned back to the guys to make sure they were ready. They both sat tall on their horses, prepared to battle it out for the win.

"Ready…set…go!" I yelled, and they launched forward even faster than before. James attacked each poll with precision, and Nils was practically galloping down the course.

It was close—too close. Each rider successfully secured all three rings on their sword, so the finish line would determine the winner. I half expected trumpets to sound as they raced forward like men in medieval times. James's jaw was clenched, and his eyes were focused, but Nils was smiling ear to ear.

I watched carefully as they crossed the finish line and the small crowd behind me cheered. It was a tie—I knew it was a tie—but that would be too easy. I wanted to have a little fun, and maybe I was drunk on my small taste of power. I couldn't let it go to waste.

"Nils wins," I yelled, to even more cheers. Nils did a victory lap around the arena, soaking up the glory. I glanced at Jenna, who now had a sour look on her face.

"Is she blind or something?" she said to the friends surrounding her, rolling her eyes. "It was obviously a tie."

I gritted my teeth and turned to Gwen on my other side.

"It was, you know," Gwen said, more quietly than Jenna. "It was totally a tie." She reached out and pinched my arm. "You're sneaky."

I shrugged, letting a small smirk cross my face before I turned my attention back to the boys. James had already dismounted his horse and was leading Lightning out of the arena.

"Good effort," I said, intentionally twisting the knife as he stepped toward me. My pulse buzzed when he met my gaze. This was too much fun, messing with him.

"Same to you, Charlotte," he said, his tone sarcastic—but not petty—as he towered over me. "You made some great calls."

"Thanks," I replied, smiling sweetly. I watched as his eyes traveled down to my exposed waist, then back up to my face in a split second. It was so quick that I almost didn't notice, but the look in his eyes told me he liked what he saw. I bit my lip.

"I'm glad to see Lightning's feeling better," I said, my cheeks getting hot. James nodded. "Me too."

We just looked at each other for a moment, and the air between us felt different.

"Well," I said, "if you ever need another ref, you know who to call."

James shook his head and chuckled. "Yeah, I'll keep that in mind."

Gwen looked at me with wide eyes as I turned away from James and walked back toward the barn, unable to contain the grin spreading across my face.

Chapter 14

I could just barely see the tall grass swaying in the back fields of the stables as I crouched in the doorway and peered through my viewfinder. I adjusted the settings of my camera and zoomed in, trying to capture the green rustling in the breeze for my photo journal.

"Charlie."

I jumped at the voice so close to my ear, feeling the hair on my neck stand up as I turned around. Ren was standing only inches away from me with a sly look on his face.

"Don't do that," I said, shoving his arm even though he was too strong to feel it. I took a few steps back and stumbled out of the shady stables and into the sunshine.

"I wanted to watch you in your element for a moment," Ren said with a glimmer in his eyes. "You look like you know what you're doing to me. Quite the professional, I'd say."

I rolled my eyes at his naive optimism. "You're an expert on photography all of the sudden?"

"Maybe not," he said, stepping closer and filling the space I'd just intentionally put between us, "but I like what I see."

I didn't know how to respond to that. I had to say something—it was my turn to speak. And I could tell my words mattered to Ren, so I had to choose them carefully.

"You love to talk about *my* career goals so much, and yet I don't know much about yours," I said.

"You're looking at them," Ren said, gesturing to the scrubs he was wearing. He only followed the dress code when he felt like it. I guessed that could be expected since his boss was his mom.

"Have you always wanted to be a vet?" I asked, genuinely curious but equally eager to shift the conversation away from my precarious future plans.

"Ever since the first time I saw my mom deliver a foal...in this very barn actually."

I watched his face light up as he described it, talking about his mom the way other boys might speak of Clark Kent.

"Well, I'm glad then...that you're getting everything you want," I said. "You deserve it."

"You speak much too highly of me for having known me for barely a month," Ren said with as much modesty as was necessary.

"I just call it as I see it," I said as I swung my camera strap across my body and turned to walk toward the office. Ren followed closely.

"So, what is someone like you doing in a barn all summer anyway?" he asked.

"Someone like me?"

"Someone creative, and who's never even been around a horse before." He chuckled. "Shouldn't you be looking for a photography internship or something?"

"Not if I want to pay my tuition," I said. "I'm already struggling to make payments on what my loans don't cover, and it's only been a year."

"Got it." Ren nodded. "That's rough."

"It is what it is," I said with a sigh. "So, get used to seeing me around here five days a week because I'm not leaving Rhode Island without some semblance of financial stability."

"Works for me," Ren said, trying and failing to hold back a smile.

I had my daily debrief with Ebony at the end of my shift, then sprinted to my car, turned the air conditioning to full blast, and unraveled the braid that held my sweaty hair. I needed this heatwave to end immediately.

I pulled down the mirror above my seat and surveyed the damage, rubbing away some stray mascara that had smudged under my eyes and hoping the sweat on my face could pass as highlighter.

I drove through the front gate and turned to head downtown—planning to go for a walk and check out an art gallery on Banisters Wharf—when my phone buzzed. I fished it out of my bag and held it to my ear.

"Hey, what's up," I said. I could just barely make out the sound of a sniffle on the other line over. "Gwen? Are you okay?"

"Hi, Charlie. I'm sorry to call like this, but do you think you could come over for a minute?"

"Yeah, of course," I said, noting that she hadn't used her usual nickname for me. "As long as you don't mind me smelling like hay. I'm just leaving the barn now, so I'm already on my way. Did something happen?"

"Um, yeah…today, Zuri came over to hang out for a bit, and we thought no one else was home since my mom's car wasn't out front, but I guess it's in the shop or something. We were in my room, and my mom walked in and saw us together. I don't know what to do." Gwen said, crying now.

"Oh, no..."

"It was awful. She ran out of the room and hasn't said a word to me since. It's been hours. She didn't even say bye to Zuri when she left. I don't know what to say to her."

"Okay, don't worry about it, we'll figure it out. Do you want me to call Zuri so we can all talk about it?"

"I don't think it's a good idea for Zuri to be around my house right now."

"Okay, I'm on my way, just hang in there. I'll be there in ten minutes tops," I said as I did a U-turn. There was a shortcut to Gwen's neighborhood by the main riding trail, I'd noticed it on my last ride.

As I left the pavement behind and turned onto a dirt road, my car started to make gurgling noises. I pushed hard against the gas pedal, but it locked up as I slowed to a stop. I made it to the side of the road just as my car completely gave out.

Of course, I would run out of gas here—at a time like this.

I'd known my tank was low, and I should've filled it up before work, but I couldn't be bothered to get out of the house five minutes earlier that morning.

Typical.

I covered my face with my hands and let out a small scream before getting my phone out to search for the nearest gas station. Maybe I could walk there?

Calling my dad was out of the question, since I knew he was holding down the fort at Briarman's until closing time. And there was absolutely no cell service. *Great.*

What did I expect, being stranded on a dirt road and all? The closest gas station I could think of had to be at least three miles away, and the barn was already two miles in my rearview. There was absolutely no way I was going to walk that far, and by then, Gwen would be wondering where I even was.

I threw my car door open and got out to search the trunk for a gas can or something—anything—to get me moving again. To my dismay, I found a pair of muddy rain boots, a sandy towel, and absolutely nothing of any use.

I closed my eyes and took a deep breath, fighting the urge to scream again, and in the silence, I could just barely hear the sound of hooves. Someone must've been coming back from a beach ride. I turned to see who my knight in shining armor could be and felt conflicted as James rode gallantly up to my car.

Why am I not surprised?

He looked even taller than usual all the way up there, and I couldn't tell if I was relieved to see him, mad that he was here to witness another one of my messes, or maybe a little bit exhilarated to have an excuse to talk to him.

"What happened here?" James asked with the tiniest hint of amusement in his voice. He led Lightning in a circle around my car, and I did my best to swallow my pride.

"Long story short, I'm out of gas and in a huge rush to see Gwen. It's sort of an emergency, and my phone doesn't have any service."

"Yeah, no one gets service out here. I'm sure Gwen will understand if you're late."

"She really needs me right now, so I don't want to keep her waiting." I ran my hands through my hair and looked around at nothing in particular.

James rode closer to my side and reached a hand down toward me.

"Hop on."

I scrunched my nose at the gesture, but he just patted his horse's back behind his saddle before extending his arm toward me again.

"I know the way to her house," he said. "I can drop you off."

"Are you sure this is safe?"

James closed his eyes and sighed.

"I already have trouble balancing on a horse by myself..." I continued.

"You'll be fine, Charlie," James said.

Charlie. My name sounded better coming out of his mouth now. Like a peace offering, or a term of endearment.

I nodded, taking his hand and getting my foot steady in the stirrup before swinging my leg over and landing behind him. He let go of my hand as soon as I was in place—not a second later—and returned his grip to the reins.

"Have you cantered before?" he asked.

"Nope."

"You better hold on tight then." He reached back, grabbed my hands, and wrapped them around his waist. I slid into place behind the saddle until there was no space left between us.

God, this summer is really putting me out of my comfort zone.

I felt James's abdominal muscles flinch as I interlocked my fingers. He smelled like a mixture of fresh linen and essential oils—probably from the all-natural fly spray he used on Lightning—and his faded blue button-down shirt was warm from the sun. I desperately hoped he couldn't smell the sweat and hay lingering on my skin from my shift that morning.

James clicked his tongue, asking Lightning to get moving, and I held on for dear life as we took off down the road.

The wind rushed past us as we raced by the beach, blue, green, and white blurring in my peripheral. I could taste salt as I gasped for air, feeling it restore me after the sweltering week.

"I get it now!" I yelled over the sound of hooves pounding against sand.

"What?" James shouted back.

"I get why you all do this!" I yelled again.

I felt James laugh.

"There's nothing quite like it," he said, almost too quietly for me to hear.

I rested my cheek on James's back and watched as we made our way down the shoreline and into a nearby neighborhood. By the time we reached Gwen's street, my arms were fatigued from holding onto him so tightly.

"Whoa, Lightning," James said, giving the reins a tug as we came to a stop at the corner.

Once we were stationary, I slowly—and somewhat reluctantly—unlatched myself from James's waist and swung my leg over the back of his horse, landing with a less-than-graceful thud on the sidewalk.

"Thanks for this," I said, glancing up at him. "I really owe you one."

"I'm pretty sure *I* owed *you* one," he said, dropping all pretense for a moment. There was something softer in the way he looked at me now. He paused for a moment before adding, "I might not be riding Lightning today, if it wasn't for you."

I nodded, accepting the white flag he was waving. I met his eyes and held them there, studying this new version of the person I had loved to hate—only I didn't hate him anymore, not even a little bit.

"Will you be okay getting home?" James said, his voice low and gravelly now.

"Oh—yeah, I'm sure Gwen will take me," I said.

James nodded, and before any more words could be exchanged, he tapped his heel on Lightning's side and took off down the road.

What just happened?

Never in my life did I think I'd ever be actually swept off my feet on horseback, yet here I was. Seemingly impossible things liked to happen in Newport, with seemingly impossible people. Before I could dwell on it all, my mind refocused on the bigger issue at hand.

Gwen needed me.

I let myself in and snuck down the hall and into Gwen's room, closing the door as quietly as possible behind me. Gwen was sitting on the edge of her bed with her knees to her chest. I took a seat in the chair by her vanity. Her face was puffy, and her eyes were red and glazed over with tears.

"So, you got home from riding today, then what happened?" I prompted, trying to get the details straight before coming up with a plan to fix it.

"Zuri and I were in here…together…and then we heard the door open," Gwen said, her expression almost blank. "And my mom was just standing there, looking confused…then upset. She ran out of the room so fast, and now, she hasn't come out of her room since. I walked by a half-hour ago, and the door was still closed. She never closes her door. I feel like I lied to her and deceived her, and I feel awful about it."

"She hasn't said anything at all?"

"Radio silence." Gwen held her face in her hands. "She's never acted like this before. You saw her the other day, she's always so…involved."

"Maybe she's just in shock?" I offered.

"Yeah, or maybe she's just appalled," Gwen said with a trace of bitterness in her voice that I didn't recognize.

"Let's not jump to conclusions," I said, but I knew it was a definite possibility. I shook my head at the thought, silently hoping that Gwen's relationship with her mom wouldn't suffer over this. I couldn't imagine the always bubbly and optimistic Gwen going through something like that.

My mind tripped over bad memories of fights I'd had with my own mother and of nights I'd spent crying alone in my room. It was strange how acute the pain still felt, even so many months and years later. There was something so impactful about the bond between my mother and me, and when it was severed, the repercussions were everywhere I looked. It haunted me long after the initial shock, showing its face in the most mundane moments—while watching an old movie or pushing a cart through the grocery store. Even when I'd convinced myself that I was over it, I never *really* was.

After about an hour of trying to comfort her, Gwen dropped me off at my car with a full gas can. She waited until my car had successfully started before taking off, not asking how I'd managed to end up on her doorstep. She was too distraught to even consider the romantic possibilities—how very unlike her.

As the sea air blew in through my open car windows, I considered the facts. It was obvious how much Gwen's mom loved her, even after witnessing just one of their interactions. I didn't want to believe that a secret like this could destroy everything between them in the blink of an eye.

The dark winding roads put me in a bit of a trance as I drove in silence, trying to come up with some sort of easy fix to my friend's problem. Parents were supposed to love their kids unconditionally, but maybe that's just something they say before they figure out the condition that would break them.

If I let my mind wander, I sometimes would think back to the good moments with my own mother. I'd still feel her warm embrace on the front porch of our house in Painesville, telling me how proud she was after a good report card came in the mail. I'd still taste the late-night ice cream runs and hear the bedtime stories she used to read to me when I couldn't fall asleep.

I let the memories in for once, entertaining the thoughts instead of just squeezing my eyes shut until they disappeared. I'd made a habit of suppressing the good times because knowing how everything had turned out had made them more painful to think about than anything else. It was easier to be mad—or just indifferent. That was another life, one before the love my mother had for me had turned conditional.

It occurred to me then, that the woman who'd raised me, who I had known my whole life thus far, was never going to be there ever again. The years would continue to pass, and we would both move in different directions, aging as we did. One day, she would be just another old woman, walking around the grocery store with her gray hair and wrinkling skin, and maybe if our paths crossed, I wouldn't even recognize her. The thought of this struck me somewhere dark and hidden in the depths of my mind.

I couldn't let the same thing happen to Gwen.

Chapter 15

Nothing could clear my head quite like starting my day at the stables. The smell of hay and fresh shavings was something I'd grown quite fond of over the past month and a half. I stepped into the shade of the barn, and before I made it even halfway down the aisle, Ebony popped her head out of her office to summon me.

"Are you occupied at the moment?" she called after me.

"Nope, just got here," I said, smiling at her. I loved it when Ebony asked for my help with things. It made me feel like I was a necessary part of this place—like maybe they needed me.

"Do you know how to braid?" she asked.

"I do…" I said tentatively. I'd grown accustomed to the unpredictability of Ebony's requests. It was difficult to imagine ever getting bored around here.

"Great, I have a new task for you today," Ebony said as she took off down the aisle, expecting me to follow. I did my best to keep up as she power-walked towards a stall where a white, blue-eyed cremello horse was munching on her morning grain.

"This is Snowball." Ebony gestured toward the horse. "Jenna is taking her to a qualifier tournament this afternoon, so I need someone to braid her mane. Apparently, there are two openings on the national team, and Jenna has her eye on one of them."

"I'm sure I can figure it out," I said, nodding as I sized up Snowball's white mane, but wondering why she needed my help when, based on Jenna's appearance each day, she definitely knew how to style hair better than me.

"Amazing, I knew you'd be the one to ask with that gorgeous hair of yours," Ebony said as she reached into her jacket pocket and pulled out a small plastic bag full of mini clear hair elastics.

"Here," she said, placing the bag in my hand. "Do one braid per inch of mane, give or take. If you have any questions, come find me."

Ebony was already walking away by the time she finished her sentence. On her way back to the office, she crossed paths with Jenna, who was sitting on a tack box, putting on her riding boots.

"Don't you look smart today," Ebony said, stopping in front of her. I listened closely, just barely making out their conversation from halfway down the aisle.

Jenna zipped up her left boot before giving Ebony a dazzling smile.

"Snowball will be ready to go soon," Ebony continued. "I'm sure you two will do great today."

"Thanks," Jenna said. She stood up and dusted herself off, even though there was no dust to begin with. "We plan on making the barn proud."

"You always do," Ebony said.

I imagined my already green eyes were practically incandescent with jealousy as I watched Ebony lovingly squeeze Jenna's arm—part of me secretly hoped that I was Ebony's favorite.

Once Ebony had disappeared into her office, I slipped a halter over

Snowball's nose, attached the lead rope, and guided her to the nearest crossties. I propped myself up on a stool and began working on her mane.

I had to steady Snowball's head every few seconds as she fought against being styled. She wasn't a fan of getting her mane tugged by a stranger.

From atop the stool, I could see everything. A few feet from me, one of the barn hands was mucking the stalls, leaving a trail of hay and shavings behind him as he pushed the full wheelbarrow toward the muck heap. Another hand was sweeping the cobblestones in front of the feed room where someone had spilled a bin of alfalfa cubes. From the other side of the aisle, I could hear water rushing into buckets, filling them up from the pipes in the ceiling. I liked that I was a small part of it all, doing my job to keep the barn running smoothly.

As I finished the fifth braid, Jeff popped out of the office and walked in my direction.

"Snowball is looking fabulous," Jeff said. His mint green riding jacket added a burst of color to the otherwise muted stables, and he winked at me as he hurried off to his next lesson.

The hustle and bustle of the barn began to fade to white noise around me as I got lost in the braiding process, so much so that I almost didn't notice someone bending down to walk underneath Snowball's crossties. I looked up just in time to catch James strolling past me.

He was surely taking Lightning to the same tryouts as Jenna and Snowball—I could tell by the perfectly tailored show apparel he was wearing. He was practically gleaming in a deep navy blazer with a dress shirt underneath and a pair of snug white pants.

"James—" I said stopping him before I could stop myself, immediately half-hoping he didn't hear me. He turned back and gave me a half-smile—a good sign. I hopped down from the stool and walked over to him.

"I just wanted to say...I appreciated your help the other day. Gwen really needed me, and I might still be stranded out there if you hadn't rescued me," I said, trying my best to maintain eye contact.

I was starting to look forward to these interactions, if only to witness the new way James looked at me—making me want to run away and stay forever all at once. I had thought maybe his disdain for me was what had made him so intriguing—that I'd only been caught up in what I could never in a million years have—but this new look in his eyes only made him more alluring. I needed to know more about what went on in that head of his.

"I'm sure someone else would've come down the road sooner or later," he said, giving in to that smile. "I hope you got your car back in one piece."

"I did. Gwen gave me some gas and drove me to it, so everything turned out okay in the end," I said, still unable to believe we were actually having a civil conversation.

"Well, good," James said.

"Yeah," I replied, not wanting the conversation to end but not sure what else I could say to lengthen it.

As James turned to leave, I felt my stomach lurch. *Don't go just yet.*

"Did you ever get around to reading *Anna Karenina*?" I blurted out, grasping at straws.

He turned back to face me again. "I finished it last night." He paused for a moment, the wheels turning in his head. "I guess that means I'll be needing a new book."

"I think that's how reading works," I said.

"Know any good bookstores in the area?" His smile was so brilliant now, I thought it might blind me.

"I may or may not have access to a ten percent off discount code at

Briarman's," I said, trying to keep a straight face.

"Hmm, that's quite a deal." Sarcastic James was irresistible. "I might have to take you up on that."

He turned and walked away just in time to avoid seeing my cheeks turn red.

On my way to the parking lot after my shift, I stopped by Dandelion's stall to give her a carrot. When I stepped inside, Gwen was sitting on a plaid blanket in the corner of the stall with her knees to her chest, folded into herself as if to hide from the world.

"What are you doing down there?" I asked, not sure if I should be bothering her.

"Hey, Charlie." She glanced up at me.

I crouched down to her level. "How are you?"

"I've been better," she said. I'd never seen Gwen act like this before. It was unsettling, since she was usually the most positive part of my day.

"Any change with your mom?" I asked.

"Nope," Gwen said, "except for the fact that she definitely told my dad what she saw because now he's avoiding me too."

I frowned.

"The worst part is, I kind of feel guilty about it all. I mean, technically, I've been lying to them about Zuri, but what else was I supposed to do? I just don't want them to hate her now…or me." Gwen covered her face with her hands.

"Listen to me," I said, prying her hands free, so I could look her in the eyes. "This is a good thing, I know it."

A flicker of hope crossed Gwen's face as she waited for further explanation.

"Think of it as an opportunity for them to finally know who you really are. Give them a few days to let the shock wear off, and I'm sure they'll come around."

There was a soft knock on the door, and we both looked up to see Zuri stepping under the stall guard.

"Is there room for one more?" Zuri asked.

"I was just heading out," I said before turning back to Gwen. "Keep me posted."

Gwen nodded.

Chapter 16

My Saturday shift at the bookstore was officially dedicated to finishing the current Austen novel on my marathon, *Northanger Abbey*. Once I reached the last chapter, I stole a fresh copy of *Persuasion*, the next book on the list, from the classics section. I was about halfway through the second page when the doorbell chimed, reminding me that I was still on the clock.

I dog-eared the corner of my page and made my way to the front of the store, ready to assist the new customer, but it was only James leaning on the doorframe, looking at me.

"Charlie," he said plainly.

"James," I said. "You came."

"Didn't I say I might?"

"I just didn't know…" My voice trailed off.

I looked at him, he looked at me.

"Are you looking for any book in particular?" I said finally.

James nodded. "A girl I know recommended something," he said, crossing his arms. "I think I might give it a try."

I was immediately jealous and struggling to keep it off my face.

"Great, and what did she suggest?" I forced a smile.

"She's partial to the classics," he said.

Of course, she is.

"She sounds smart," I said.

"Yeah, I imagine so. I don't really know her that well yet." James chuckled. "She's always going on about Jane Austen. Something about the female perspective and all that."

I felt my cheeks turn pink as I realized, and a strange wave of relief washed over me—the girl was me.

"So," he said, seeing that I'd finally caught on, "which novel do you think will convert me to the Austen fan club?"

"Hmm…" I looked him up and down, sizing him up as if to fit him for a suit rather than help him pick out a novel to read. "One might take the obvious approach and suggest *Pride and Prejudice*…"

He closed his eyes and sighed.

"…but I think you could do well with *Sense and Sensibility*. It's always been my personal favorite," I finished.

James nodded, considering this. "I'll trust you on this one, but if I hate it, you might not be able to *persuade* me again." His lips curled into a grin as he said this Austen-themed pun.

"Ha ha," I said flatly. "Follow me."

I escorted him to the classics section and found his book on the top shelf, standing on my tiptoes to reach it.

"Here," I said, handing it to him. James took the clothbound novel from my hand and opened it to read the synopsis on the inside cover.

"Don't—" I blurted out, almost snatching the book from him.

"What?" he laughed.

"It's more fun to go into a story blindly," I said. "It's a much better experience for the reader."

James snapped the book closed. "If you say so."

I couldn't help but feel strange talking to him like this, like we could just forget the way things had been between us—as if none of it had even happened. Our relationship had changed so much in the past few weeks, it was almost too difficult to keep up with. I'd only just started to allow myself to appreciate the things about James that had originally irritated me: the way his height made me feel small when I stood next to him, the way he looked effortlessly perfect each day, the power in that rare smile of his—the one he'd only recently stopped trying to hide from me. The air around him used to feel cold and unforgiving, but now he radiated a warmth that made me want to lean in.

"So, what is it about Austen?" James asked, giving me a curious look. "Why have you dedicated your whole summer to reading her books?"

I bit the inside of my cheek and looked up at him—it was a good question.

"She was such a keen observer," I said, looking thoughtfully at the display of her complete works in their clothbound covers. "Her characters are such accurate depictions of human nature, and even though her novels were written hundreds of years ago, they still ring true, even now."

"So, you find her stories to be relatable?" James offered.

"Definitely—in a way. There's a hopefulness throughout her novels that I find reflects the way I see the world. Like how a person can show up in your life and change how you see everything around you. Or how a room could have just been a room before, but now with someone in it, the room feels different entirely."

"A place is only as special as the people who inhabit it," James said.

"Exactly." I nodded. "I like that her characters exist primarily in a state of longing and anticipation—always wondering and waiting to see their love interest…I think I like that part of love stories the most. Maybe that's really the best part of love, I don't know."

"You don't think there's something to be said about life after the wedding?"

"How can I be optimistic about it when I've seen a marriage crumble right before my eyes?" I said. "And Jane never actually married…I feel like maybe that might have preserved her from witnessing the ugly reality that can sometimes follow the happily ever after. Nothing will ever be as good as one hopes it might be…so why would I want to read stories about disappointment?"

"But what's the point of anticipating the main character falling in love, if you don't believe it could truly last?" James asked, almost laughing at the contradiction in my reasoning. "What's the point of obsessing over romance, if you believe it to be so unreliable?"

"Maybe I like the idea of love more than the reality of it."

"Maybe you've just never given the real thing a chance," James said with a half-smile.

I felt myself blush and turned my face away to conceal it. He was right, I knew he was right. But maybe I didn't want to toy with love at the risk of my romantic illusion being shattered forever. What if nothing in life could ever rival the way fictional love made me feel?

"Do you mind if I hang out here for a bit and get a head start on reading?" James said, holding up the book. "I don't have to be at training for another hour, so I've got some time to kill."

"Yeah, sure—of course," I responded, looking around for a nook he could occupy. "We don't really have any chairs or anything…"

"I'm good with the floor," he said, walking deeper into the store. I followed behind him as he took a seat against a bookshelf across from the register.

"By the way, how is training going?" I asked. "I saw that you went to that tryout the other day with Jenna, right?"

James looked up at me and smiled. "Yeah, it went well. Lightning is making me really proud this year."

"I'm glad," I said as I settled back into my chair. "Okay...well, I'll just be here...if you need anything."

I opened my book and tried my best to focus on its pages. After a few minutes of hard work, I started to tune out my surroundings and found myself back in the world of *Persuasion*. The only thing tethering me to reality was whatever song by Bach that played softly from the speakers mounted in the corners of the store. My dad only allowed classical music in Briarman's because he said it was the best to read to, which only helped to romanticize the present moment. *Thanks, Dad.*

My mind wandered a bit, remembering my parents telling me stories of how they'd fallen in love so many years ago. They had both been avid readers—my dad obviously still was. They had dates at the local library, just sitting on the floor together in the poetry section. I remembered my mother saying that they would sit shoulder to shoulder, reading love poems to each other and sharing pages of their private journals. How could something that began so beautifully have ended so horribly? How could I ever know what would last and what was already doomed from the start?

As I fell deeper into my book, suppressing my spiraling thoughts, I felt as though I was being watched. I glanced over the top of my page and caught James's eyes on me. He held my gaze for a second before returning his eyes to his book.

"What?" I asked.

His low chuckle was almost inaudible. "What?"

"You were watching me," I said, smiling now.

"Yup." He glanced at me again.

"Why?"

"You just look so…serious," James replied. He paused for a moment. "It's cute."

I covered my face with my book.

"Stop distracting me," I said into the binding that concealed me. It was difficult to focus on reading when life was becoming more interesting than the pages of my book.

Chapter 17

With each riding lesson, I could feel my confidence building and my abilities growing. Last week, Jeff had taught me how to post while trotting, and I was somehow able to get around the arena twice without losing my balance while riding a fifteen-year-old horse named Blaze.

As I walked toward the office to check this week's riding agenda, I hoped Jeff had reserved Blaze for me again. It was easier for me to make progress on a horse once I'd begun to trust them. It made me feel safer to push myself further outside of my comfort zone.

When I stepped into the office, Ebony was on the phone but gestured for me to come over to her desk.

"Oh no, that doesn't sound good," she said into the receiver.

I stood there and pulled on a loose thread on my sleeve, waiting for her to explain who she was talking to.

"Yes, absolutely, don't worry about it. Just make sure you call us with an update on Pistachio." She hung up the phone and sighed.

"That was Jeff," Ebony explained. "I'm sorry to do this so last minute, but he has to cancel your lesson for today. His dog isn't feeling well, and he's already on his way to Dr. Aki's clinic. I would find you a sub, but all our trainers are booked."

Ebony scanned the schedule once more before giving up. "Sorry, hun," she added, reaching out and stroking my arm. It was so warm, so motherly, that I was temporarily taken aback.

"That's okay," I said, trying to mask my disappointment. I was really enjoying riding these days. "I just hope Pistachio is okay."

"I can cover her lesson," James said, stepping into the office. He must've overheard us talking from the aisle. "I've got some time before training."

Does James even give lessons?

"That's very kind of you, but you're not on the payroll anymore," Ebony said. "Have you even taught a lesson since that beginner's class last summer?"

"I haven't, but I don't think I've suddenly forgotten how to ride… or instruct." He was cocky and charming, and it surprised me how unintimidated he was by Ebony, who I couldn't imagine speaking to that way.

"Charlie is approaching intermediate level now. Can you handle that?" she asked.

"I think we'll manage," James said with a grin, meeting my eyes for the briefest moment. "We don't want her to lose her momentum now, do we?"

"If it's okay with Charlie, it's okay with me," Ebony said, conceding. She looked at me, then back to James. "But we're going to have to pay you in cash."

"Works for me," James said. "Charlie?"

I stared back at him, unable to pinpoint exactly how we had ended up here. I didn't have any desire to show off my subpar riding to someone who had been competing since pony camp—especially since his opinion mattered to me more than I liked to admit.

"C'mon," James said with that intoxicating smile. "It'll be fun."

"Okay, yeah...why not?" I replied, unable to say no to him. Why had I been so eager to get James to stop hating me? It was so much easier to understand him then. Now every move he made was more disorienting than the last. It was starting to make my head spin.

James turned to leave, expecting me to follow him out of the office, and I shot Ebony a look that pleaded for help as I rushed to catch up with him. She only laughed and shook her head.

Once we were in the aisle, James led me to a stall belonging to a five-year-old horse named Spike.

"Alright, why don't you get him tacked up and meet me outside," he said, leaning against the stall and tapping Spike's nameplate.

"Uh, I think you might have the wrong horse," I said, giving James a sideways glance.

He shook his head. "Jeff has been way too easy on you. Even Ebony said you're almost intermediate now. I think it's time to kick it up a notch."

I couldn't hide the panic in my eyes, which only made James laugh.

"Come on, Charlie, you can definitely handle this," he said, imploring me to give in. He stepped closer. "Just give it a try. I promise you'll have fun."

"Okay," I said finally, taking a breath. "But you better not laugh at me if I fall off."

James was already backing away as I said this, giving me no time to change my mind. The smile on his face continued to both perplex me and fill me with an odd, sunny feeling. I would never be able to trust first impressions again.

With more caution than usual, I led Spike to the nearest crossties, groomed him, and tacked him up. As I clipped my helmet in place, I said a quick prayer to the universe to keep me from breaking anything important.

When I finally led the horse outside towards the arena, James was sitting on the top rung of the fence. He stepped down and waited for me to come closer, taking a pair of sunglasses that hung from his shirt and putting them on.

He looked good. The sleeves on his button-down were haphazardly rolled up to his elbows, revealing tan arms and defined veins. His jeans were black, and his sneakers were white—too white to be in a sandy arena. I guessed he hadn't changed yet for his afternoon training. It was intimidating being near him, as usual, but still, I found myself looking forward to seeing him one-up himself with every encounter we shared. An impossible task, yet somehow, he managed it each day.

James took the reins from my hands and led Spike to the mounting block. He held the horse steady as I swung my leg over and settled into the saddle. James checked each side and carefully adjusted my stirrups, making sure I was secure before instructing me to start riding along the perimeter of the arena. He directed me from the center, telling me to pick up the pace and get Spike up to a trot.

"Keep your heels down," he shouted. "Find the rhythm, then go with each bounce. Don't fight it, we aren't posting yet."

I tried my best to do what he said, but as soon as I changed something new, I'd forget to maintain the previous adjustment. James didn't seem bothered by how many times he had to repeat the same instructions—he was much more patient than I would have assumed—and each time I got something right, his face lit up.

"Alright, now try posting," he said. "Just like Jeff taught you, rise and fall with the outside leg." He patted his thigh as an example.

All I wanted at that moment was to impress him. The horror stories and dangerous warnings about riding seemed to fade from my mind, and suddenly, I was fearless.

I sat deeper in the saddle and kept my arms steady as I found the rhythm of Spike's trot. I felt myself falling in sync with the horse, and something clicked between us. I could sense him anticipating my next command before I even told him where to go. My legs felt strong as I lifted myself in and out of the saddle, and I no longer felt nervous or unsteady. Instead, I used the bouncing motion as momentum, absorbing the impact and lifting off the horse's back with more purpose than ever before. I squeezed my heels into Spike's sides, working our way up to a collected canter.

I knew I'd finally done it. I'd reached a level of understanding that I had never been able to get to before. Something within me shifted, unleashing my potential as a rider. James could see it too. After a minute, he told me to slow down to a walk and cool off. I did as I was told even though I had the urge to go faster and take off down to the beach, leaving the barn and James in my dust. Maybe I could even get up to a gallop or jump the fence? This unstoppable feeling was like a new drug coursing through my veins. I finally understood why this was so addicting.

All in good time, I told myself as I got Spike to slow down and circled back over to James's side.

"It doesn't feel like that with a twenty-year-old trail horse now does it?" he said, grinning with satisfaction. I shook my head, unable to stop the smile that was taking over my face. He had been right after all.

After a few more laps around the ring, James called it and gestured for me to meet him by the entrance. I slowed to a stop and prepared to dismount. Spike was by far the tallest horse I'd ridden so far. I looked down from the saddle, trying to figure out how to best maneuver myself to the ground.

I swung my leg over the saddle, but as I twisted to hop down, my other foot got caught on the stirrup. Before I could fall, I felt James's hands grab my waist. He carefully lowered me to the ground, his arms holding me close as I slid down his chest and landed directly at his feet. Once I was securely on the ground and had not made an absolute fool of myself, I realized he was still holding me. His breathing was heavier than usual, and my eyes scanned upward until they met his.

The world around us seemed to have slowed. A soft breeze brushed past, and a few loose strands of my hair gently swirled outside my helmet. James was looking at me in a way that electrocuted my senses. A current ran through me, a surge of energy that was entirely new. He was so close—it felt like maybe he was seeing too much of me. Then it all became too much, too fast. I pulled away, looking anywhere but his eyes.

The world began to move at a normal pace again, and I unclipped my helmet and shook my hair out. I watched as James took a restorative breath and cleared his throat, turning away for a moment before looking back at me.

"You did pretty great out there," he said, his voice doing that gravelly thing again.

"Thanks. I might have to work on that last part," I said, trying to break the tension that lingered in the air, but my mind carefully filed away the compliment.

As we made our way back to the stables, Ren stepped outside and draped his stethoscope over his neck. His smile faded a bit as his eyes landed on me and James.

"Hey," I said as we approached. I was smiling too wide, adrenaline still coursing through my veins.

"Hey," Ren responded politely. "What're you guys up to?"

"I took over her lesson for today," James replied, but he was looking only at me when he said it. He patted Spike and added, "You should've seen these two working together. They were great."

"I wish I could've been there," Ren said, his gaze shifting from James to me. His tight-lipped smile and blank expression were dead giveaways—he didn't like how close James and I were getting. Afterall, only a few weeks ago, Ren would've likely been the one to give me the lesson.

"You'll have to give me a few pointers sometime," I said to Ren.

"Yeah, for sure, Charlie." Ren nodded at me and then at James, as if to excuse himself.

A tiny piece of my heart broke every time Ren saw me and James together. I hated the idea of hurting him, but James and I had *actually* had fun today—more fun than I'd had in a while—and nothing could distract me from that.

Chapter 18

I had more energy than usual the next morning, so I decided to go on a jog around town before my shift at the stables. As much as it went against all my previous beliefs, it actually felt good to be up so early.

Who have I become?

A soft mist settled just above the harbor, a result of the chilly morning air colliding with the warm summer water. It looked like something straight out of a gothic novel—too bad I'd already finished reading *Northanger Abbey*.

I turned onto Banister's Wharf and noticed a small dog running around at the end of the dock next to a waterfront coffee shop. As I approached to get my daily caffeine fix, the dog ran towards me and jumped up on my shins, its little paws playfully scratching at my leggings. I bent down to pet my new friend as the owners came out of the cafe.

"Pistachio, get down," one of them said between sips of his iced coffee. "I'm so sorry, she won't bite, but she's always excited when she meets new people."

"Pistachio?" I said, remembering the name. I looked up to see the second man removing his sunglasses. Jeff grinned at me.

"Hi, Charlie," he said with a smile before turning to the man beside him. "This is my husband, Ben. Ben, this is one of my most promising students."

"It's nice to meet you," I said, reaching out to shake Ben's hand, but he went in for a hug.

"I've heard so much about you," Ben said as he pulled away from me, holding me at arm's length, so he could get a good look. "You're even more gorgeous than Jeffy described."

I shot Jeff a look before turning my attention back to his husband.

"Thanks," I said, trying to accept the compliment that I definitely didn't deserve at the moment. My hair was in a tangled ponytail, and I was still wearing the t-shirt I'd slept in.

"So, this is the famous Pistachio," I said, picking up their dog and giving her a squeeze. She barked happily, grateful for the attention. "I heard you had to take her to Hana's yesterday. Is she doing okay?" I searched the dog in my arms for any obvious afflictions.

"Jeff is a total hypochondriac when it comes to her," Ben said. "Pistachio hadn't eaten her dinner the night before, so he was worried something might be wrong. Hana checked out our little tree nut and said everything was good to go."

"Turns out she just had a bit of gas," Jeff said matter-of-factly. "Most likely from the bean chili leftovers I slipped her at lunch."

"She wasn't the only one…" Ben teased, giving his husband a look. Jeff nudged him with his elbow and laughed.

"I still feel bad about missing your lesson," Jeff said, turning back to me. "Should we reschedule it for this week? I think I have some time on Thursday evening."

"We've got book club that night," Ben said, then turned to me. "I'm sure he's just trying to use this as an excuse, rather than telling the group he didn't read this month."

"I read four chapters already!" Jeff said.

Ben patted his husband on the arm. "Well, then you have plenty of time to catch up before the meeting."

Jeff rolled his eyes. "I guess I'm all booked out this week. Let's find some extra time next week to make up for it."

"That won't be necessary," I said, hoping he didn't feel too guilty—his canceling on me was maybe one of the best things that happened so far this summer. "James covered my lesson, so you're off the hook."

"James?" Jeff said.

"Yup," I assured him.

"Really?"

"Uh-huh," I said. "He volunteered when he overheard Ebony and me talking."

"Wow," Jeff said, his smile turning into a mischievous grin. "I had no idea you two were so close. James going out of his way to help you…for him, that's practically a declaration of his affection."

I felt my face heat up as I looked around to make sure no one had overheard.

"Don't you think you might be jumping to conclusions on that one just a bit?" I said in a whisper.

"Oh, my sweet, naive Charlie," Jeff said, pulling me in for a side embrace. "He's totally smitten with you."

I blinked at him. "You can't be serious."

"I heard about what happened with Lightning the other week. A boy never forgets about the girl who saved his horse."

"How poetic," Ben chimed in, looking off into the distance and placing a hand on his heart.

"You guys have it all wrong," I said and stepped back from Jeff's friendly embrace. "Seriously, James and I are barely even friends, nothing more."

But as the words escaped my lips, looking at their hopeful faces, I knew it was a lie.

✳✳✳

The weather was perfect for riding—not too hot but not too chilly either—so I knew the riding team would likely be at the barn today, using this opportunity to train. I'd put some makeup on and brushed out my hair after my run just in case I ran into anyone during my shift.

I sat on a stool inside the tack room and pulled a croissant out of my bag. I needed to get some breakfast in my system before my shift started, and the coffee shop from earlier had offered a nice selection of pastries. I was only on the second bite when I heard something in the aisle. I peered outside and saw Jenna grooming Snowball in her stall. Across the aisle was James, leaning up against the wall.

"I saw you at qualifiers, Jenna. It's gonna be you," James said.

"Yeah, well, there are two spots, so who do you think that leaves room for?" she said, gesturing to him in between strokes brushing her horse's mane.

"We'll see about that," James muttered. "I need to focus more, if I'm going to consistently clear the five-foot jumps before the final round."

"You'll do it," Jenna said without an ounce of doubt in her voice. She placed her brush back in her grooming kit, stepped into the aisle, and sauntered right up to James. "I know you will."

Only a few inches remained between them now, so close that she could probably smell his clean linen scent. James stood perfectly still, his face hardened slightly, like he was trying to control himself.

"And then we will have the rest of the year together to do this…" Jenna said as she leaned in, stood on her toes to reach him, and pressed her lips to his.

James seemed surprised, his eyebrows shooting up, but then he pulled her closer and kissed her back.

My appetite disappeared, and my hands were almost shaking as I tossed the croissant back into the bag. I was about to turn away, not feeling the need to torture myself any further, when James snapped out of his trance and pushed Jenna away from his chest.

"What was that?" he said, breathless. His face was stern.

"What?" Jenna replied sweetly, ignoring the obvious hurt in his voice.

"What about your boyfriend?"

"Luca?"

James nodded, looking more and more irritated by the second.

Jenna put a sad pout on her face. "He broke up with me."

I could have sworn I saw a flash of amusement in James's eyes, but it was gone too soon to tell.

"So, you thought this," James gestured between the two of them, "could happen again, now that you're alone?"

"Why not?" Jenna said.

James scoffed, but it came out as more of a laugh. He turned away from her.

"Why are you fighting this?" Jenna asked, her voice becoming harsh. I got the feeling she was used to getting exactly what she wanted, when she wanted it.

James's expression shifted to something more offended than angry. "You thought you could just come back here and what? I'd be waiting for you? How pathetic do you think I am, Jenna?"

"Well, when you put it that way…" She seemed to be almost enjoying the rise she was getting out of him, like he was her puppet on a string, ready to dance when she said so. "You can't look me in the eyes and tell me you don't miss me."

"That's not really the point, is it?" James breathed. I watched as his eyes flitted back to her lips for a moment, fighting the pull she had over him. "I'd be an idiot if I didn't know exactly how this would end…again."

"Come on, James—"

"It's not going to happen this time," he said firmly.

Jenna looked shocked as James walked away, but the glimmer in her eyes looked a lot like respect.

James continued down the aisle without looking back, and before he could get close enough to see me, I pulled myself against the wall of the tack room, just out of sight.

***

"Have you eaten yet?"

I flinched, not realizing anyone was around, and turned to see James leaning against the door of the stall I was in as I emptied a bag of fresh shavings onto the floor.

"No?" It came out as more of a question. I could still feel the croissant from that morning churning in my stomach.

"I'm grabbing takeout in town, if you wanna join," he said, as if this was a normal thing for him to ask me. I paused for a second, remembering what I had overheard earlier.

Is he doing this to prove something to Jenna? I glanced around to see if she was nearby, watching us, but she was nowhere in sight.

"Okay," I said, crumpling the now empty shavings bag in my arms and pulling it to my chest.

"Great," James said, tilting his head towards the exit. I shoved the shavings bag in the nearest garbage can and followed him to the parking lot.

The car filled with the scent of tortillas and fresh salsa as we drove from our lunch pickup spot on the wharf toward the coastline on the other side of the island.

"Where are we going?" I asked.

James kept his eyes on the road as he said, "Have you been to Second Beach?"

"I think so...isn't it the one off the main trail?"

"Yup. It's my favorite place on the island, just far enough from town that it usually stays pretty quiet during the weekdays."

"Is that why you like it?"

"Actually, yeah," he said, glancing over at me. "Are you calling me a loner?"

"Those were your words, not mine," I said. It was strange how easy this felt—getting lunch, talking to him.

"I'm not a fan of crowds," he said, cracking a smile. "Not that you would understand, living in the city and all."

"I've only lived in a city for a few months, it's not like I was raised there," I said. "I'm much more comfortable in places like this." I gestured towards the gleaming sea that stretched before us.

"Good to know," he said, catching my eyes again before returning his focus to the road.

As we pulled up to the beachside parking, I couldn't blame him for his assessment of the place. It was relatively vacant, and the view was breathtaking. For a second, I almost considered running into the waves and swimming as far as my legs could take me.

Instead, I carefully pulled the takeout containers from the bag in my lap and handed James his lunch. He rolled down the windows, letting the sea breeze drift in with the sound of seagulls squawking in the distance and the rush of waves over the rocky shoreline.

The food was delicious—not that I noticed. I was too preoccupied with James's presence next to me in such close quarters. Every crunch of my tortilla chips only added to my nervousness, but James didn't seem anxious at all. He was halfway through his lunch before I managed to take three bites.

It was hard for me, impossible even, to grasp that James wanted me to be there next to him. That he was the one who asked me to join him in the first place, which he hadn't had to do. No one was forcing him. Maybe I was just overthinking it all.

"I've been meaning to say," James said, interrupting my internal monologue, "it really bothers me how I treated you during your first few weeks here."

I took a sip of my iced tea and glanced over at him.

"I can be a real dick sometimes, and I never properly apologized for that," he continued.

I blinked, trying to think of something to say. This would have been a very different conversation, if he'd said it a few weeks ago. I wasn't mad at him anymore.

"You shouldn't take all the blame. I mean, how dare I offer a horse a carrot without written permission from its owner first?" I said, trying to keep a straight face. "I don't know *what* I was thinking."

"I know what I was thinking," James said under his breath.

"Oh?"

"Yup," he said plainly.

I waited for him to elaborate, but he wanted me to ask for it.

"And…" I said.

He paused for a moment, looking out at the ocean, then turned back to me.

"I was thinking, where did this girl come from, and why did she have to show up and distract me when I should be focusing on my training."

"Sure…" I said. "And yet, you practically ignored me."

"If I liked you less, I might be able to talk about it more."

"Did you just quote *Emma*?" I turned to him, laughing now. "Someone's been reading a little too much Jane Austen."

"Her stuff is actually pretty good," he said, cracking a smile. "And it's the truth."

I had no idea how to respond to that. A familiar voice crept into my head as I stared out at the ocean. *Run*, it said, *before you say anything you'll regret.*

It wasn't likely that I could escape in the middle of lunch, so I pushed the feeling down until it was almost hidden from my mind and glanced over at James. My eyes wandered to his lips as I remembered Jenna had kissed him just this morning, then I looked away.

"You didn't make it easy to ignore you either," I found the courage to say. "Even when I tried to hate you, my efforts seemed to have the reverse effect. Now, I think I like you instead."

My eyes were glued to the ocean waves, but I could feel James's reaction next to me. I'd never said anything remotely forward before. To some, it might've been nothing to write home about, but to me it felt incredibly difficult to say. I glanced at James again who was unabashedly looking back at me.

"Really?" he said, his eyes staring too deeply into mine. There was a glint of arrogance in them now, and I wasn't so scared anymore. It didn't feel wrong to be looked at like that by him, the way it usually did with other guys. If I was a dark storm after all, then James was lightning and pouring rain. I didn't have to hide myself from him.

He knows too much, echoed the voice in my head, but still, I replied, "Yeah, really."

We had said how we felt, exposing a piece of ourselves and putting it out there, making it real and tangible, and it was normal. Nothing happened. We were both still sitting there, eating lunch by the ocean. Only now, I knew that James liked me, and he knew that I liked him back.

By the time we pulled into the barn parking lot, it was already two o'clock. As we stepped into the stables, I saw Ebony leaving her office and walking towards us.

Were we gone for too long? My mind started grasping at excuses as Ebony smiled at me.

"Just the girl I was hoping to see," she said. "I have something I'd like to discuss with you."

James gave me a nod that said, *see you later,* before continuing down the aisle. His hand gently grazed my shoulder as he left my side, making my pulse hum throughout my body. I turned my attention back to Ebony and tried to focus.

"I was scrolling through Facebook last night and saw that you posted some photos you've taken this summer," she said.

"Oh…" I wasn't anticipating that. "Yeah, photography is a bit of a hobby for me."

"Have you considered making it into more than just a hobby?" she asked. "Your stuff is great, and you must have a nice camera. The quality is amazing."

"Thank you," I said, looking at my shoes. "That's really nice of you to say."

"I was thinking, maybe you could take some photos of the barn? Something we could put on the website?"

"Sure—yeah, I think I could do that," I said.

"We would compensate you, of course," Ebony added.

"Cool," I said, nodding and doing my best to act somewhat professional. I could really use the money.

"The weather is supposed to be nice on Monday. Why don't you ditch barn duties, and I'll organize the riding team for a photo op instead," Ebony said.

"Sounds good," I replied, excited about the opportunity but equally terrified that I'd somehow screw it up.

Chapter 19

The cobblestones were cold against my knees as I struggled to reach the lowest panel of wood on the stall door before me, polishing it with citrus-scented oil and an old rag from the tack room. My fingers had started cramping after the third stall, but I was determined to finish at least one side of the aisle before my shift ended. So far, I hadn't seen any of my friends around the barn, so I had fewer distractions than usual. I knew Gwen had a shift at the cafe that morning, but I wasn't sure what everyone else was up to. Maybe it was the rainy weather that was keeping them away.

Just as I finished scrubbing the last door and pulled myself into a standing position, I saw Zuri stepping into Sophie's stall with a bag of carrot sticks. She didn't look sad—not the way Gwen had lately—but she looked tired.

I tossed the dirty rag I'd used into one of the laundry bins in the tack room and put the oil away under the sink before finding my way back to Sophie's stall. I pulled a peppermint out of my back pocket as I unhooked the stall guard and stepped inside.

"I brought you something," I said to Sophie, unwrapping the mint and smiling at Zuri. The horse took the candy from my palm, leaving behind some alfalfa dust that was stuck to her nose from her morning grain. I wiped it off on my jeans.

"Here I am trying to teach her to make healthy choices," Zuri said as she held up the bag of carrots. "She's going to start liking you more than me."

"No way, you're still her favorite," I joked. "I'm just like…her cool aunt."

Zuri laughed, but her brown eyes were still clouded with something else.

"Any updates from Gwen?" I asked, hoping for some good news but sure I wouldn't get any by the looks of things.

"Did she tell you about the Dad Derby?" Zuri asked.

"She mentioned it a few weeks ago…why? Did something happen?" I'd almost forgotten about it. The event must've gone on over the weekend while I was at the bookstore.

"Her dad never showed up," Zuri said, rubbing her horse's nose. "Gwen was crushed."

Oh, no. It felt like a gut punch just imagining Gwen standing there, waiting for him.

"Where is she now?" I asked. "Still at work?"

Zuri checked her watch. "She should be heading home soon. I wish I could go over and see her, but I just can't."

"They won't let you come over?" I asked.

"They never said so outright, but it's not even that. It's like…a place of mind. Like I would feel…ashamed? I can't go back to that."

I couldn't imagine Zuri being anything other than her vibrant self. It felt strange to even consider that she'd had to come out—or doubted herself in the first place. She was just Zuri, and she loved Gwen. It was simple.

"How long have you been out?" I asked.

"About a year, but I knew for a while before that. My mom took it really well, but that didn't mean I wasn't still scared to tell her," Zuri said. "I can't even imagine what I would have done if she had iced me out like this."

As I heard things from Zuri's perspective, I realized that I'd really taken for granted the ease of being straight. I loved to harbor self-pity for my lack of a love life, but in reality, I had so much less to worry about than my friends did. I couldn't imagine how I would handle it if I had another layer of judgment and confusion from the world—I was already confused about it all. Why couldn't people just accept that any form of love was something to cherish? Why was it still so hard for me to accept any form of love for myself?

"Maybe this will turn out to be a good thing," I said, giving Sophie a scratch under her mane. "Gwen was putting off telling them, and now you guys don't have to keep it a secret anymore."

Zuri smiled at me, but it was weak. I wished for something to say that could alleviate her stress, but I knew that nothing could—no words from me, at least.

※※※

My dad stopped by the bookstore during my Saturday shift to help me organize a large shipment of cookbooks that had arrived the night before. It was nice to have some time with him since life had gotten pretty busy lately.

We started at the back row of the store, unboxing the baking books and placing them on their designated shelves. Halfway through my first box, I got distracted by a British pastry book and sprawled myself out on the floor, lazily flipping through the recipes.

"What do you say we ditch this and go make some trifle instead?" I asked, turning the book around to show my dad a photo of the English dessert.

"If you can somehow make it vegan, I'm in," he said, cracking a smile.

I spent the next hour filling him in on the current happenings at the barn and explaining the dynamics of the social scene I'd somehow fallen into—it truly baffled me how easily I had made friends in Newport. The conversation quickly found its way to Gwen's situation with her parents.

"Gwen's dad didn't even show up to the derby," I said as I reached down and arranged a stack of books on the lowest shelf, "—the one he wins every year!"

My dad shook his head.

"I just don't get why they're acting like this," I continued.

"You have to keep in mind, these people are from an entirely different generation. Things were different when we were growing up," my dad said.

I stood up to grab another stack. "It must take a lot of effort to be that stubborn."

"Oh, and you don't know anything about being stubborn now, do you?" My dad raised an eyebrow at me.

I rolled my eyes. "I just hate doing nothing while my friend is upset."

"Hopefully, her parents will come around soon," he said. "Make sure you tell Gwen that she's welcome to come over or stay with us anytime she wants."

"I will," I said, glancing at him. "But there's just something so wrong about this whole thing. How could her parents even consider not talking to their daughter just because she's dating Zuri?" My volume was rapidly increasing as I got more and more agitated.

"Not everyone was raised the way you were, Charlie. The ideals we are taught growing up can be hard to shake."

"I know—but can't they at least try to be happy for her?"

I was cut off by the sound of a stack of books falling to the ground, so distracted by the sound of my own voice that I hadn't heard any customers coming in.

When I turned around to see who it was, I could feel the color draining from my face. Gwen's mom was crouched before me, gathering the books at her feet. As soon as she had a handle on them, she placed the pile on the counter, turned around, and walked out of the store without a word.

I just stood there with my jaw open as I watched her leave. I hated seeing Pam like that. When we'd met a few weeks prior, she'd been so enthusiastic and loving. Now, she looked distant and pale, like she'd been ill. A part of me wasn't even sorry that she had heard what I had said—she probably needed to hear it—but the rest of me felt like the biggest idiot on earth.

"That was her mom?" my dad asked.

"Uh-huh," I managed to say as I stared blankly at the door. My own mother's face flashed in my mind. I remembered how she would look when she was disappointed with me. The memory throbbed in my head, pushing me over the edge.

I took a few deep breaths and tried to compose myself, but despite my efforts, each breath came faster and faster.

The doorbell rang again—this time I heard it. At the most inopportune time imaginable, in walked James looking strikingly handsome, as per usual. With all the excitement of the afternoon, I'd completely forgotten that he'd said he might stop by and fill me in on his progress with *Sense and Sensibility*.

James's smile shifted to a frown as he discovered me in the back of the store. He made his way toward me as I slid down a bookshelf and pulled my knees to my chest.

"You okay?" James got down to my level, eyeing my dad, as if to wordlessly ask if I needed medical attention.

My chest continued to rise and fall at an increasing speed, and my breath couldn't seem to catch up. I imagined this was what a panic attack was supposed to feel like, but I wasn't sure how to make it stop.

"Charlie, why don't you take a break? You and your friend can step out back for some air," my dad said. He was at my side now, his forehead scrunched with worry as he helped me stand up.

I made my way to the back door, brushing my hands along the shelves on each side to ground myself. I pushed the door open and felt the humid air rush in as I stepped into the back alley. Leaning against the weathered wooden panels, I covered my face with my hands and tried to regain composure.

"Hey," James said once the door had closed. He stepped closer to me and in a hushed tone asked, "What's going on?"

"I messed up," I said, my voice muffled by my hands.

"It can't be that bad."

I lowered my arms and looked up at him. I couldn't believe he was seeing me like this. I couldn't believe I was even acting like this.

"I just made such a fool of myself in front of Gwen's mom," I said between short breaths. "I think I made things even worse for her at home. Maybe if I just stayed out of things, I wouldn't be humiliating myself all the time." I wrapped my arms around my chest and stared at the ground, searching for some solace in the cobblestones beneath my feet.

"Her parents found out about her and Zuri?" James asked.

I looked at him. "You know about them?"

"They don't hide it well."

I nodded. "Her parents won't even talk to her about it."

He shook his head. "That sucks."

"Gwen and her mom are so close, and I just don't want her to lose that because that kind of thing wasn't easy to get over. I mean it *isn't* easy—I assume." I cleared my throat. I hadn't really talked to anyone about my mom since I'd arrived in Newport, and I hadn't wanted to. Especially with everything James had gone through—*actually* losing his mom—it felt wrong talking to him about this stuff. I couldn't tell if my sadness was even justified in comparison to his.

But James had noticed what I'd said. I watched his face change.

"Did something happen with your mom?" he asked, his voice a near whisper.

I tried desperately to hold it together, but when I nodded, a single tear betrayed me and slid down my cheek. I tried again to force my breathing to slow down, but it felt impossible. My vision blurred as my eyes welled up without my permission, and it all became too much to keep inside anymore. Even as I tried my hardest to hold back the floodgates, my heart pounded out of my chest, and my lungs refused to slow down.

Suddenly, I was sobbing, and I didn't even know why. Was it the indignity of the encounter with Gwen's mom? Was it the fear of making things harder for my friend at home? Or was it something else? Something I'd fought to keep locked away in my subconscious for too long. It had been fighting hard to be set free, waiting for something to unleash it.

The tears were coming too fast to wipe away, but I tried to anyway, gasping for air as my breathing started to level. I couldn't believe that James—of all people—was witnessing this. We were finally getting to a good place, and now here I was, scaring him off. But when I looked up, he was still standing there, watching me. He stepped even closer, looking at me with empathetic eyes.

In and out, I tried to keep track of my breathing, but my thoughts continued to spiral and tears continued to stream down my face. My mind raced with a private screening of all the unpleasant memories I'd been suppressing. Betrayal and anger coursed through my veins, trying to reach the surface. I was filled with the misery of missing someone that didn't even exist anymore—not in the same way. She still lived and breathed, but she wasn't the person I'd thought she was. Could it be possible to miss the person someone used to be? Was it harder to lose someone that way than someone who was actually gone? At that moment, it felt like the same thing.

All of a sudden, James was holding my face in his hands. He hesitated for a moment, his brown eyes searching my face for some kind of permission, before kissing me. The abruptness of his mouth on mine stunned me, forcing my chest to relax. His lips lingered for a moment, taking a breath before pulling away and studying my reaction. He appeared almost boyish for the first time since I'd met him—all wide-eyed and unsure.

The kiss had felt strange at first. It was new and unfamiliar—so much to take in all at once. But as soon as he backed away, I wanted his mouth on mine again.

"Sorry," he said, his breath warm against my cheek.

"It's okay," I whispered.

What was I thinking about before? I was taken off guard just enough to ease my mind.

"You were so stuck in your head," he said, reaching for my hand and rubbing his thumb aimlessly against my palm. "I had to do something."

I brushed my fingertips over my lower lip and looked up at him, trying to find something—anything—to say, but my mind was suddenly blank. When I went to wipe my eyes with my sleeve, I realized my tears had stopped.

I'd never actually had anything like this before—I was way out of my depth. All the guys I'd kissed in the past had been nothing more than a rite of passage, checking off a milestone toward social maturity, more contrived from a sense of obligation than from passion.

But it was different with James. I felt like I had drifted too far from shore—my feet couldn't touch the bottom anymore. I had been comfortable before, with my feet firmly planted on the ground. I couldn't lose what I never had. But being comfortable was as dull and meaningless as it was easy. This felt so raw and real, and I knew real things could hurt me.

I looked up at James, and something had shifted in the way he was looking back at me—like I possessed the answer to a question he was dying to ask. It wasn't just my heart on the line anymore. My stomach tightened as I fought against every instinct I had screaming at me to run away.

For a moment, everything seemed to hang in the balance. The space between us was full of potential, and it was my choice to decide what would happen next. Before I could weigh my options and change my mind, I reached for James's shirt, my fingers grasping at the soft fabric, and pulled him closer. I kissed him again, trying to convey everything I couldn't find the words for, and I felt a smile on his lips as he kissed me back.

Chapter 20

Since the incident earlier in the day, I had been trying to get in touch with Gwen to warn her about my loudmouth. Her phone must've been off because none of my texts would deliver, and all my calls were going straight to voicemail. Part of me was relieved to wait a little while longer to admit what I had done. My head hurt just thinking about it.

I was equally distracted by pangs of regret rolling through me in waves as I thought of what had transpired between me and James. My mind felt like the impact zone, wiped out by shame spirals from all sides. *His eyes, his lips, his breath.* It came back to me in flashes. I squeezed my eyes shut and breathed through it. He was so close, I had nowhere to hide. He could see way too much of me. I felt suffocated as I remembered it, but still, I was counting down the seconds until I could see him again.

I was sitting on the couch at home, wrapped up in a blanket with the six-hour version of *Pride and Prejudice* playing on my laptop when Gwen finally called me back. My mind was miles away, barely even watching, when my phone buzzed under the covers.

"Hello?" I answered.

"Hey, Charles." Gwen's voice came through the receiver, and she didn't sound upset—I took that as a good sign.

"Gwen, I have to tell you something…and you're not going to be happy with me," I started to ramble. Before I could lose my nerve, the words spilled out. "Your mom overheard me talking about your situation with my dad. I was at Briarman's, and I didn't hear her come in. I feel *so* awful, Gwen. I won't forgive myself, if I made things worse for you and—"

"Charles, breathe," Gwen said. "It's okay."

"It is?"

"Whatever you did or said, it actually helped. My mom came home this afternoon and texted me and my dad for a family meeting. We finally talked about what happened, and they actually apologized for taking so long to process everything."

I breathed a sigh of relief.

"My mom said she was just sad that I hadn't opened up to her sooner," Gwen continued. "She was more upset that I had been lying to her than by the fact that I was dating a girl. Both my parents said they were going to try to learn more about my 'community'—which was kind of weird—but they seemed pretty sincere. My dad was so upset about missing the Dad Derby that he promised to take me out for ice cream this weekend, just the two of us, to make up for it. I don't think Zuri will be sleeping over any time soon, but I actually feel relieved that they finally know."

"Oh my god, Gwen, that's so amazing, you have no idea. I was killing myself with worry over this," I said, feeling a weight lift off my chest.

"Me too," Gwen said. "And now, I don't have to keep secrets anymore. I don't have to keep lying to them." I could hear her smile through the phone.

"Oh, I almost forgot—" I said. "My dad wanted me to invite you over for dinner tonight. He's cooking, and he says there's more than enough veggie burgers to go around."

"Well, when you put it like that, how could I say no?" Gwen said with a laugh. I hadn't heard her laugh in days.

I rolled onto my stomach and opened my messages on my phone.

Crisis averted, I texted James, hoping he'd saved my number.

I knew you couldn't have done anything that bad, he replied.

***

Gwen barely made it through the front door before I smothered her in a hug. I hadn't even realized how much I'd missed her—the real her.

"I appreciate the enthusiasm, Charles, but you're cutting off my air supply," Gwen said as she tried to escape.

"It's good to have you back," I said as I pulled away, a smile taking over my face. She knew what I meant.

My dad was setting the table as we rounded the corner into the dining room.

"You must be Gwen," he said, reaching out to shake her hand. "What a treat to meet two of Charlotte's new friends in one day."

"Dad, it's just Charlie. No one calls me by my full name here," I said, trying to change the subject.

"Another friend?" Gwen raised an eyebrow at me. "Do you mean to tell me that your dad met Zuri before me?"

"Oh, no," my dad clarified. "Charlotte introduced me to a young man from the barn earlier today…what was his name?"

"Ren?" Gwen asked.

"No, that wasn't it…" my dad continued.

"James," I said quietly, avoiding eye contact with both of them. This was not how I intended for this conversation to go.

"James?" Gwen repeated a bit too enthusiastically.

"Yup," I said, unable to think of a way to explain it in front of my dad. Instead, I just stared at her, my eyes pleading for her to drop the boy talk.

Gwen shot me a clever smile. "So how about those veggie burgers?"

"They're almost ready," my dad said on his way to the kitchen to grab the buns and sugar-free ketchup. Only he could find a way to make burgers seem healthy.

Once we were sat for dinner, I had to admit that my dad's veggie burgers weren't half bad. In fact, they were almost enjoyable—or maybe it was just the company.

"So, Mr. Briarman, have you come by the barn yet to see your daughter train?" Gwen said. "I think she's got a bright future ahead of her on the Seahorse team, if she'll have us."

"I haven't yet," my dad said with a smile. "But I'd love to stop by sometime and check it out for myself, as long as I wouldn't be in the way."

"Oh, not at all!" Gwen said, with a sneaky grin. She was up to something. "I'm sure Ebony would be happy to have you visit the stables."

"I'd actually like to meet Ebony since Charlotte has told me so much about her."

"Dad—"

"For sure," Gwen interrupted me before I could interject. "You know, Ebony is absolutely stunning, about your age too, give or take a few years, and very single…"

Oh, Gwen. Always the matchmaker. I couldn't even be irritated because I was too happy seeing her back to her old self.

My dad laughed and leaned back in his chair.

"I'm sure Ebony doesn't want to get involved with a recent divorcé, but I appreciate the thought, Gwen," he said.

She waved her hand, as if to shoo away the idea. "Don't sell yourself short, Mr. B. I have a good feeling about you two."

I laughed and shook my head, but imagining my dad dating again, maybe even in a happy relationship, made my heart warm.

The three of us sat in the dining room for over an hour, chatting and laughing as my dad and Gwen fell into a conversation about veganism and the climate implications of eating meat. She gave him a few new tips about sustainable living and single-use plastic as he printed out his favorite meatless Monday recipes, and by the time we cleared the dishes, I was afraid that my dad would want to adopt Gwen and replace me.

"Thanks so much for dinner, you guys." Gwen beamed at us as she slid her denim jacket over her shoulders. She turned to my dad and added, "I'll bring you a few of my reusable straws next time I come over."

"Looking forward to it. And don't forget, you're welcome here any time." My dad gave her a knowing look.

"Don't tempt me with a good time, you won't be able to get rid of me," Gwen said before turning back to me and holding her arms out for a hug.

"Don't forget," she whispered in my ear as we embraced, "we have a *lot* to catch up on."

She had no idea.

Gwen pulled away and added, "I'll see you tomorrow at the barn photoshoot," then winked at me before heading down the porch steps and to her car.

Chapter 21

By the time Monday morning rolled around, my excitement for the barn photoshoot had shifted to nervousness. I was already awake when my alarm went off, scrolling through the virtual mood board I'd created and double-checking that my camera batteries were fully charged. No one from the stables had seen my photos before, and I knew this was my chance to prove myself to them—to show that I was more than just the girl who mucked out their horses' stalls.

It felt strange not throwing on my normal barn attire as I slipped into a pale blue sundress and pulled on a pair of white converse. After brushing my teeth and putting on some mascara and lip balm, I pulled my hair into a high ponytail and made my way downstairs. My dad had a green juice waiting for me on the counter when I walked into the kitchen.

"Morning," I said, noticeably more chipper than I used to be at this hour.

"Excited for today?" my dad asked.

I glanced at him over his newspaper. "Mostly just nervous."

I grabbed a piece of bread from the counter and popped it into the toaster as my dad got up and gathered some ingredients to blend a smoothie.

"Here, you can bring this one to Gwen," he said, placing a cup on the counter and adding a metal straw. "And tell her I got some reusable straws from that market she suggested."

"I'm sure she'll love that," I said, rolling my eyes and shoving the last bite of toast in my mouth. I grabbed my keys from the wall, swung my camera bag over my shoulder, and reached for the two drinks on the counter before running out the door.

"Have fun today," my dad called after me.

"I'll try," I yelled, running down the steps as the door swung shut behind me.

The barn was bustling with excitement by the time I arrived, with everyone grooming their horses and polishing their riding boots. I rounded the corner of the second aisle and immediately bumped into Ren.

"Look at you, all professional with your camera," he said warmly, but I watched as his eyes quickly took me in from head to toe.

"No scrubs today?" I said, taking note of his seersucker button-down and khakis.

"Nope," he said. "Ebony has requested my presence at the photoshoot. She says it will be good for barn PR to show that we have trusted medical professionals on-site at all times."

"Should I break the news to her that you're only the assistant?" I teased.

"Very funny," he replied, nudging my arm as I walked away.

Gwen and Zuri were grooming their horses with curry combs when I found them in the first aisle. They both had their hair pulled back into low buns and wore navy blue blazers with tan riding breeches.

"You both look incredible," I said as I patted Dandelion on the nose.

"I'm *so* excited to finally have some updated photos of me and Sophie to post," Zuri said. "The last time we had a photoshoot, she was still mostly gray."

She pulled a hairbrush out of her grooming kit and began to detangle Sophie's white mane.

"My mom says she's going to print the photos out and get them framed for the living room," Gwen added.

No pressure.

"Oh—Gwen, I almost forgot." I held the smoothie out to her. "My dad made this for you. He wanted me to point out the metal straw. He really took what you said about the sea turtles to heart."

Gwen gasped and took a sip.

"Mmm, strawberry banana," she said before passing it to Zuri to share. "Make sure to tell your dad I said thanks."

"For sure," I said as I ducked below their crossties. "I'm gonna head outside and start setting up."

As I passed the wash bay, I saw Jenna standing with her arms crossed, glaring at her horse who had definitely rolled in her stall overnight. Snowball was covered in dirt and stains, even sullying her snowy white mane. That would take a good shower to fix, and luckily, I was off the clock.

Over by the first stall, James was diligently scrubbing a stain out of Lightning's coat, and as I passed by, I could smell the essential oils he'd sprayed to keep the flies away for the shoot. He glanced up at the sound of my footsteps and smiled, making my stomach do a somersault.

I will never get used to that.

I hadn't seen him since my minor breakdown at the bookstore, and

I wasn't even sure where we stood now. All I could seem to do was stare back at him and let out a small laugh, and just as I opened my mouth to finally say something, Ebony called my name from outside. James shrugged as if to say, *we can talk later*, and I walked away hoping my smile communicated that I was, in fact, very glad to see him.

When I stepped onto the back field, I inhaled the sweet smell of freshly cut grass and exhaled some of the tightness in my chest. Ebony had gone all out to get the barn in tip-top shape for today—the whole place was practically sparkling. The white picket fence was gleaming from a fresh power wash, the grass had been mowed as recently as that morning, and the paddocks had been picked until they looked as if they'd never been used. Blue ribbons hung from each door, and everything had been swept and polished to perfection.

After doing a few test shots of the lighting and adjusting my camera settings to get the exposure right, I was ready to get started.

My first shot of the day was of Gwen and Zuri with their horses. The familiarity of my subjects helped me to relax a bit as I snapped the first few photos. Other than their horses' inability to ignore the grass below them, they proved to be good models. Next, the riding team members each took turns posing with their horses, giving them a kiss on the nose, or jumping on them bareback for a photo. I could feel Ren standing behind me, watching as I worked, and I tried my best not to think about my every move being monitored, even by friendly eyes.

James stepped forward for his solo shots next, and Lightning followed obediently behind him. I started with some full-body photos, taking my time to find the right angle—which wasn't hard since James didn't seem to have a bad side. I caught myself peering through the viewfinder for a few extra seconds before snapping each picture, trying and failing to hide the smile that had crept onto my face. I moved closer, positioning Lightning and James right beside each other to get a shot of just their eyes. I'd found the photo idea on Pinterest the night before and immediately thought of James's dark and brooding gaze—plus, he was conveniently tall enough to stand eye-to-eye with his horse.

As I approached them, I noticed a few strands of James's hair were out of place, falling onto his forehead. For a moment, I forgot about the people watching me and combed my fingers through his wavy locks until they were right again. I felt a swell of anticipation as James smiled down at me. Even up close, he looked perfect—but that wasn't really what drew me to him anymore. I felt like I was starting to truly know him—what was going on inside his head, what he might be thinking at any given moment. For instance, I could tell he was enjoying the attention I was giving him, almost leaning into my hand. I broke away and tried to refocus.

When I turned around to get a shot from farther back, I was met with Ren's green-eyed gaze. His cheery disposition had shifted to something more jealous, and I hated that I knew it was because of me. I wished I could conceal it from him, but then again, how could I? Ren was my friend, and I cared about him, but James was more. I couldn't hide that or pretend otherwise, no matter how much I wished to spare Ren's feelings. It was written all over my face.

We made it to the final shot, which would be for the heading of the barn website, and I lined up the entire group along the freshly washed white fence, feeling my heart swell as I looked at each of them. I could recall a pleasant conversation with almost every friendly face that stared back at me. In such a short amount of time, I'd become so attached to all of them. It felt strange to think back to a time when they weren't part of my life. Even Jenna squeezing herself close to James's side couldn't bring me down.

A small cloud rolled in and covered the sun for a moment, shifting the light, and James glanced at the sky.

"Maybe we should wait for the light to come back," he said, squinting up at the clouds.

Before I could nod in agreement, Ren spoke.

"I'm sure Charlie could figure that out for herself," he said. The tone of Ren's voice struck me with its distinction from all our previous interactions, though shrouded in sarcasm and paired with a short laugh, I could tell he was upset. It made me uneasy—like maybe his even temper had been a façade, or maybe I'd been deceived by my own perception of him.

I took a breath in and out. I tended to overreact to these types of moments—running far away from even the slightest of inconsistencies in people's behavior. Not everyone was going to change on a dime like my mom had. People were allowed to be in a bad mood. Ren was only trying to stand up for me, this wasn't a big deal. I forced my mind to lay down its weapons and be sensible about this.

I chipped away at the nail polish on my thumb that I'd painted for the occasion and glanced at James, whose eyes were narrowed in confusion, as if to ask, *where did that come from?* I gave him a look that said, *don't worry about it.*

"It's fine, Ren," I said, giving him a polite smile and trying to ignore the pit in my stomach. A small part of me yearned for the simpler times when nothing had changed between any of us—when I had just been the new girl whose heart belonged to no one. Back when I thought no one could ever have it in the first place.

Chapter 22

When I rolled over in bed to turn my alarm off the next morning, I realized it was actually my phone ringing that had woken me up.

Who could possibly be calling before six in the morning?

I squinted at the screen, unable to look directly at the bright light so soon after waking up, and blindly accepted the call.

"Hello?" I said, my voice tired.

"Were you still asleep?" a familiar voice replied.

"James?" I said, half-convinced that I was dreaming.

"Don't you have to be at the barn by seven?"

Does he know my schedule?

"And your point is...?" I said, fighting the urge to slip back to sleep.

"That's in an hour."

"An hour and ten minutes," I corrected him, checking the time. "Forty more minutes to sleep, twenty to get ready, and ten to drive there."

"Someone's a morning person," James teased.

I didn't have it in me to come up with a witty response before the light of day.

"So, you called for…" I mumbled.

"I wanted to ask if you'd like to get dinner with me tonight."

I jolted up in bed, suddenly very awake.

"Tonight?"

"Yes," he replied.

"Just me and you?"

James laughed. "I'd prefer it that way."

"Okay," I said. "I should be free—I think."

"Don't make any schedule adjustments on my account," he said.

I rolled my eyes and tried to ignore my heart pounding in my chest.

"I'm available," I said. "What time should I meet you?"

"I'll pick you up at seven," he said with a laugh before hanging up.

Since I had been roused way earlier than usual, I decided to go to the barn early and take a quick trail ride to start my day. Ever since my lesson with James, I hadn't been nervous to ride alone anymore. I tacked up Caramel, and we made our way down the path that led toward the woods.

Golden light flickered on the leaves that still glistened with morning dew as we trotted down the dirt trail. I led my horse further into the woods in search of my favorite resting spot—a grove of elm trees tucked away by a small pond. Whenever I'd passed it before, I liked to imagine Colin Firth's Darcy swimming there like in the pond at Pemberley.

As I approached the grove, Caramel's ears pinned back, and she let out a nervous whinny. I looked around to see what might've spooked her, and my eyes landed on a chestnut mare standing in the shade, then on a pile of clothes rumpled at the horse's feet. Before I could fully grasp what I was seeing, James emerged from the water. This time, he wasn't wearing his green swim shorts, in fact, he was wearing absolutely nothing at all.

My hand shot up to cover my face as I gasped, mortification coloring my cheeks. The sound of Caramel's hooves got James's attention, and his eyes shot to mine before I could back away unnoticed.

"Charlie?" James said as he shielded himself behind his horse. His still-visible face appeared to be much more amused by this than I was.

"I didn't think anyone was out here," I shouted as he pulled on his boxers.

Stepping out from hiding, he yelled back, "What happened to you getting up at 6:30?"

"I received a call this morning that rudely woke me up, so I had no choice but to embrace the extra half hour," I said, trying my best to seem unphased—my mind wouldn't allow me to so easily move on from what I'd just seen.

I dismounted and walked over to James, with Caramel following behind me.

"I didn't mean to interrupt you…like this." My eyes drifted slightly down and then back up to meet his eyes again.

"You mean, it wasn't your intention to find me swimming naked this morning? I'm glad we cleared that up," he said, holding back a grin.

My cheeks flushed, and I turned my face away from him, trying to appear immune to his effortless charm—I was so obviously afflicted.

"I'll just be going then," I said, putting a foot back in the stirrups and grabbing the reins.

"Or you could join me?" James said as he backed toward the edge of the pond and dove in. Ripples extended in every direction as he resurfaced and smiled at me, shaking his hair out like wet dog. I looked down at my outfit—leggings and a T-shirt—and shook my head at him.

"C'mon, it's like bathwater in here," he shouted.

I glanced at the trail I had intended on exploring during my ride, then back at James, weighing my options. This was a bad idea, but it was one of those bad ideas that would make me swoon if I read it in a novel.

Screw it.

"Turn around." I gestured for James to look away, which he did without hesitation, and tied Caramel's reins to a branch next to Lightning. I pulled my shirt over my head and shimmied out of my tight pants before stepping to the edge of the water and dipping a toe in.

I slowly lowered myself into the pond, and James was right—it felt amazing. My head sunk beneath the surface, and I felt my nerves seep out of my body. I reemerged, taking a breath, and saw that James had turned back around and was watching me now. His shoulders were just visible above the surface and beads of water dripped down his neck.

We both stayed silent for a moment, just wading in the shimmering pool. I watched James's chest rise and fall with each breath he took. He stared at me over the water—sunlight reflecting off the surface and illuminating his features—and I was struck by the feeling that his undivided attention produced in me. I had to look away.

"Why do you do that?" James asked.

I stole another glance at him. "Do what?"

"Why do you hide away like that?"

I bit my lip and fought the urge to turn away again.

"I don't know what you mean," I lied.

He shook his head. "It feels like you're running from something every time I look at you."

I blinked at him but didn't let myself move.

"Maybe I am," I said, practically under my breath.

James moved closer to me. "Why?"

I bit the inside of my cheek. "I don't know."

James closed his eyes for a second, considering something. "You never told me what happened with your mom."

"I don't really want to talk about that," I said, each word weighing heavily on my tongue before being spoken.

James was silent for a moment, then found my eyes again. "It's scary how the more you love someone, the more they can hurt you."

I had to look away as I took a shaky breath and said, "Yeah."

James was only a few inches from me now. I could feel the gravity of his presence prickling under my skin. He looked solemn, like he had figured me out somehow, and everything was fragile all of a sudden. James closed the gap between us and brushed a piece of my wet hair off my cheek. I looked up at him, meeting his dark stare once more, and this time, I allowed him to study my face, his eyes tracing every feature until his gaze settled on my lips.

My breath caught.

Suddenly, small ripples appeared all around us. I looked up to see clouds rolling in as James lifted his hand out of the water and caught a droplet of rain. Within seconds, it was downpouring.

"What the hell?" I shouted over the violent pitter-patter.

James looked up at the sky and let out a hearty laugh.

"That's Rhode Island for you," he yelled, shaking his head. "My horse has a very ironic fear of thunderstorms, so we should probably get back to the barn."

"Okay!" I said as James backstroked to the edge of the pond. I dove below the ripples and swam after him. As I pulled myself up onto the mossy shore, my foot slipped. James grabbed my arm to steady me.

My eyes stared at the place where he was touching me, scanning upward until I found his face. A soft smile pulled at his lips, and he stepped closer just as a crack of lightning lit up the sky.

James reached for my hand, and we ran to grab our clothes. My T-shirt clung to my skin as I pulled it over my now-soaked sports bra, and there was no chance of getting my leggings back on while I was drenched. Without wasting time, I pulled on my boots and got back on my horse.

James was already clothed and back in the saddle, waiting for me before taking off. He raised an eyebrow at my bare legs and chuckled. He pressed his heels into his horse's sides and brought Lightning to a trot. I followed him closely as we made our way back down the path toward the barn.

"Here, pass me the reins," James said as he dismounted. "I'll take Caramel in." He peeled off his windbreaker and tossed it at me.

"*Thank you,*" I mouthed at him, pulling the jacket over my arms. It was long on me—enough to hide my underwear and cover part of my exposed thighs. I turned to run into the locker room, but it was too late. Ebony was coming toward us, eyes wide as she took in my unkempt appearance.

"Do you have any idea what time it is?" she asked.

I shook my head—I'd left my phone in the tack room that morning. James nudged my side and held his arm out to me. I read the watch on his wrist, and my stomach dropped.

7:34 am.

"I'm *so* sorry, Ebony. I forgot my phone in the tack room, and then we got caught in a storm, and I totally lost track of time."

As if being half-naked in front of my boss wasn't enough, I had to be a half-hour late to work too?

Ebony shook her head. "Don't let it happen again."

The disappointment in her voice hit me harder than it should've.

"And please go put some clothes on," she finished.

I nodded, feeling shame warm my cheeks. But as I turned to sprint into the girl's locker room, I caught James grinning as he watched me walk away.

***

My hair was still wet from the shower when James knocked on the door to pick me up for dinner. I ran downstairs to get to the door before my dad could, and when I opened it, James was standing there in a linen button-down and faded black jeans.

I smiled at him before remembering to feel embarrassed about our morning encounter.

"You look nice," he said, taking note of my lilac wrap dress that I'd hoped he'd like.

"Thanks," I said. "So do you."

He smiled and gestured towards his car in the driveway. "After you."

James took me to the same restaurant I'd gone to with my dad since I'd mentioned that I liked it. As we sat at a table for two by the window, I tried to ignore the gnawing feeling in my stomach. No one had ever taken me to dinner before—it sort of felt like I was trying to act older than I was.

James, on the other hand, seemed quite at his leisure. I hoped he couldn't sense my ridiculous paranoia. *Why does he even want me here? Do I even want to be here?* He took a sip of water, then placed the glass back on the table. I focused my attention on the condensation forming a ring on the tablecloth. He picked up the menu, I fiddled with my silverware. He took a breath, I took a breath. He glanced at me and raised an eyebrow, I averted my gaze.

"Gwen seemed back to normal at the photoshoot the other day," he said as he returned his eyes to the menu.

"Yeah, she's been better since talking to her parents about everything." I forced a smile. It suddenly felt impossible to act normal. I looked at the menu, pretending to be hungry.

"I'm glad," James said. After I didn't respond, he looked up at me. "Charlie?"

"Mhm?"

"Are you okay?" I could hear a laugh in his voice as he tried to be serious.

"I'm fine," I said.

"You seem nervous."

I looked down at my fork.

"You don't have to be," James said, finding my gaze somehow, his eyes sincere.

I cleared my throat. "I just…don't really do this that often."

"Dinner?"

I took a breath and smiled. "Yes, dinner," I said, feeling a few bricks crumble and fall from the wall guarding my heart. I glanced out the window at the Newport bridge, and Jamestown didn't seem quite so far away anymore.

About halfway through our meal, a group of twenty-something guys spotted us from the bar.

"James! What's up man?" one of the guys said, fist-bumping him.

"I see summer's been treating you well," said another guy as he shifted his eyes to me and then back to James. I fidgeted in my seat, feeling like we were on display.

"It's been good so far. What about you guys?" James responded, then glanced at me, as if to say, *ignore them*.

"Spending most of our time prepping for the final round of tryouts.

Only two weeks away," said the first guy. "We miss you on the team, bro, it's not the same since you graduated. How's your training been going?"

"Just the usual, about an hour a day. I'm trying not to overwork Lightning before it counts," James said.

"What's the tryout for?" I asked, looking from James to his friends.

"The World Equestrian Games," said the second guy. "They have two last-minute openings on the team this year. Half of the Brown team made it through qualifiers."

"It's nothing," James said, shooting his friends a strange look.

"Well…we should probably get back to the group," the first guy said. "Text the chat after the final round. I'm sure you and Lightning will kill it."

"They always do," his friend said as they turned back to the bar.

I looked at James, waiting for him to elaborate.

"That sounds like a cool opportunity," I said after a few moments of silence.

"If I qualify," he said plainly.

"Your friends seem to think you will."

"It doesn't matter what anyone thinks. It all comes down to how we jump on the day." The tone of his voice was harsh again, like when we'd first met.

"Well," I said, finding his eyes, "if you need anyone to oversee your training, I know someone who could give you a few pointers."

James took a breath.

"I wasn't aware that you were in the business of coaching now," he said, his emerging smile sending a warm wave of relief through me.

"I could try to squeeze you in for an afternoon session this week," I said, "but it's gonna cost you."

"Oh yeah?"

"Yup. Looks like dinner is on you this evening," I said with a grin.

After dinner, we drove to Second Beach. Being in the car with the windows down and the radio playing seemed to ease my nerves a bit. A red sunset colored the sky and reflected onto the water below. James glanced at me as he parked the car.

"I'm sorry if things were a little weird with the guys from school," he said.

I forced my mind not to jump to conclusions and waited for him to continue.

"I get kind of crazy with this competition stuff," James added. "My mom was on the national team."

I worked up the courage to reach for his hand, carefully rubbing my thumb back and forth as I listened.

"It's just—I've made it this far. I need to finish this, even if she isn't here to see it. It's what she always wanted for me…it's why she bred Lightning. I can't let her down." His attention seemed to drift.

"You never told me what happened to her," I said quietly.

James looked at me with a pain so deep in his eyes that I felt it in my bones. Then he blinked, and it was hidden again, somewhere behind the mask he wore each day, pretending it didn't hurt as badly as it did.

"Riding accident," he said. "Three years ago."

I closed my eyes. "James—"

He held my hand tighter for a moment, like he was bracing himself for the memory.

"You can always come to me," I said, "if you want to talk about her."

I looked up at him, and his face was lit with a red glow. He nodded and leaned closer to me, his chin nestling my hair.

"You smell good," he breathed, quieter now.

"Thanks," I said, taking a mental note of the shampoo I'd used.

James looked at me, and his eyes did that thing again, brimming with depth and anticipation—like a small part of him was afraid.

Then he leaned in and kissed me, lightly at first. His lips were warm on mine. My hand found his face, then his hair. His dark waves felt soft as I ran my fingers through them.

"I'm really glad you're here," he whispered in between kissing me and breathing.

"Me too," I said.

We stayed like that—wrapped up in each other, closer than we'd ever been—until the red sky went dark.

Chapter 23

Waking up early no longer felt like a chore. I found myself stirring in bed before my alarm, even skipping my morning coffee, not needing a jolt of caffeine to keep me awake. I'd gotten to the barn early every day that week and had one thing on my mind.

Where is he?

I no longer had control over my gaze, my eyes searching up and down the aisles, turning my head at every chestnut horse or flash of brown hair in my peripheral. The pull James had over me was magnetic, and I was done fighting with myself to resist.

As I brushed the cobwebs off an empty stall in the third aisle, I could hear someone training in the outdoor arena. I peeked over the windowsill to see James expertly leading his horse over the fences. Lightning soared over each jump, making it look easy. I loved how relaxed James looked when he thought no one was watching him. I wanted to capture it.

I slipped out of the stall and glanced at the clock hanging on the wall. 12:45 pm. Ebony would be back from her lunch hour in fifteen minutes.

I rested my broom against the wall and sprinted towards the back doors, looking around to make sure none of the other stable hands could see me. Lunch hay needed to be distributed soon, and they'd be annoyed with me if I didn't pull my weight. I turned to check one last time as I passed the tack room, and without looking where I was going, I crashed into someone. My palms broke my fall on the cobblestone floor, and I pushed my hair out of my face before looking up.

Jenna stood over me, her immaculate riding clothes gleaming in the afternoon light and her fringe framing the smug look on her face.

"There you are," she said, extending a hand to help me up. I looked at her, confused, but accepted her hand. Her grip was tight and cold, not unlike her tone of voice. Her riding boots gave her a few extra inches of height, which helped her to look down at me as she said, "I need you for something."

I blinked at her, still a bit jostled from my fall.

"Snowball is being an idiot this morning," Jenna said. "She rolled in her paddock, and I need her to be squeaky clean for my tryout today. You can use the purple shampoo in my grooming kit and—"

"Jenna," I interrupted. She narrowed her eyes at me, as if I was the first person who'd ever dared to speak over her.

"What?"

"I already have a list of chores from Ebony today, and I was just going on my break," I said. "I'm really sorry, but I don't have time to help you."

"Very funny." Jenna blinked and gave me a tight-lipped smile. "You know, my boarding fees are what pays for all those Cavalleria Toscana knockoffs of yours," her icy gaze scanned me up and down. "So, I'm pretty sure that means you have to do what I say."

"Excuse me?" I felt my cheeks heat up—I wasn't sure if it was from anger or embarrassment.

"Unless you want Ebony to hear about how you've been slacking off lately…"

"I think Ebony can form her own opinion of me," I said, dusting off my hands and backing away from her.

I quickly grabbed my camera bag from the tack room and made a run for it. Once I'd made it outside, I exhaled a sigh of relief and crept under the bleachers near the arena.

James was still training, so concentrated on the course that he hadn't noticed me.

Perfect. I snuck my camera between two bleachers and started snapping pictures as he and Lightning cleared the fences. His eyes were focused as he led his horse around to each of the jumps.

As he made his way toward the end of the course, James got close enough to hear the shutter of my camera. His eyes shot to me, and I gave him a small wave before crawling out from my hiding spot. James just laughed and shook his head, clearing the final jump before leading Lightning over to where I was now sitting on the top rung of the fence.

"So, in your expert opinion," James said, "how did we look?"

"I have no complaints," I replied with a half-smile.

"Want to show me how it's done?"

I scrunched my nose at him. "What?"

"Hop on," James said, tilting his head towards the space behind him.

"But you're in the middle of training."

"I think I deserve some extracurricular activity after that last round," he said, reaching a hand toward me.

I shrugged, giving in way too easily, before taking his hand and using the middle rung of the fence to mount his horse. If this was just an excuse to get closer to me, I fully embraced that. In fact, I couldn't believe I hadn't thought of it first—proximity to James was quickly becoming my top priority these days. I wrapped my arms around his waist and clasped my hands together to steady myself as James dug his heels in and brought Lightning back into a canter. I held on tight as we raced around the arena, feeling James's lungs expand and contract with each breath he took.

We rose and fell in tandem against the saddle, and I could feel the adrenaline rushing through me. Riding had felt scary and difficult before…but with James, it was thrilling. As I got more comfortable, my grip on his waist loosened and my hands drifted to my sides, letting my thighs hold me in place.

Just as my arms let go, Lightning switched directions, and our diagonal pattern changed with it. Suddenly, I was off the rhythm and instantly tensed up, which only made my seat bouncier. I tried to reach for James again, but it was too late. One second I was on the horse, and the next, I felt myself plummeting to the dirt below.

The wind whistled in my ears as the world blurred into indistinct colors around me. The only tangible thing in view was my brown hair flowing freely around my face.

I forgot to put on a helmet.

Then everything went dark.

✳✳✳

I reluctantly opened my eyes and squinted against the blaring sun above me, feeling the side of my head throbbing as I regained consciousness. I felt a lump already forming as my hand surveyed the damage. Lightning was tied up to the fence, and I realized my head was in James's lap, recognizing the familiar feeling of his hand holding tightly to mine.

"Charlie—" James said with quiet urgency.

"What happened?" I said weakly.

"You blacked out for a few seconds after you fell." His eyes were clouded as they moved all over my face. "How do you feel?"

"I don't know," I said, still getting my bearings. "Not great."

"We should get you to the hospital," James said, helping me sit up.

"What? No—I'm fine. I just need a minute."

"Charlie, we need to get you checked out," he said, but when I looked up at him, he seemed far away. "Head injuries are no joke."

How could I argue with him on that? He knew better than anyone.

James lifted me in his arms and carried me to the passenger seat of his Jeep. I winced as the sound of the door slamming sent a shooting pain to my temple, and I could tell James noticed as his face went from pale to ghostly.

I reached for his hand. "I'm fine, I promise."

He squeezed it back, but his eyes were glued to the road as we drove off.

After a few minutes of filling out paperwork, a nurse came over to us in the waiting room of the hospital.

"The doctor will see you now, this way." She pushed the wheelchair they insisted I use into an empty room. "She'll be right in."

James paced back and forth as we waited, glancing at me with each turn, as if to make sure I was still alive.

"Don't make this harder for yourself. I'm fine," I insisted. "Look."

I attempted to push myself upright in the stretcher I was now laying on, but James rushed to my side, grabbing my arm and holding me in place.

"Please just rest."

"James, look at me." I took a breath and forced a pleasant expression. "You don't have to worry."

A blonde woman in a white lab coat stepped into the room and closed the door behind her, shutting out the noisy hum of nurse chatter and oxygen machines.

"What do we have here," she said, grabbing a clipboard from the side of the stretcher.

"She fell off a horse," James said. "She was out for a few seconds."

"Let's take a look," the doctor said, smiling at me. She took a small flashlight from her pocket and shined it in and out of my eyes. "Hmm... your pupils are acting up a bit."

"Do you think she has a concussion?" James said, moving closer to my side.

"Can you close your eyes for me?" the doctor said. "Now put your finger to your nose."

I complied, finding my nose with minimal effort.

"Okay, you can open again," she said. "Any headache or nausea?"

"No nausea, but my head hurts a little."

She took a few notes on the clipboard before turning her attention back to me.

"Well, luckily it looks like you only have a minor concussion, but you still need to monitor your symptoms for the next few days and let us know if anything changes. Anything abnormal could be a sign of something more serious." She glanced from me to James. He nodded.

"You should avoid strenuous activities and try not to concentrate on books or computer screens for the next ten days." The doctor reached for a pamphlet on the wall and handed it to me. "This will tell you all the dos and don'ts for the next week and a half. If anything changes, don't hesitate to reach out. It's always better to be safe than sorry with this kind of thing."

James took my hand in his and gave it a squeeze.

"Just take it easy for a few days," the doctor concluded. "We can schedule a follow-up in ten days to make sure everything's good, okay?"

"Okay, I can do that," I said, nodding. When the doctor opened the door to leave, I saw my dad searching the hallway.

"Dad?" I said, my eyes narrowing. I turned to James. "You called my dad?"

James ignored the question, instead saying, "Mr. Briarman—we're in here."

I pushed myself up on the stretcher and twisted so my legs hung over the edge. After taking a steadying breath, I forced myself into a standing position, trying my best to ignore the pounding in my head.

"Dad, before you say anything, I'm fine. It's only a mild concussion, nothing serious," I said in a rush, realizing that James must've called the store to get ahold of him. "Please don't be mad, okay? I know I promised you I'd be careful. I messed up. I'm really, really sorry."

My dad looked at me with teary eyes and said, "All I want to do is to make sure you're okay." He wrapped his arms around my shoulders, my head nestling against his chest, and planted a kiss on my forehead. "Please just wear your helmet from now on, so I don't have to worry about you all the time."

He looked relieved, but I couldn't understand why he wasn't angry with me. He had warned me about this—I wasn't wearing a helmet. I was being reckless and irresponsible. And he was just *worried*?

"Let's get you home," my dad said, taking the pamphlet from my hands and leading me toward the door. We walked to his car with James following closely behind us, and when my dad opened the door for me, I stopped him.

"I just...I have to talk to James first," I said. "It'll only be a second."

My dad nodded and got into the driver's seat, closing the door to give us some privacy. James was waiting patiently, leaning against the side of his car as I walked over to him, trying to ignore the ashamed look on his face—this wasn't his fault.

"Hey," I said quietly.

He was only a few feet in front of me now but still seemed far away, not even looking at me.

"I'm sorry if this…brought back any bad memories for you." I cringed at my words. "I don't really know how to talk about this with you, and I'll probably just say the wrong thing, but…I could tell how scared you were in there, and I feel awful that I caused that."

James looked incredulous.

"Charlie, you can't seriously be apologizing to me right now," he said, running a hand through his hair and taking a breath. "I should have *never* let you get on a horse without a helmet on. Especially at your level."

I felt a pang in my chest. *Of course, he still sees me as the pathetic, nineteen-year-old amateur that I am.*

"It was my responsibility, not yours," I said. "And I'm going to be fine."

James stepped closer and reached for my hand.

"Listen to me," he said, taking a sharp breath. "If anything had happened to you—"

"But it didn't."

"But if it had…" He glanced back at the hospital. "It's scary how fast good things can be taken away. One day, someone's there and the next… they're not."

I searched for the right words to comfort him but came up blank.

"I can't lose another person to a riding accident," he said, quieter now.

I blinked back the saltwater in my eyes.

He continued, "You of all people understand how it feels to not have your mom around anymore."

My heart ached as I looked up at him. I really did understand, but we had never talked about it after he brought up my mom in the pond. I couldn't bring myself to explain to him that my mom hadn't actually left me—not really. I had left her.

"I can't go through something like that again," he breathed.

I reached for him, trying to find a way to prove that I was okay, but I knew it wouldn't help. He knew better than most how painful loss could be. He had to carry the fear of it with him every day. I pulled him closer to me and looked up into his sad brown eyes.

"I'm not going anywhere," I whispered. "I promise."

Chapter 24

The days started to drag on now that I had absolutely nothing to do. My one and only task was to rest, which wasn't easy when all I wanted was get back to work. I yearned for the days at the barn and the bookstore. I missed reading. It had only been four days, but it felt like an eternity. James visited almost every day on his way home from training, and Gwen and Zuri had made the rounds, but what I really wanted was my freedom back.

I rolled over in bed and groaned into my pillow, sick of staring at the ceiling, and laid there until I heard a knock on my door frame.

"Ren?" I said after turning to see how it could be—I wasn't expecting any guests today.

Ren stood outside my bedroom door with a small potted plant in his hand. Half of me was happy to have company to entertain me, while the other half of me remembered that I had no makeup on and that my hair was most likely a disaster. I tucked a few loose strands behind my ears and sat up, but Ren didn't move from where he was standing.

We hadn't talked in a while—not since the barn photoshoot. It kind of felt like he'd taken the hint and backed off after seeing me with James, but it was good to see his face again.

"I hope I didn't wake you," he said.

"Ren, it's noon." I gestured for him to come in.

"I've—we've missed you at the barn," he said.

"Probably not as much as I miss seeing you guys," I replied with a sigh. "I've been so bored laying around here all day."

"I brought you something that could help with that," Ren said, piquing my interest. I patted the comforter next to me and pulled my legs out from under the covers into a crisscross position.

Ren placed the plant on my nightstand and carefully took a seat on my bed, pulling a Walkman radio out of his jacket pocket and handing it to me.

"Here," he said, letting a small smile crack his otherwise earnest expression.

"Uh…thanks?" I said as I took it from him, flipping it over in my hands.

"One more thing," he said, fishing something out of his pocket. "I know you only have one more book left on your Austen list after finishing *Mansfield Park* last week, and I don't want you to stop your marathon just because you can't read right now."

He placed a cassette in my hand with *Sanditon* handwritten on the label.

"The last thing she wrote…" I trailed off, feeling a lump in my throat as I realized how much he must have paid attention to my ramblings this summer.

"Someone made an audiobook of it, even though it's unfinished. They published it anyway, I guess," Ren said.

"Thank you so much," I breathed, wrapping my arms around his neck in a hug. He froze for a second, then pulled me closer.

"I never asked you before, but how did you get so into Jane Austen anyway?" he said as he pulled away. "Not interested in giving other authors a chance?"

I set the gift down on my nightstand next to the plant and turned back to Ren. "I don't know…probably from my mom. She gave me a copy of *Pride and Prejudice* as a kid, and I guess I really liked it."

"Do you miss her?" he said, likely realizing by now that she didn't live here.

"We don't really talk anymore," I said. "I guess reading these books sort of helps me to remember how things used to be between us. Sometimes, I feel like she was an entirely different person back then."

Ren nodded, and there was a brief moment of quiet.

"Have you been feeling any better?" he said, steering the topic to something else, as if he could sense that I didn't want to talk about it further. "I heard it'll be almost two weeks 'til you're back at the stables."

"I have a checkup in a week, then I'll be right back to it. I can't afford to miss any more work, if I want to buy textbooks next semester."

"Plus, you have to get back on the horse," Ren teased. "You don't want to lose momentum on your training."

"Yeah…for sure," I said. I wasn't dreading getting back to riding, but I'd be lying if said I wasn't hesitant.

"I still can't believe this happened," Ren said. "I mean falling off is part of the sport, but you always ride the older trail horses. You couldn't have been going very fast, and your helmet should've protected you."

I swallowed. "I wasn't wearing a helmet."

Ren gave me a puzzled look.

"Charlie, as much progress as you've been making, you're still a beginner. Jeff should've never allowed that during a lesson." He shook his head. "It's barn policy."

My stomach tensed. I thought Ren of all people had noticed how well I was doing with my training, but of course no one really took me seriously.

"I wasn't having a lesson," I clarified, not looking at him.

"Then why were you in the arena?"

Should I tell him?

I knew hearing that I had been with James would only make Ren upset, and I didn't want to pour salt in the wound that I had caused in the first place, especially after he'd been so thoughtful. But my head was throbbing, and I didn't have the energy to come up with a lie.

"I was riding with James," I said, wincing at Ren's visceral reaction to the name. He stood up from the bed and turned away from me.

"You were riding James's horse without a helmet on?" Ren said, his voice wavering between jealousy and disappointment—and maybe a hint of fear for how much worse it could've been. My fingers pulled at the edge of my blanket, and I tried not to look at him.

"What was he thinking?" Ren said under his breath, pacing now in the limited space in my room. He ran his fingers through his black hair and turned back to me. "This would have never happened if—"

"Don't," I interrupted him.

"—if you had been with me," he finished.

I closed my eyes and took a breath.

"This has nothing to do with you or James," I said, a stern warning creeping into my voice. It felt so wrong arguing with him, but it felt even worse letting James take the blame. "I'm the one who got on the back of a horse without a helmet on, and I'm the one who let go. I'm the only one responsible for what happened."

Ren just shook his head.

I stood up to face him. "I'm an adult, Ren, and you're treating me like a child."

"I am well aware that you're an adult, Charlie." Ren's eyes looked sad all of a sudden, clouded with something more than just this fight. "Trust me, I don't need a reminder."

"Well, then please start acting like it," I said, taking a shaky breath. The pain in my head had returned with a vengeance.

Ren's gaze swept across my face, and he took a step closer to me, looking too deeply into my eyes.

"Charlie," he said, quieter now, "I feel like I've been pretty obvious this summer, but I think I'm going to need to just come out and say this…"

I felt my stomach drop, knowing full well what he was about to tell me—only I didn't want him to. I didn't want to have to tell him that I cared for someone else the way he cared for me. I didn't want to subject him to the pain of unrequited feelings. And most of all, I didn't want to lose him as a friend.

"I like you, Charlie—a lot," he said. "I think you're smart, and witty, and cooler than you give yourself credit. And you're so beautiful that I haven't been able to take my eyes off you since you stumbled into that stall and almost fell on top of me."

"Ren—" I said, feeling myself blush as a piece of my heart broke, but he stopped me.

"I'm not blind, I've seen the way you look at James. But I think if you gave this a chance, we could be good together." His eyes searched my face for a reaction. "I don't want you to give me an answer now. Just promise me you'll think about it, *really* think about it, then you know where to find me."

I just stood there, blinking at him, unable to string a sentence together, as Ren nodded once and turned to leave my room, closing the door behind him.

As much as I tried, I couldn't put my whirling thoughts to bed. Ren's face was there, even when I closed my eyes, staring at me with his heart in my hands. I knew I had led him on in some ways over the course of the summer—but I didn't know how to explain that I did like him back, only not the way he wanted me to.

I slowly sat down on my bed, holding my fingers to my temple and took a slow breath in and out. My usual remedy for overthinking was still off-limits for the next week—how inconvenient it was that I was strictly forbidden from reading or watching anything during recovery, right when I needed it the most. I would've done anything to sink into someone else's reality for a few hours and forget about all this.

I groaned as I reached over to my bedside table for the Walkman, feeling guilty for using Ren's gift, knowing that I was inevitably going to hurt him.

I slipped the headphones over my ears and pressed play as I sank into my mountain of pillows. Since the novel was unfinished, I wasn't sure how long it would take to get through it, but I didn't care. The words started flowing into my ears, and my attention began to drift to the trials and tribulations of an entirely different Charlotte in an entirely different seaside town. Suddenly, I was in *Sanditon*.

Chapter 25

For once, I was more than happy to keep to myself for the day. My dad made breakfast and brought me a plateful as I was waking up. I ate it in bed while I pondered what I could do to get through the next few days as painlessly as possible.

As I took a bite of syrupy vegan pancakes, my phone buzzed next to me. I felt my whole-body tense up—there were too many people I was trying to avoid these days. This time, it was only Ebony, so I accepted the call and held my phone to my ear.

"Hello?"

"Charlie," Ebony's soothing voice came through the receiver. "How have you been feeling?"

I set my breakfast plate on my bedside table and cleared my throat.

"Better," I said. "Nearly recovered, I think."

"I'm so glad to hear that," Ebony said. "And if I wasn't so worried about you, I would be lecturing you about breaking barn policy and being reckless, but I'll save that for once you're fully healed."

"I'm so sorry, Ebony," I said quietly. "It will never happen ever again."

"Good. Since that's out of the way, I wanted to ask you something."

"Okay," I said, sitting up straighter.

"We have an event coming up, we throw it every year to raise money for riding scholarships—have any of your friends mentioned it to you?"

"No, I haven't heard anything yet."

"It's our annual Barn Ball at Rosecliff—you know the mansions, right? It's the best night of the season, everyone wears black tie, all the women in long dresses, and men in suits, dancing the night away. It's always quite a spectacle."

"Oh…wow," I whispered. It sounded like a dream—or a scene out of every regency novel I'd ever loved.

"I just had a thought this morning, how wonderful it would be if we had a photographer to document the night since everyone will be looking their best," Ebony said. "It's next Friday, and I know your recovery should be done by then, so I thought you'd be just the girl for the job."

"I'd love to," I said quickly as visions of dancing and ballgowns and James in a suit swirled in my mind. "Thank you so much for thinking of me."

"Great, it's settled then," Ebony said. "Now, you get some rest, we need you back at the barn soon. Our stable hands are lost without you."

I closed my eyes and smiled.

"I'll be back before you know it," I said before hanging up the phone.

After finishing my breakfast and bringing my dishes down to the kitchen, I put on a bathing suit and headed out to the backyard. My beach blanket billowed in the breeze as I spread it out on the lawn and took a seat next to the birdbath. I laid on my back, put on a pair of sunglasses, and pulled a tattered Cavaliers cap over my eyes for a little extra protection from the glaring sun. With my headphones on, I fumbled to press play on the Walkman next to me.

The chapters flew by as I listened to more of the audiobook that Ren had given me. I squeezed my eyes tighter under my shades as I replayed his declaration in my mind. I thought back with regret to every moment I'd likely encouraged his affections: our run-in at the grocery store, when we'd caught the runaway horse, when we talked in the indoor arena. Maybe I'd looked at him too long or given him too many compliments. I hated that the friendship I'd grown so fond of had been so badly misinterpreted.

I took a deep breath as the British audiobook narrator introduced chapter twelve. Even though I was only a small fraction into the story, Charlotte Heywood's adventures were already bringing me solace. She was so observant and sharp-witted, always coming up with the perfect comeback when chatting with the ridiculous Sir Edward and seeing through everyone's facade as she navigated her new surroundings. I finally discovered what a compliment it was to be her namesake after all.

My mind wandered further from reality as the plot thickened. After a lively conversation with Mr. Tom Parker about the miraculous benefits of sea bathing for one's health, Charlotte and Mrs. Parker made their way to Sanditon House to see the very rich and very rude Lady Denham. They had also just encountered an attractive gentleman by the name of Sidney Parker. I could already sense a romance brewing between Sidney and Charlotte and was eager to see what would happen next.

The chapter came to a close and I waited for the narrator to introduce the next one, but there was only silence. I looked over at the Walkman, and it had stopped. I had reached the end—and what an abrupt ending it was. Just like that, it was over, with all its building plotlines and developing characters never to be revisited by Austen again.

The sudden and inconclusive end of *Sanditon*—and Jane Austen's entire literary collection for that matter—left me in a somber mood. How could I simply move on from this after dedicating my whole summer to reading her work? And for it to end with no end at all? It felt wrong. All that was left to do was to assume what could have been.

I reached for my phone to distract myself and check my messages from the afternoon, using the lowest brightness setting as to not hinder my recovery too much. The most recent text was from James, reminding me that he was coming over tomorrow to watch *Sense and Sensibility* with me. I'd convinced him to do so by saying that I would keep my eyes closed and just listen to the movie, so it wouldn't technically be breaking any rules. I'd seen the film enough times to know exactly what would be happening on screen anyway, plus I was much more interested in watching James's reactions.

No word from Ren. I sighed and looked at the sky. I hadn't been expecting to hear from him, but the silence was only a reminder of how things had already changed between us.

Chapter 26

My dad was standing at the entrance of my room when I woke up the next morning. I rubbed my eyes, adjusting to the light flooding in through the open curtains, and saw him leaning against the doorframe with a mug in his hands.

"I didn't mean to wake you," he said, his voice soft.

I stretched my arms and sat up. "You didn't."

"Coffee?" He held out the mug for me to take.

I raised an eyebrow at him. "Are you encouraging my caffeine addiction?"

"It's decaf."

"I should've guessed," I said as I accepted it. I took a long sip, feeling it warm me up. "Were you watching me sleep?"

"No," he lied. "Just making sure you were still breathing."

I nodded, placing the mug on the table next to my bed. "Everyone needs to calm down," I sighed, leaning back into my pillows. "I'm fine."

My dad took a seat on the edge of my bed and shook his head.

"You don't understand this yet, but it's impossible to stop worrying about your children. As soon as they're born and you hold them in your arms, it becomes your full-time job to worry. Twenty-four hours a day, seven days a week."

I looked at him, a bit thrown off by his misty eyes. He was always supportive, but I never considered that he was *that* concerned about me. It was interesting to think about how he had watched me grow up, through every phase of my adolescence, and now was seeing me as an adult going to college. I hadn't considered how surreal it must be to watch someone develop into the person they were meant to become—but my mom had been there too, through all of the same moments. How could it be that she'd stopped caring?

"Why did you wait so long to get a divorce from Mom?" I said, taking another sip of my coffee.

My dad gave me a look that said, *where did that come from?* We didn't do this very often—talk about that sort of stuff—but I wanted to know. I just never really thought to ask him before.

"I didn't want to make a mess of things at home, you know, right as you were applying to college and getting ready to start your life." He sighed. "Maybe a part of me hoped that if we waited long enough, things could go back to normal between me and your mom, like they used to be."

"Like at the library?" I asked. "When you'd read together?"

He nodded and smiled, but his eyes were far away, revisiting old memories.

"We just aren't those people anymore," he said. "It's a shame."

I always found it incredibly difficult to picture my parents in love, but I knew they must've been at some point, or else I wouldn't be in this mess.

***

Even though James was hesitant about me defying the doctor's orders, he still came over to watch *Sense and Sensibility* with me since he'd enjoyed the book so much.

As we watched the movie, I suppressed my need to comment on all my favorite moments—I wanted to see how they affected James first before sharing my opinions. Would he feel Marianne's sorrow when Willoughby left? Would he be fond of Edward's friendship with Margret?

Watching these adaptations and reading these books often reminded me how timeless the human condition could be. As I grew up, I always related to Elinor Dashwood. She struggled so much to express her feelings, keeping them locked away until she couldn't contain them anymore. I thought maybe if Jane Austen had put words to how I felt, hundreds of years ago, it might not be so impossible to overcome.

"So," I said, my eyes on the ceiling, "will you be attending the annual Barn Ball next week?"

"Well, that depends," James said. "Will you do me the honor of reserving your first dance of the evening?"

"You'll have to ask my father's permission, since technically he's my plus-one for the night." I laughed without looking at him. "But I'd like that."

"I'm sure he won't mind."

"You've never told me about your dad," I said, turning to face him. "Will he be at the ball too?"

"Not likely," James said, a somber look creeping onto his face. "He's been pretty reclusive these days."

"Makes sense," I said, quieter now. I didn't know how much he wanted to talk about it, but I wanted to understand him better. "Are you two close?"

James closed his eyes and took a breath. "We used to be, but ever since the accident, we kind of act more like roommates than family. I think I remind him of her, which only makes things worse."

"It's hard," I said, "feeling like you're all on your own."

"Yeah," James said, meeting my eyes for a moment before turning back to the screen. "It really is."

The light from my laptop flickered on James's face as he watched. Without taking his eyes off the film, he took my hand and intertwined his calloused fingers with mine, mindlessly caressing my palm with his thumb, sending a buzzing feeling throughout my body. I breathed in and out and stared at the wall, but all my focus was directed at where our hands were touching. It still felt so foreign to me, being with someone, in any capacity really, but I wanted to be good at it.

After a few minutes, James caught me staring at him. He smiled, and although my head still ached, I felt a wave of warmth wash over me.

"Is your dad around?" he asked.

"Nope," I said. "He's at the store all day."

"Good," James said.

"Why's that?" I said, nudging his leg with my foot.

James laughed under his breath. "Because that means I can do this."

He gently stroked my cheek with this thumb, and then his mouth was on mine. He kissed me softly at first, his lips gentle and warm. When my hands found his face and I kissed him back, something roused in him. He lowered me down on the couch and kissed me deeper, making his way down my neck.

"You're missing the movie," I said between breaths.

"I'm more interested in what's going on in reality," James said as he made his way back up to my lips. "Unless you don't want to."

"No," I said, meeting his eyes. "I do."

Suddenly, we were intertwined in a way we hadn't been before, our legs twisted up in the blankets, his breath hot against my cheek. His hands grazed the small of my back, moving up my shirt. My hands were lost in his dark hair. I started to feel dizzy—and not from the concussion. The minutes passed as I fell deeper into the haze.

I could feel my independence seeping out of my body and being replaced with reliance. His body pressing against mine made me feel less lonely than I'd ever been, and now that I'd had him like this, I didn't want to let go. Yet, at the same time, I was struck with the fear that he might feel the same—that he might need me now, too.

I clutched his shirt and pulled him closer, trying to silence the shouting in my mind. *What if, one day, we don't feel this way about each other anymore?* I knew it was inevitable, nothing stayed exciting forever. I thought back to slammed doors and fights in my Ohio house growing up. The thought of James and me ending up like that was too much for my senses. *What is the point of starting this, if I already knew how it will end?* I kissed him harder, desperately trying to convince myself to enjoy it, but it was no use.

I pulled away, pushing myself up off the couch and reaching for my coffee mug. I needed an excuse to be alone for a second.

"Do you want anything to drink?" I said as I stepped into the kitchen, avoiding James's confused eyes and trying to forget what I'd just felt.

"I'm all set," he replied, his voice deeper than usual and a bit rough.

I poured my coffee and sat on the edge of the counter, taking a slow sip.

"You're phone's ringing…" I heard James say over the sound of the film.

When I went back into the living room, the atmosphere had shifted. James was no longer lounging on the couch where I'd left him. He was sitting upright with his feet planted on the floor and his eyes staring past the computer screen. My phone was resting in his hands.

"Who called?" I asked, feeling my palms begin to sweat. He took a breath and looked at me.

"It was your mom," he said.

"Oh."

"If you call back now, I bet she'll still be on the phone. Maybe you can still catch her?" he said, holding the phone out to me. I took it from him and slid it into the back pocket of my jeans.

"Let's keep watching the movie," I said. "Lucy was about to reveal that she and Edward have been secretly engaged this whole time."

"Charlie, you don't have to pretend to be calm about this." James searched my face for an explanation. "I know it must be shocking to hear from her out of the blue like this."

I turned away from him, trying to think of what to say. My relationship with my mother, or lack thereof, had always felt like a touchy subject with James.

"Maybe she wants to mend things between you two," he said, his naivete making my stomach hurt.

"It's not the first time she's called," I said finally.

His eyes narrowed. "I thought you told me she wasn't in your life anymore."

"She isn't."

"Why is she calling you, then?"

I took a slow breath in through my nose. *Just talk to him about it. He will understand.*

"I don't know," I said, turning to face him. "And I don't really care."

I could hear the bitterness in my voice—this topic always unleashed the worst version of myself. Betrayal and hurt crept up my throat, threatening to pour out of me. I didn't want to deal with this here.

"You don't care?" James said, matching my tone.

"No."

"You have the chance to fix things with your mom," he said, "and you're just going to throw that away and ignore her?"

My chest tightened as I felt my walls shoot up. James was crossing a line that he didn't understand. He didn't know the full story, and maybe it was my fault for not telling him.

"You don't know what you're talking about," I said. I hated talking about this with him.

"Yeah, I have no idea what it's like to lose my mom," he said, visibly upset now.

"That's not what I meant," I said, quieter now. I crossed my arms, trying to hold myself together.

His mother had supported him and loved him unconditionally.

"All I know is, if I had any chance to talk to my mom again, I would take it," James said. He stood there, in front of me, and suddenly, his height made me feel incredibly small. "I can't believe you're being so stubborn."

His words felt like a knife in my chest because, in a way, he was right. But he also didn't know my mother or the emotional roller-coaster I'd endured over the last four years. I just couldn't bring myself to get back on and start it up again.

James knew what he'd said had hurt me, I could see it in his eyes—but now, *he* was being too stubborn to back down. I didn't move from where I stood, scared that if I did, I might run away from the conversation and never try to resolve it. Instead, I looked at the floor and tried my best to explain myself.

"My mom stole a lot of money from me this year," I said. "She left me with years of college debt ahead of me and betrayed my trust beyond repair. Not to mention the years of pretending I didn't exist, unless it was convenient for her. And now, here I am, working every day at the barn and at the bookstore, just to somehow make enough money to stay in school for the next three years." As I said this, I realized that this information wouldn't be enough to convince him. It probably sounded petty and frivolous, and I wasn't ready to tell him the rest—the real, clinical reason why everything had fallen apart.

"I should go," James said, grabbing his jacket from the arm of the couch, and before I could decide whether or not to object, he was already out the door.

***

I couldn't spend another second in that house after James left. I paced back and forth in the living room, racking my brain for ideas of where to go as the events of the last nine days played on a loop inside my head.

Being new in town severely limited my options of where I could escape to. I could go to Gwen's, but then I'd have to explain why I was so upset. I did *not* want to talk about it yet. I could go into town, but it was getting late, and I might run into my dad.

My phone screen lit up my face in the now-dark room. Nine o'clock. I knew a spot where no one was likely to be hanging around at this time of night.

My headlights lit up the stables as I pulled into the parking lot, and the beams of yellow light softened at the edges as my eyes welled up. I turned off my car and blinked the tears away, unwilling to let myself break yet. The lot was empty except for two cars I didn't recognize.

The horses were in their stalls for the night. Some poked their heads out to assess the noise as I walked down the second aisle. I found the door that led to the back of the yard and slid it open. The night air was cooler than usual now that it was August, hinting at the impending autumn weather. I took a deep breath in and felt the chill seep into my lungs. Somehow, I had gone from not wanting the summer to end to dreaming of October days back in Boston, far away from all of this.

I reached the fence surrounding the first paddock and climbed up to the top rung, hanging my legs over the edge. For the first time all summer, I took a moment to look up at the stars. The lack of ambient light on the island made them shine so much brighter here than they did in the city. The big dipper stretched across the sky—the one I always used to look for while stargazing in Ohio. It looked exactly the same somehow, even though I was miles away from home—the home that wasn't home anymore.

Warm tears escaped from the corners of my eyes, falling down the sides of my face as I continued to look up. A part of me felt awful thinking about how upset James had looked standing in my living room—the desperation in his eyes, the longing for the chance to talk to his mom again. I understood where he was coming from, but I couldn't feel the same way about my mom. Tears streamed down my cheeks faster now, and I used the edge of my sleeve to wipe them away. It made me so angry that she still had the power to make me cry, even when I thought I was over this.

"Charlie?"

I turned to see Ren standing behind me. *Of course.*

"Are you okay?" he asked. "Shouldn't you be resting?"

I let out a pitiful laugh and looked down at him. "I've had enough rest for a lifetime."

"Did something happen?"

"No. It's nothing," I said, jumping down from the fence. I had to get out of there.

"Hey." He stepped towards me. "Come here."

I stood there and let Ren wrap his arms around me. He pulled me so close that I could hear his heart beating beneath his T-shirt. The soft cotton brushed against my cheek, and I took a deep breath in and out, letting myself sink into him.

"What are you doing here so late?" I asked, my voice muffled by his chest.

"I was on a vet call," he said, "but that's not important."

He held me for a minute, not asking questions. I felt my pain melt into him, focusing only on how warm he felt in the night air and how the smell of him was making me feel less isolated. We stood there in silence, surrounded only by the sound of distant crickets.

After a little while, Ren pulled away, but I didn't want him to. I wanted to stay in his arms for as long as I could. It felt safe there. Hidden. He stared at me like he was waiting for me to speak, but I didn't want to speak.

"Are you going to tell me what happened?" he whispered.

"I don't want to talk right now, okay?" I looked up into his eyes and begged him to leave it alone.

"Okay," he said.

Our eyes were locked for a second too long, and I knew I was sending the wrong signals, but I didn't have it in me to stop what would happen next.

Ren leaned down and kissed my tear-soaked cheek, then found my lips. And after a second, I kissed him back—not because I'd changed my mind about him, but because kissing him made my brain stop. I didn't want to think anymore, and his mouth on mine made everything disappear for a moment. Ren lifted me by my waist, and I wrapped myself around him.

Maybe I needed to see what it would be like. Maybe I wanted to hurt James for hurting me. Or maybe I was just as bad as my mother, leaving a path of emotional destruction in my wake, perpetuating the pain that I carried with me, even when I knew it was hurting the people I loved.

"Wait," I said, pushing myself off his chest. I turned around and ran my fingers through my hair. *What am I doing?*

"Did I do something wrong?" Ren asked.

I was vulnerable, and he was trying to comfort me. That's all.

I turned back to face him.

"No," I whispered. "No—no, it was all me."

"Charlie—"

"I'm so sorry, Ren," I said as I grabbed my keys from the grass below. "I have to go. Please don't tell anyone about this."

Ren nodded as I turned and ran into the barn, doing my best to wipe away my tears and any evidence of what had just transpired. As I sprinted down the aisle, I could've sworn I saw Jenna in Snowball's stall, but I ran past without taking a second look.

Chapter 27

I pulled into the first empty parking spot I saw at the hospital, eager to get my follow-up appointment over with, and speed-walked through the front doors. After a few minutes of anxiously twiddling my thumbs, a nurse came into the waiting room and called my name, gesturing for me to follow her into an exam room.

"So, Charlotte, how have you been doing?" the doctor asked as she closed the door behind her.

"Not great," I said without thinking. "But my head is feeling much better."

"Let's assume we're speaking only in terms of your concussion for this check-up," she said as she made a note on her clipboard. "So, still no nausea? And has the throbbing gone away?"

"Yup, my head feels back to normal. And I haven't had any headaches in the past three days."

"All good signs," she said with a smile. She quickly shined her mini flashlight in and out of my eyes again and took note of my reaction. "I think it's safe to say that you've recovered nicely. I'm officially clearing you. You're all set to go."

I breathed a sigh of relief and stood up. At least that was taken care of.

As I walked back to my car, I felt my phone vibrating in my pocket. When I looked at the screen, my stomach sank.

Can we talk?

It was James. And I didn't know if I was ready for that conversation yet. He didn't know about what had happened between Ren and me the night before, and I wasn't prepared to talk about it yet. I could feel the guilt forming a pit in my stomach, plus I was still upset about what James had said to me—I didn't like how easy it was for him to hurt me.

I can't today, I replied.

I slid my phone back into my pocket and slipped into the driver's seat, shutting the door behind me. Maybe that would hold him off until I figured out what I even wanted him to say.

When I got home, my dad was sitting in the living room with a copy of *The Catcher in the Rye* in his lap—his go-to read when he was stressed about something.

"There's mail for you," he said.

"Thanks," I replied, but I wondered who could have sent me something here—I hadn't given anyone my new address.

I made my way into the kitchen and reached for an ivory envelope on the table. I didn't need to flip it over and see the return address to know who it was from—I would recognize that red wax and vintage stamp anywhere.

I felt like jumping out of my skin, feeling violated that my mother had reached me somehow, even as I did everything I could to shut her out. I didn't want to hear from her—she didn't deserve it. Still, I held the letter tightly in my hand as I made my way upstairs to my bedroom, closing the door behind me before tearing it open.

> *Charlotte,*
>
> *Since you've been ignoring my calls all summer, I did the only thing I knew would get through to you. Who knows, maybe even this method has failed me, and this letter is currently burning in your father's fireplace or tossed into the kitchen garbage with the rest of the junk mail. But if you are reading this, I hope you're doing well.*

Letter writing was a lost art that my mother refused to let die. I remembered playing with her sealing wax and stamp when I was young, imagining that one day I'd send a letter of my own, confessing my affections to a love interest or staying in touch with a faraway friend. My mom used to tell me as a child that she would send me letters once I moved away to college—that we'd be pen pals. That obviously hadn't panned out as I'd once hoped.

I could feel tears threatening to spill over as I continued reading— the letter was written in the voice of the mother I'd once loved. She was probably having a few good days on the upswing of her everchanging mood. She was smart. She knew exactly what to say to evoke something in me, to make me miss her and resurface the pain that I'd learned to live with. She was once again reminding me of what I'd lost.

> *I know you don't want to hear from me, and for good reason—I can't say I blame you for your silence. But I just need you to know that I'm sorry, not just for the money, but for everything. I hope that, one day, you can find it within yourself to forgive me.*
>
> *Mom*

A guttural sob erupted from so deep within me that it scared me a bit. She wasn't allowed to do this—she wasn't allowed to be sorry now. Sorry didn't bring back the years when I felt like an outcast in my own home. Sorry didn't erase the nights I'd spent alone, crying in my room. Sorry didn't change the way I couldn't handle the way Ren looked at me or the fact that I couldn't enjoy dinner with James. Sorry didn't change the way I was drawn to those who treated me poorly or how I couldn't trust anyone who actually supported me.

This apology was for her and her only. All it did was absolve her guilt while making things even harder for me. I crumpled up the letter and threw it away, catching a glimpse of myself in the mirror.

My reflection startled me. Black streaks of mascara bled down my cheeks from my bloodshot eyes, and my nose was red and raw. I used the sleeve of my shirt to wipe it all away.

Stop crying. You're better than this.

The truth was, I was better than that. I had moved on with my life, and in some ways, I knew I would forgive my mother in time, but I would never forget what she did, and I would never be able to let her back into my life.

I stood up from my bed, pulled my tangled hair into a messy ponytail, and made my way downstairs, stopping only to grab my keys before walking out the door.

I turned my key in the ignition and rolled down my car windows to catch my breath. Since I was officially cleared for regular activities, I knew exactly where I wanted to go.

I parked on the street outside the gated entrance to the stables, willing to take all the necessary precautions to not see the people I was avoiding. I followed the fence that lined the property for a few hundred feet before deciding it was a safe enough spot to enter. With my helmet in one hand, I gripped the wood panels of the fence with the other. White paint flakes scratched against my palms as hoisted myself up to the top rung, swung my legs over, and climbed down the opposite side.

I was in.

I scanned the yard, trying to find the least populated barn entrance, and my eyes landed on the back door near the second aisle—Caramel would be in her stall by that door. If I could manage to sneak inside, I could get the horse tacked up and get back outside without running into anyone.

The grass in the farthest field had been neglected for a few weeks, so weeds and wildflowers scratched my knees as I trudged toward the back paddocks. The sky was overcast—perfect weather for a ride—and my heart raced at the thought of getting back in the saddle. After the last few days, I was itching to do something reckless.

The door was open just a crack when I got there, and I peered through to investigate.

All clear.

Barely moving the door, I slipped through and tiptoed toward Caramel's stall.

"Hiding from someone?" a voice said a little too loudly.

I turned to see Jenna standing there in gray riding pants and a white long-sleeve top with a navy vest. She looked smug, but that wasn't far off from her usual expression.

"No," I said unconvincingly before going back to gathering Caramel's tack.

"For a girl who's supposed to be on house arrest, you sure do show up here a lot," Jenna said, making sure to brush my shoulder as she passed me. I ignored her comment and just kept moving.

"Hi, Caramel," I whispered as I stepped into her stall. Her ears perked up. *At least someone is happy to see me.* I quickly secured her saddle and bridle before sneaking out the door.

We trotted off in search of an opening in the fence, but from the back door, there weren't any in sight. The only gates were near the busy parking lot or the back paddocks, which were also occupied. I couldn't risk running into James…or Ren. I wasn't sure which would be worse.

"C'mon." I clicked my tongue and got Caramel moving again. She listened without me needing to dig my heels in, which I greatly appreciated since I was wearing sneakers—not the most ideal footwear for the occasion, but this had been a spur-of-the-moment decision. I took a deep breath and tried to think of another way out, but all I saw were fences everywhere I turned. Then I spotted it—a small stretch of stone wall, not very tall, probably three feet or less, and out of sight from any onlookers at the barn.

Before I could come to my senses, I brought my horse back to a trot, then to a canter, moving in a wide circle to gain momentum. I could feel cold sweat on the back of my neck as I aimed us directly at the wall, heading faster and faster toward it. I'd watched my friends jump over fences much higher than this all the time—how hard could it be? My stomach dropped as I lifted myself out of the saddle and leaned forward, signaled for Caramel to jump. I squeezed my eyes shut and felt the ground fall away from beneath me as we flew through the air.

When we hit the ground on the other side, my legs relaxed, and I fell back into the saddle with a sloppy thud. I wouldn't be winning any shows with my form, but I'd done it—I'd actually jumped the wall!

I gave Caramel a solid pat on the neck before we took off down the dirt road toward the beach.

The air felt thick and salty on my skin by the time we reached the shore. I unlatched my helmet and let my hair blow in the wind—at least I was wearing it this time.

On the other end of the beach, I spotted a patch of trees. Caramel trotted towards the shade, and once we reached it, I pulled back on the reins and looked out at the ocean. Today wasn't particularly hot, but it was humid—it felt more like I was swimming in the air than breathing it.

I dismounted and tied the reins to the closest branch. Caramel started munching on a patch of grass as I looked around. There was no one here, not for the whole stretch of the beach, so I slipped off my shoes and pulled my t-shirt over my head, tossing it on the ground.

The sand was hot on my bare feet as I sprinted toward the ocean. My toes reached the water first, sending a jolt up my spine. It was refreshing—but not too cold. By late August, the water had plenty of time to warm up in the scorching Rhode Island sun. I trudged deeper and dove headfirst into an oncoming wave. Water rushed past me, combing through my hair as I swam against it. I resurfaced on the other side and gasped for air, exhilaration coursing through my veins.

My mind was finally at ease as I waded in the water, tasting salt on my lips and feeling sand between my toes. It seemed Tom Parker had been right after all about the healing effects of bathing in the sea. I started to laugh, swimming and splashing around all by myself, feeling a sense of relief as the water washed away the past few days.

After some time floating on my back and watching the clouds, I reluctantly swam back to shore, leaving a trail of droplets behind me in the sand as I walked back to Caramel's side. Exhausted, I pulled my clothes back over my now-damp skin and slipped my shoes on my sandy feet.

My legs felt like sandbags as I mounted my horse straight from the ground, and my skin pinched on the saddle flaps as we trotted back down the beach—that's what I got for riding in shorts. It didn't bother me though, in that moment, nothing could. My swim had left my chest feeling lighter and my mind feeling clearer. I was somewhat ready to return to my life.

When I got back to the barn, I threw caution to the wind and took the usual entrance, rather than risking the wall again. The top half of my shirt was soaked from my wet hair, and I was sure I looked like a mess as I led Caramel toward the door and dismounted. I slipped inside, without looking around this time, and ran into Zuri cleaning her reins in the tack room.

"Hey," I said, feeling a bit out of place after my two weeks away from the stables—almost like the first day of school after summer break.

"Charlie!" Zuri's face brightened at the sight of me. She took the saddle from my hands and put it away on its rack before pulling me into a hug. "How are you feeling?"

"Mostly relieved," I said. "I got the all-clear this morning."

Zuri pulled away and her eyes scanned my wet clothes.

"You just couldn't wait to get back to it, could you?" she said, laughing. "Did you go for a swim or something?"

"Ten days is a *very* long time to be stuck inside," I said, smiling at her. "I took Caramel out for a trail ride, and the ocean looked too inviting not to go in."

"Well, you were missed here at the stables," Zuri said. "Mostly by two gentlemen in particular…"

I felt my muscles tense up at the reminder of the mess I'd made.

"James has been more aloof than usual—if that's even possible—and Ren hasn't been making quite so many vet check-ins these days," Zuri said with a grin.

I bit the inside of my cheek and turned to hang the bridle up with Caramel's tack.

"Hey?" Zuri said, her voice softer now. "Are you okay?"

I turned around to face her again. I couldn't decide if I wanted to talk about it yet, but I was sick of letting everything that had happened occupy my brain. Maybe it would be good to get it out.

"No, not really," I said. "I think I really messed things up."

Zuri took a seat on the bench against the wall and patted the spot next to her.

"What happened?" she said as I sat down.

"It's just that…" I paused. "James and I got into a fight."

Zuri listened patiently as I did my best to untangle my thoughts into somewhat coherent sentences.

"It was stupid because neither of us did anything wrong really, but he found out about my mom. And I can't blame him for getting upset, with everything that's happened to him, but it still hurt. What he said to me. He said I was stubborn, and I think he meant it, even if he didn't mean to say it. And the worst part is, I think he might be right."

I could tell that I wasn't making much sense, but I didn't know how to explain it any better.

"Your mom?"

I looked at Zuri, realizing she didn't have all the information either.

"It's a long story."

"I've got time," she said.

I looked away, unsure if I was ready to open this up. I'd never really spoken about my mother's illness to anyone—not even my friends from back home. I'd tried not to think about it while I was in Ohio—like ignoring the issue would make it go away, but it never did.

I took a breath and looked at Zuri again.

"My mom was diagnosed with borderline personality disorder when I was fifteen," I said in a near whisper, as if being quiet would make the information less revealing. "She didn't want to listen to her doctors, she always thought she would be fine and that she could work through it on her own, even when she was far from it. She refused to seek treatment, and things just got worse and worse until eventually…everything sort of fell apart."

Zuri put a hand on my shoulder. I took a breath and continued.

"We don't talk anymore—and James knew that part. But he didn't know that my mom has been trying to contact me all summer. I think it hurt him to see that I had a chance to fix things with her since he can never talk to his mom again."

"Charlie, I'm so sorry," Zuri said, her voice gentle. "I had no idea you were going through anything like that. Why didn't you tell us?"

"I hate talking about it," I said, crossing my arms tightly against my chest, as if to keep myself from unraveling any further, but it was no use. Once the words started tumbling out of me, it was impossible to hold it in any longer. "I sometimes feel like I can never really react normally to things that are normal for everyone else. I feel so hot and cold sometimes, and I shut down so easily…like at the smallest sign of trouble, I just freeze up and disappear. And I used to be okay with it, like maybe it was protecting me or something, but now I just feel like I'm hurting people… like I have something wrong with me, and I can't deal with things. I'm not sure if I'll ever be able get close to people, because I can't handle it…the ups and downs, how unstable it all feels…I don't know if I'll ever be able to really trust anyone again."

Zuri pulled me in for a hug as tears started sliding down my cheeks.

"I'm really glad you told me this," Zuri said into my ear.

I exhaled into her hair and focused on the feeling of her polyester riding shirt against my skin.

"I think James will understand if you explain it to him," Zuri said as she pulled away. "I'm sure he'll apologize for everything he said the next time he sees you."

I stared at the dusty tack room floor. "I'm not sure he's the one who needs to apologize."

"What do you mean?" Zuri nudged my leg with hers.

"I kissed Ren."

"What?" she said in a loud whisper.

"He kissed me really—but it took me *way* too long to stop it."

"Where? When?" Zuri looked at me with wide eyes. She always had been rooting for us to get together.

"Last night," I said, swallowing hard. It hurt my head just thinking about yesterday's events. "Here, at the stables."

"Oh my god…" Zuri breathed.

"I know." I covered my face in my hands, trying to force the memories away.

"So…how was it?"

"It was nice—I mean it was Ren, of course, it was nice," I said, peaking at her through my fingers. "But I stopped it before anything else happened. And then James wanted to talk this morning, but I totally blew him off. What am I even supposed to say to him?"

"What do you want to say?" Zuri asked.

"I don't *want* to tell him what happened. I feel like it will ruin everything."

"Charlie," Zuri said, sitting up straighter and folding her hands in her lap. "It already happened. You can't change that now by ignoring it. The truth always comes out, so before it does, why don't you just do the right thing and apologize?"

I took a breath and nodded—she was right. If I pretended it never happened and never owned up to my mistakes, I would only be following in my mother's footsteps.

"You're right," I said, pushing my hair behind my ears. "I have to tell him."

Zuri gave me a soft smile. "See, you're already facing conflict head on," she said. "You should be proud of that, no matter the outcome."

"Thanks," I said, and I really meant it. Having Zuri there made it a lot easier to want to do the correct thing for once. I was dreading it, yes, but somehow, I already felt lighter—like the burden was lifting off my back just by choosing to do what I knew, deep down, was right.

"Oh—I almost forgot! I heard that Ebony hired you to photograph the ball at Rosecliff this year," Zuri said. "That's great!"

"Oh, yeah," I said, remembering that in just a few days, everyone I had been avoiding would be in the same place, and I was obligated to be there too.

"I'm *so* excited," Zuri said with a smile. "It's always the most fun night of the summer, and I'm so glad you'll be there this year too. I'm sure you'll love it since you're into all that Regency era stuff."

"It honestly sounds like a dream," I said, forcing a smile and trying not to dwell on my impending confession. It really *did* sound like a dream. Plus, people were actually taking my photography seriously, and the money Ebony was paying me would cover the cost of my books for my next semester, at least. I needed to focus and make sure the event went perfectly. Maybe I could wait until after the ball to come clean about everything to James. I didn't want to risk getting swept up in the fallout just when I had to show up and be professional. What was a few more days of avoidance?

Chapter 28

I could tell that Zuri had filled Gwen in about my boy drama as soon as I stepped into Coastal Toast, and I was relieved. I wasn't in the mood to explain it all again. Gwen shot me a wide-eyed look as she finished up with the customer ahead of me, and I scanned the chalkboard menu behind the counter. The special of the day was French roast with French toast—Gwen's navy beret and striped shirt were starting to make more sense.

"Next in line, please," Gwen said, smiling at me. "What can I get for you?"

"Hi." I glanced at her through my eyelashes. "I'll have an iced cold brew please."

Gwen grabbed a cup and scribbled my order and a smiley face on the side. When I reached into my bag for my wallet, she stopped me.

"It's on the house today, Charles."

"Thanks." I smiled at her, put a few dollars in the tip jar, and turned to sit down.

"Oh—wait," Gwen said, stopping me. "I almost forgot to ask, have you decided what you're wearing to the ball on Friday? Zuri told me you're taking photos for it, and I can't believe we haven't gone shopping or anything, but with you recovering and everything that's happened lately, I totally forgot to mention it to you."

"I'm not sure if I have anything fancy enough to wear," I said, biting my lip and thinking back to the limited items in my closet that I'd managed to ship from Ohio. I definitely didn't have any spare ball gowns lying around. "I might just grab whatever I can find at the boutiques in town. I'm sure they'll have something."

"Actually," Gwen said, "you should look no further because I ordered two dresses just in case one didn't fit me, so you can totally wear the other one if you want."

"Really?" I said, grateful that I might not have to go out and spend money that I didn't have. "Are you sure?"

"Of course! Someone needs to wear it, and Zuri already has a dress. Plus, it would look perfect on you. It will definitely bring out the green in your eyes."

"You're a lifesaver, Gwen." I said as I breathed a sigh of relief—one less thing for me to worry about.

"I'm pretty sure that's your title," Gwen said with a grin as she poured some milk into my cold brew.

I laughed as she handed me the coffee, then took a seat in my usual spot by the window. I pulled out my laptop, slid in my SD card, and opened up the photography files from the barn shoot. Ebony had said she trusted me to choose the best ones to edit for the website, and they were due by the end of the week. Now that I could finally look at screens again, it was time to get to work.

I clicked through the memory card files, starring the photos I liked as I drank my coffee. When I reached the individual shots of James, I felt the pit in my stomach worsen. It was the first time I'd seen him since we fought—even though it was just a picture. His face, the one I'd grown so fond of seeing, stared back at me through the screen, and I felt a wave of guilt envelop me. I clicked through the images as fast as possible and tried not to notice how his brown eyes caught the light.

I moved on from the shots of James and landed on shots of Ren, feeling a second rush of guilt wash over me. I clicked through pictures of Ren's warm smile and kind eyes, faced with the choices I was making and the trouble I'd caused. The other night at the barn felt like a blur of regret and bad decisions. I had screwed up for real this time, making Ren collateral damage in the tornado that was my life. I felt so out of control, so scared to get hurt again that I was the one hurting people. I was starting to hate myself for it.

***

I sat at a red light on the way home from the cafe, considering the two directions of the intersection before me. The right turn would take me home, where I should be going. The left would take me to Dr. Aki's office, where I knew Ren would be working his afternoon shift. I found myself switching my turn signal back and forth, unable to decide, when my phone lit up in the cupholder next to me.

Can you at least let me apologize in person? I feel like a total dick after the other night.

James again. I desperately wanted to pick up the phone and fix things with him, so we could go back to normal, but I had to sort something else out first.

When the light turned green, I turned left.

When I arrived at the doorstep of Hana's office, I went to knock, but the door opened before I had the chance. Ren was on his way out, pulling his arms through a windbreaker as he ran into me.

"Woah—" he said, startled. "Sorry, I—"

"Hi, Ren," I said, nervously tugging on the sleeves of my shirt.

"Charlie...hey." Ren gave me a half-smile, like he was glad to see me but knew why I'd come.

"Can we talk for a second?"

"Yeah, of course." He led me around the side of the building for some privacy. "What's up?"

I took a steadying breath and forced myself to meet his eyes.

"Ren—I've thought a lot about what you said the other day." I paused, trying to work up some courage. "I need you to know that I care about you so much...you were one of my first friends here...and you've always made me feel so welcome, like I was an important part of this place, even when I felt like a total idiot."

Ren's eyes softened as he watched me struggle to put my words together.

"You've been nothing but sweet to me, and I know that I've made things confusing between us. I've sent you the wrong signals because I like talking to you and I like being around you, but the other night at the barn...it was so selfish of me to kiss you back. I should've never done it, knowing how I feel about James."

My eyes welled up, and Ren took a small step closer, as if his instinct was to comfort me, but then he restrained himself.

"I sometimes think that maybe if I'd never met James—"

"Don't—" Ren said, stopping me before I could say something I'd regret. "I just...I can't hear that right now."

I nodded, wiping the tears from under my eyes.

"I just don't get why you suddenly like the guy so much," Ren said with a soft, hollow laugh. "You told me he brought out the worst in you, and that you thought he hated you."

"I don't know why," I said. "Maybe because he gets me somehow… after everything he's gone through."

Ren nodded, and I turned away for a moment, unable to look at him.

"I hate that I've done this," I said, gesturing between us. "I hate myself for hurting you, and I'd understand if you hate me now, too."

"I could never hate you, Charlie." Ren shook his head and looked at me with glistening green eyes. "But I'm going to need some time."

Chapter 29

When I opened my eyes on Friday morning, I tried not to think about everything the day would entail. My phone buzzed on my nightstand as I sat up in bed.

I need to talk to you about something, Charlie.

James again. Somehow, I'd managed to avoid him since our fight, ducking into empty stalls when I saw him at the barn and dodging his calls and texts all week. I knew it was selfish. I needed to face him eventually and own up to everything, but I couldn't bring myself to do it before the ball. This opportunity was too important to mess up. I needed to focus, and confessing my mistakes to James beforehand would make that impossible.

After the ball, I texted back.

I set my phone down and sighed. Even though I'd daydreamed about attending a ball for most of my life, I couldn't wait for this day to be over.

The afternoon sped by as I organized my film rolls and tested my lenses, wanting to make sure that I was fully prepared to take hundreds of photos for Ebony that evening. I'd decided on shooting the ball on 35mm film to give the photos a more sentimental and old-fashioned feel, hoping that when I developed them, everything would turn out how I'd wanted them to look. It was a bit riskier than shooting digital, but I knew that if I could get the lighting right and choose the correct lens, it would be worth it. The stakes felt higher today, like any faith I had in my photography skills hung in the balance.

Gwen had dropped off my dress the night before, and it was hanging on my closet door, still in the bag. I hadn't been able to bring myself to try it on yet, too nervous about everything else to even think about how I'd look.

I took a shower and blow-dried my hair before going over it with a curling iron and pulling it into an updo, using Kiera Knightley's hair at the Netherfield Ball as a reference. I quickly did my makeup—some mascara, blush, and lip gloss mostly—then painted my nails with black polish. Once I was otherwise ready, I unzipped the dress bag to reveal an emerald-green, floor-length, silk gown.

I couldn't help but gasp at the sight of it and was almost too afraid to put it on, with the off chance that I might spill some punch or fall onto some grass. I couldn't believe that Gwen hadn't chosen this one for herself.

I carefully took the dress off the hanger and stepped into it, pulling the zipper into place before turning to see myself. When I glanced at the mirror, I was immediately struck by how elegant I looked. My makeup was minimal but gave my skin a healthy glow, and my pinned-up hair and off-shoulder neckline showed off my arms and collarbones. The dress was cinched at the waist, then flared out into wide pleats until it reached the ground. I studied my reflection, adjusting the gown and pinching my cheeks, and I didn't feel so out of place in Newport anymore. Tonight, I looked like I truly belonged here.

It made me a little bit sad as I realized that this dress would be wasted on a night when I would be avoiding James, but at least he would see it from a distance.

After putting on my heels, I packed up my Pentax K1000—the film camera my dad had given me from his photography stint in the 80s—and headed out. My dress billowed around me as I made my way downstairs and rounded the corner into the kitchen where my dad was waiting in his tuxedo.

He looked at me, speechless, and brought a hand to his heart.

"You like it?" I asked with a small smile.

He got up and pulled me into a hug, careful to not mess up my hair, and said, "You look beautiful, Charlotte."

I'd spent so much time that summer feeling angry about falling out with one of my parents, but my other parent had been there all along. Even though things would likely never be fixed with my mom, I still had my dad, and somehow, that had become enough for me.

My dad offered to drive so I could scroll through my mood board on my phone one more time in preparation. The sun began to set as we passed through town, and when we pulled onto Bellevue Avenue, the houses got larger and my nerves started to spike. *How am I going to manage to photograph an event this large? What if I don't get the lighting right? What if my film is expired? What if I chose the wrong lens?* Then I started to spiral about the social obstacles of the night. *What will I say when I see James? What if I run into Ren? How am I going to hide from everyone for the whole night?*

Before I knew it, we were pulling into the driveway, and I looked up to see the most beautiful house I'd ever laid my eyes on. Rosecliff mansion stretched before us with white terracotta tiles, Baroque-style windows, and intricate black gated doors at the entrance.

My dad drove up to the front, and a man in a suit and white gloves opened my door for me.

"Let's have some fun tonight," my dad said, his expression soft and his tone sentimental as I gathered the bottom of my dress in my hands and prepared to step out of the car. Maybe he had noticed how hard that had been for me lately.

I turned back and smiled at him, dazzled by my surroundings and a bit less worried than I had been a moment prior, and said, "I'll try."

With that, my dad tossed his keys to the valet, and we were left standing under a pair of glowing lanterns as chatter and music spilled out of the doors before us.

Another man opened the door for us, and my dad and I stepped inside and followed the maroon carpet that led toward the ballroom. Each wall was adorned with old paintings, and white marble statues seemed to mingle with the guests.

Before we could reach the entryway, Ebony emerged from the ladies' room, and her eyes landed on us. She wore a black, floor-length gown, simple and classic, with a diamond necklace that glinted in the light as it rested on her chest.

"Charlie, you look amazing," Ebony said as she took in my appearance. "You're bound to break some hearts tonight in that dress."

"I hope not," I said almost too quietly to hear, then turned to my dad. "Dad, this is Ebony."

"It's great to finally meet you, Mr. Briarman," Ebony said as she reached out to shake my dad's hand.

"Please, call me Steven," my dad said. "And the pleasure is all mine. I've heard so much about you."

"All good things, I hope," Ebony said, shooting me a clever look.

My dad laughed. "All great things. Charlotte's had a lot of fun this summer at the barn."

"Okay…maybe we should find the ballroom," I said before he could divulge anything that might make me look overly enthusiastic.

"Right through those doors," Ebony said as she pointed toward a gilded entryway. "I'll check in with you later, Charlie."

When I entered the ballroom, I was immediately overwhelmed by the reality that I was, in fact, attending a ball. I took a small breath and smiled to myself, trying to enjoy it, even with the potential chaos that lingered just below the pretty surface. The ivory walls protruded with columns and intricate detailing, and on the ceiling, there was a painting of a beautiful blue sky with whisps of clouds floating about, while two gilded chandeliers hung down to light up the room.

The dancing had already begun as people waltzed and spun around the hardwood floor. I recognized most of the boarders and riding team members standing amongst people, whom I assumed to be their parents and siblings. There were also many strangers roaming about, likely donors to the riding scholarship or locals that simply enjoyed attending the annual ball.

My dad nodded at me, as if to say, *go do your thing*, before making his way to the bar. I scanned the crowd, searching for moments to photograph—and for people I needed to avoid. I'd always preferred candid photos to posed shots, so this environment was perfect. There was so much movement and excitement as people flirted and gossiped while they danced. It was fascinating to me how photographs could preserve these fleeting moments in time, and I felt so lucky getting the chance to be there to capture them.

Through my viewfinder, I spotted James across the crowd with a scotch glass in his hand, talking with Nils. He was dressed in a full tux with a pleated white dress shirt, patent leather oxfords, and a black bow tie. He looked unreal, as if I had conjured him up somehow while wishful thinking over the years. I zoomed in with my lens to get a closer look, spying in plain sight.

James had a smile on his face, but his eyes were clouded with something—possibly stress from being ignored for a few days, or maybe just from the strain of social interaction. It was hard to tell. I snapped a picture, unable to move my lens without capturing him in the romantic evening light.

I was already feeling nostalgic for the moment I was still in, knowing in a few short weeks, I'd be back at school. The thought pulled at my heartstrings as I looked around at everyone I'd become accustomed to this summer. I knew that eventually it would all be just a memory pasted to the pages of my photo journal, and my first summer in Rhode Island would become merely a warm recollection to hold onto during the winter months in Boston. *But not yet.* For now, the days were still hot, the air was still salty, and the people I'd started to call my friends were still right in front of me.

I lifted my camera to my eye to take one more picture of James, only to catch his gaze on me. He turned to Nils and was seemingly trying to wrap up their conversation. I turned to find anyone else to busy myself with and spotted Ren, his half-smile barely masking the wistful look in his eyes. He was dressed almost identically to James, only with a long tie, and he nodded at me and raised his glass before turning in the opposite direction. I couldn't help the lump in my throat when I saw him like that, keeping his distance from me, even though I knew I was to blame for that look on his face. I hung my camera around my neck and headed toward the front hall, needing a moment to myself.

After a few minutes and a few deep breaths in the ladies' room, Zuri walked in, wearing a striking purple gown with a halter neckline and a column silhouette. She grabbed a hand towel from the counter and held it to her face.

"You okay?" I asked, catching her attention.

"Oh—hey Charlie," she said, turning to face me. "I'm just a little anxious."

"Not a fan of dancing?"

"It's not that," she said, tapping her fingers nervously on the counter. "I just haven't seen Gwen's parents since they found out about us. I know they said they were cool with it, but I just don't want them to treat me any differently than they used to."

I stepped closer and gave Zuri's arm a gentle squeeze.

"If they want to make things weird, then that's their problem," I said, trying to comfort her.

"I know, but Pam is like a second mother to me…I can't imagine her not liking me anymore."

"Have you seen Gwen yet?" I asked, realizing I had yet to show her how amazing the dress she'd lent me had turned out.

"Yeah, she's over by the grand piano with her mom. She just texted me to come and find her."

"I can come with you, if you want. Strength in numbers?"

"Thanks, but I have to do this on my own." She took a deep breath and smoothed out her dress before heading out the door. I waited until she was fully outside before following close behind. I wanted to be nearby just in case something went wrong.

Zuri bravely made her way through the crowd toward Gwen's family. Gwen's mom and dad were chatting with another couple while Gwen stood a few feet away in a golden gown with an empire waist, staring at the floor. She was the very picture of modern glamour meets regency era, and I could finally understand how she found a dress to top the one I was wearing. With her blonde curls falling at her shoulders, the gold suited her better than the green would've.

As I watched Zuri move closer to them, I realized that, if my friends could handle this, there was no reason for me to be concerned about my drama tonight. Their situation required a lot more courage than mine did.

Gwen spotted Zuri first from a few feet away, and I watched as Gwen's parents turned to see Zuri standing there, ready for whatever reaction they gave her. The distance and crowd between us made it harder to read their expressions, but after only a moment of hesitation, Pam broke into a wide smile and held her arms out for a hug. Relief washed over Gwen's face as Zuri embraced her mom. They pulled away, both smiling, and began to chat as if nothing had ever happened.

A single tear rolled down my cheek as I watched, but I quickly wiped it away before snapping a picture of the moment—more for my friends to cherish than for the website. Then I kept moving.

After taking group shots of most of the families that board at the stables and chatting with Jeff and Ben on the ballroom floor, I grabbed a cup of punch from the bar and made my way to one of the windows on the edge of the room. Conveniently, both James and Ren were tied up in conversations with riding team investors and horse owners, so I let my guard down for a moment. As I switched out my roll of film, I saw Jenna out of the corner of my eye. She lingered by the refreshments, reaching for a salmon puff before a woman who looked too much like her not to be her mother shook her head and tossed the hors d'oeuvre in the trash.

"You don't want to look bloated in that dress," the women said.

Jenna's face reddened as she reached for a glass of champagne instead and brushed past her mother to join Nils on the other side of the room.

My dad found me a few minutes later and offered me some crudités from his plate.

"I'm not hungry," I said. "But thanks."

I scanned the crowd again for possible danger zones, only to find James making his way toward me. I was about to turn and make a run for it, when Ebony reappeared at my side.

"Having fun?" she said, smiling at my dad and I.

"I'm just focusing on taking photos tonight," I said with a forced laugh as James got closer. "Strictly here on business."

"Oh no, no, no," Ebony said. "I won't have you working the whole night away on my account. You are at a ball, so you have to dance."

She looked around for possible suitors, and her eyes landed on James, who was only a few feet from us now.

"James!" she said with wide eyes, possibly a bit buzzed from the almost empty champagne glass in her hand. "Why are you walking around while there are ladies here without dance partners? I insist that you take Miss Briarman out onto the floor."

"My thoughts exactly," James said as he found my eyes. "Charlie?"

"James," I said quietly.

My dad smiled at us. "James, it's good to see you again."

James nodded. "Likewise, Mr. Briarman."

I reluctantly put down my camera and took James's hand as he ushered me to the center of the ballroom. Out of the corner of my eye, I watched as my dad offered his hand to Ebony for a dance as well, which she readily accepted.

"You look stunning," James said, his voice close to my ear as he placed a hand on my waist and led us across the floor.

"Thanks," I said, looking up at him. "You look…perfect."

He just stared at me for a moment, studying my face, and holding his tongue, like he wasn't sure what to say first after so many days apart. I indulged myself for a second, staring back into his dark eyes, startled by how much looking at him felt like coming home.

"Charlie," James said as he carefully spun me around and caught me in his grasp. "Where have you been?"

I swallowed and looked out at the fellow party goers surrounding us.

"I've had a lot on my mind," I said, finding his brown eyes again. "I'm sorry, I shouldn't have been so…distant. It's just…we have a lot to talk about."

"Yeah, we do," James said. "But you're not the one who should be apologizing. I get why you needed space. I feel awful about what I said the other night. I know I overreacted about everything with your mom. I just wish you would've told me sooner, so I could've understood better."

I shook my head. "I understand why you reacted that way."

"That doesn't make it okay," he said. "I never want to take out my problems on you."

"James." I paused, taking a steadying breath. "I've been meaning to tell you something too…"

There was no avoiding it now. It was time to face the music.

"Before you do, there's something I need to say first," James said, holding me close as we moved across the floor. "I just found out that—"

Before James could finish his sentence, Nils tapped his champagne glass with a spoon, and the room went quiet. James's brow furrowed, and he turned away from me to look across the room at his friend. The live pianist stopped her performance and the crowd's conversations lowered to a murmur before going silent. Nils, always happy in the spotlight, smiled widely at everyone.

"I'd just like to take a moment to tell everyone some incredible news," Nil said to the crowd.

James clenched his jaw, and his hands held my waist tighter for a moment before he released me, dropping his arms to his sides. Whatever this announcement was about, it looked like he already knew.

"As all of you probably know, the national riding team had vacancies this year and held final tryouts last week to fill the two spots."

How could I have forgotten? James had mentioned it weeks ago, but I didn't think they would've chosen someone this soon. My palms began to sweat as I smoothed out my dress where James's hands had been.

"I'm very happy to announce that two of our very own riders have been chosen for the team," he said, clapping his hands and encouraging the crowd to join in.

Two?

"Let's hear it for Jenna and James!" Nils shouted, gesturing towards his friends as the crowd broke into applause. The sounds of cheering and clapping reverberated around the room and overwhelmed my senses.

I felt like I was being torn in half. On one hand, I was happy for James—he'd been training all summer for this opportunity—but on the other hand, he would be spending *a lot* more time with Jenna because of it.

"So, it seems this has turned into a bit of a going-away party. They leave tomorrow to start training, so make sure to say your goodbyes tonight," Nils finished.

My stomach dropped. *Tomorrow?* James had never said anything about cutting the season short in Newport if he made the team.

"We're gonna miss you guys," Nils added, loudly enough for everyone to hear. He was smiling across the crowd at James, making his way towards us with Jenna in tow, but the only person James was looking at was me.

"Congratulations," I said softly, blinking back the tears welling in my eyes as I forced myself to look up at him.

"I tried to tell you, Charlie. All week, I tried to talk to you about it," he said in a rush.

I took a breath and attempted a smile. "I'm happy for you, really, I am."

I didn't want to talk about this here, not with Jenna breathing down my neck and Ren watching from nearby. I didn't want to think about saying goodbye to James tomorrow, and the void he would leave behind. I didn't want to think about how abruptly my Rhode Island summer was coming to an end.

"Can we go somewhere and talk about this?" James said more quietly, moving closer to me. Before I could respond, Jenna interrupted us.

"Charlie, why don't you take a picture of James and me," she said, pulling James to her side, "since we won't be hanging around here much longer."

"Sure," I said, ignoring the pit in my stomach. I retrieved my camera from the windowsill as Jenna posed next to James, who was struggling to muster a smile.

"Just think," Jenna said to James as I snapped a few pictures, "with the two of us traveling and training together, it will give us plenty of time to reconnect, won't it?"

"You know it's not going to be like that," James said, stepping away from her and back towards me.

"Oh…wait," Jenna said, her eyes animated as she turned to me. "You didn't tell him, did you?"

My blood ran cold. *She wouldn't.*

"Tell me what?" James said, turning his attention from Jenna to me, but I stayed silent. Jenna took it upon herself to fill in the blanks.

"About her and Ren," she said, twisting the knife. James turned to Ren, who was standing just behind us now, and then back to me, waiting for some sort of explanation.

"Jenna, don't," Ren said.

James looked at me in disbelief as he tried to put the pieces together. "Charlie, what is she talking about?"

"They totally hooked up the other night at the barn," Jenna said matter-of-factly. Then, with a smile, she added, "You guys look really cute together. The vet and the stable hand, how quaint."

"What?" James said, his eyes narrowed, and I couldn't tell if he was more angry or hurt.

"That's not what happened," I said, mentally punishing myself for not planning a better explanation. *I should've remembered Jenna's ominous comment the other day. I should've told James already.*

Jenna looked at me with mock sincerity on her face. "That's what it looked like…"

"C'mon, Jenna, we barely even kissed," Ren said.

"You actually kissed him?" James said to me, his eyes begging me to contradict him.

I searched for the right words, but with everyone watching, it felt impossible to find anything to say that could fix this. "No—I mean yes, but it wasn't like that."

James's eyes changed when I said that. He wasn't looking at me with warmth like he had over the past few weeks. Instead, he gave me a cold, almost expressionless stare, like he didn't even know me at all. Like any trust he had in me was gone. My stomach lurched—we were back to square one.

"Just let her explain," Ren said, but James wouldn't listen.

"I don't want to hear anything from either of you right now," James said. I reached for him, but it was no use. My fingers barely brushed against his cufflinks before he backed away from my touch and strode out of the ballroom and into the night.

Chapter 30

It suddenly occurred to me that night, as I watched James walk away, that my mother may have known what she was doing by naming me after Charlotte Heywood. *Sanditon*'s abrupt ending closed a chapter that Charlotte wasn't done exploring. There were so many plotlines brewing and so much potential for love and adventure, all cut short.

I could relate.

After James left the ball, I must've called him at least ten times, but he never answered. I texted him too, begging for a chance to explain myself, but still got no response. Once I saw that he had read my texts and didn't care to acknowledge them, I just let my phone die, sick of incessantly checking it just to be disappointed. I left my uncharged phone on my desk for the night, not bothering to set an alarm, and attempted to get some sleep.

After hours of tossing and turning without relief, I peered through the curtains of my bedroom window to see if it was still dark outside. It was dark, but a hint of morning light glowed in the sky. I let out a frustrated breath, longing for the convenient unconsciousness of sleep as visions of James's face haunted me.

James had sparked something within me over the course of the summer that I hadn't recognized in myself. I thought back to the gravitational pull I felt towards him, knowing that by this time tomorrow, I'd be yearning for someone hundreds of miles away. The hours and days I'd spent hiding from him felt wasteful now. I could hear my heartbeat in my ears, like a ticking clock, counting down the seconds until he would be gone.

It was all my fault—I felt the weight of that now—and I wanted desperately to escape from it, to distract myself with running back to Boston and blocking out all the mistakes I'd made over the summer. But I could see now how cowardly that would be. It sounded like something my mother would do.

I got up from my bed, tore a blank page from my photo journal, and rummaged in my desk for a pen. Taking a deep breath, I sat down to write.

Mom,

I received your letter, and I want you to know that I forgive you. I'm doing okay here, and I'm trying to move on from everything that happened. I hope, for your sake, you are getting the help you need.

Charlotte

I sealed the letter with some red wax I still kept in my desk drawer, flipped it over, and wrote my old home address on the back. Before I could change my mind, I quickly slipped on whatever riding clothes I could find in the dim light of my room and grabbed my keys.

I pulled into the Post Office parking lot and stepped out of the car, closing the door behind me. Only my headlights lit up the still-dark sky as I stepped toward the mailbox. I took a deep breath and slid the letter through the slot. Deep down, I knew I wasn't over it yet—the emotional abuse I'd endured, the fact that a house was worth more to my mother than her own daughter—maybe I never would be. But for now, I needed to find peace with what had happened and let it go.

The sky was a light gray by the time I stepped into the empty stables, joined only by the horses who poked their noses into the aisle to see who had arrived.

I made my way toward Caramel's stall after collecting her saddle and reins from the tack room and searched for a clock on the wall to tell me the time. It was past five in the morning now, only a half hour until sunrise. I'd gotten close a few times, but I had yet to catch the whole sunrise that summer on the beach. Caramel was tacked up in no time and ready to go, so today was the day.

I saw someone walking down the first aisle as I mounted my horse outside and squinted my eyes to see who it could be, but it was only Gwen. I waved at her as she stepped into Dandelion's stall, then continued down the aisle. Once we were outside, Caramel and I took off down the road toward the ocean.

By the time we reached the sand, the sky had lightened to a faint orange color. I hopped down from Caramel's back and kept hold of the reins as I surveyed the beach. It was peaceful being there while it was completely empty, just how James liked it. I took a seat in the sand next to my horse and let out a deep breath, replacing it with briny sea air.

Maybe this summer had been just a big mistake. Yes, I'd desperately needed to make money, and I had no choice but to come to Rhode Island, but maybe I should've just kept to myself. It was so exhausting getting attached to people just to have them ripped away. I was sick and tired of missing people.

The sand was still chilly from the night air as I laid back, letting some of my stress melt into the ground beneath me. I closed my eyes, trusting that Caramel wouldn't step on me, and focused on the sound of each crashing wave and the water rustling over rocks in the shallows. These noises had become the soundtrack of my summer—seagulls squawking, hooves galloping against sand, grass swaying in the breeze. I would miss the natural symphony of this place.

But I hadn't just been imagining the galloping noise in the distance—I'd ignored the sound at first, but it only got louder. Reluctantly, I sat up and squinted down the beach, only to see a chestnut horse racing down the shoreline. As it got closer, I could see that it was James riding toward me.

The moment seemed to last forever as he got closer and closer, his white dress shirt from the night before untucked and billowing in the wind—looking very much like a regency novel come to life. I finally understood what Captain Wentworth meant in *Persuasion*, when he said he was 'half agony, half hope'—only today, my hope was wearing thin.

"Whoa," James said to Lightning, pulling up on the reins to bring his horse to a stop. He dismounted with urgency, dropped his reins in the sand, and stepped toward me. I stood up to meet him, a bit flustered since I thought I wouldn't be seeing him again for months.

"I've been trying to get a hold of you for hours," he breathed, and for the first time all summer, I noticed a bit of facial hair on his usually clean-shaven face.

"My phone's been dead since last night," I said, trying to remain calm as my heart ached at the sight of him.

I studied his face, trying to memorize the features I'd grown so fond of seeing that summer before he would be taken from me—but I knew my attraction to him was about so much more than how he looked now. It was the way he understood a part of me that I could barely understand myself. It was how he read similar books and liked my favorite movies. It was how he didn't give his smile away to just anyone but gave it to me. It was how he always had a smart comeback and how he made every moment with him feel like a work of fiction. His outside appearance was simply icing on the cake, appreciated but not entirely necessary in the end.

A part of me was glad just to have the chance to see him one last time before he left. I wanted to reach out to him, to wrap myself up in all that he was for another moment, but I kept my distance.

"Did you not get my texts last night? Or see any of my calls?" I asked with hurt in my voice.

James looked out at the ocean and took a breath before returning his gaze to me. "Yeah, I did. And I'm sorry for ignoring you, but what would you have done in my position?"

He had a point.

"I probably would've shut you out, too," I admitted, knowing it was the truth.

"I mean, you ignored me for days, just for me to find out that you—" he paused, suppressing the frustration rising in his voice. "—you kissed someone else."

Yet again, I was faced with more pain that I had caused. I felt my walls shooting up as my instincts screamed at me to spare myself the effort of trying to fix this.

"Why are you here, then?" I asked.

"Ren stopped by my house last night."

I looked up at him. "He did?"

James nodded. "He said that he was the one who initiated things the other night and that you stopped him and said it would never happen again." He looked at me like he was waiting for some type of confirmation.

"It wasn't all his fault," I said. "I was really messed up about our fight, and I didn't exactly discourage him—but I did stop it, and I was going to tell you after the ball. I promise, I was going to come clean about everything."

James nodded, but I could see the hurt in his eyes as my betrayal hung in the air.

"I keep making mistakes," I continued. "I don't know why I did it, because we had something really good between us, and I screwed it all up. I was hurt and scared, and I'm so sorry that it even happened at all. I told Ren that I only feel that way about you."

James's expression softened.

"We've both made mistakes this summer," he said, "trying to push people away just to avoid moments like this, and yet, it caught up to us anyway, didn't it?"

I looked down at the sand beneath my feet, struck by how well James understood me.

"I hate how much time I wasted staying away from you," I said, looking up at him as tears spilled down my cheeks. "And why didn't you tell me you would have to leave so soon for training if you made the team?"

"I didn't know," he said, shaking his head. "I just found out that I made the team two days ago, and they told me an hour later that the training schedule was moved up by a month. I tried to tell you, but you weren't answering my calls. Then, at the ball, it was impossible to get anywhere near you, and by the time Nils made his announcement, it was too late. I didn't want you to find out that way. I wouldn't do that to you intentionally, you know that, right?" His eyes searched mine.

I nodded, knowing again that I had been the problem there.

"And then after Ren stopped by my house, I texted and called, but you didn't answer. This morning, I stopped by your house, and your dad said you'd already headed out for the day. Luckily, Gwen saw you this morning, or I would've had no idea where you went." James's chest rose and fell as he tried to explain himself in the limited time we had. "I'm sorry for bombarding you like this, but I had to see you before I left. My flight is in a few hours."

It all made sense, yet it made no difference.

James stepped closer to me, and I basked in the feeling of him, knowing all too well that it would be gone too soon. He reached for my hands, his skin warm and weathered from years of gripping reins, and I felt everything all at once. Regret for all the days I'd wasted. Shame for hurting Ren and shutting James out. Gratitude for finally finding a place and people that felt like home. Nostalgia for what was still surrounding me, knowing that it would soon be just a memory. I longed to capture it in a photograph, but nothing tangible could hold this feeling. James's hands grasping mine made me feel something deep within me—that maybe, for once, I truly wasn't alone.

The horizon faded to a peach color as the sun peeked over the ocean, and I felt James's hands tighten around mine. I could tell he didn't want to let go just yet, but he had to. I looked up into his melancholy brown eyes and was unable to come up with the words to express how much this was killing me. I let go of his hands and wrapped my arms around him, holding tightly to his chest, his arms pulling me closer as his heartbeat ran wild.

It was strange to know that how strongly we both felt for each other had no bearing on the fact that we were to be separated for the foreseeable future. He would be busy, training, and living his life with the team until the tournament, and I would be in Boston taking classes. Neither of us could give up what we had planned, and we shouldn't have to.

I held on to him a little longer, my thoughts enveloping me. This wasn't supposed to happen like this, and maybe it shouldn't have happened at all. It was so inconvenient to fall in love for the summer when everything was so temporary. Where was our happy ending like in all the stories I'd read? Where was the running off into the sunset, credits rolling kind of feeling? That kind of love was impossible—it didn't exist.

I pulled away and looked up at him, my hair blowing gently in the breeze. We were still so close—only inches away—and I wanted him to kiss me, but that would only make things harder. Instead, I slowly untangled myself from James and stepped back, letting the electric feeling he produced in me seep out of my body and into the space between us.

"Will I see you at Christmas?" he asked, choosing the words that were easier than goodbye.

I nodded, giving him a weak smile. James brushed his thumb against my cheek and tucked a stray piece of hair behind my ear, his eyes pouring into mine for only a moment more before he reached for the reins in the sand. He mounted his horse and stole one last look at me before digging his heels in and galloping away.

All at once, he was gone, and I was left standing alone, just as I had always been. I sank back down to the sand beneath me, letting myself feel the ache that filled my chest. It felt like a bruise—painful, but not entirely in a bad way. There was something sweet about it, like something memorable had to have happened to leave such a mark.

This summer had broken me, but in a way it had also healed something deep down, hidden away inside me. It was almost hard to believe that it had happened in real life and not just in the pages of a book I'd read. And now, the chapter was ending, and it was all coming to a halt.

Epilogue

How strange it was to feel like barely any time had passed since I'd unpacked, yet here I was filling my suitcases to go back to school. Over the last few weeks, I had returned to my normal routine, but it wasn't quite the same. Not without James.

Ren and I had barely spoken since the ball, and I couldn't really blame him for it. I missed seeing him around, but it was probably easier for him to stay away. When I wasn't in a riding lesson or working at the stables or the bookstore, I spent most of my remaining time with Gwen and Zuri. Keeping busy made the days pass by quicker, but try as I might, I couldn't hide from the fact that Newport lacked its usual luster in James's absence.

I slid my photo journal into my backpack and tried my best to get it closed. The journal had doubled in thickness since I'd arrived in Newport that May, bursting at the seams with memories from this summer. The week before my departure, Ebony sent out a barn-wide email with the link to the new and improved website featuring my work. I'd clicked on it immediately, curious to see which of my photos had made the cut.

When the webpage had loaded on my screen, it revealed dozens of images from the barn shoot, the ball at Rosecliff, and even some photos I'd taken in between. I was stunned, and for the first time since I could remember, I felt truly, undeniably proud of myself.

When I said goodbye to Ebony after my last shift at the stables, I had to hold back tears. She was the reason I was even there. She had taken a chance on me and given me the opportunity to start over for the summer, and I would be forever grateful. As she gave me a hug, she made me promise that I'd be back next summer, saying that the barn wouldn't be the same without me. Ebony and my dad had gone on four official dates since the ball, and I could tell by the way my dad constantly wore a smile how happy it was making him. I liked the idea of Ebony being around more, and it was too soon to tell, but it felt right that she could eventually become a new part of our little family. Plus, I wanted my dad to have good people around him while I was away. I hated the thought of him being all alone in this house.

Now, as I stuffed a few pairs of sneakers into the outer compartment of my suitcase, I heard a knock on my door. I turned down the music on my phone and pulled my bedroom door open to find my dad standing in the hallway.

"Charlotte, there's someone here to see you," he said.

Behind him, Ren was making his way up the stairs and toward my door. My dad smiled at me, then went back downstairs to give us some privacy.

"Hi," I said, not quite sure what to think about him showing up like this.

"Hey," Ren replied, standing across from me in the hallway. "Sorry to barge in on you."

He looked as friendly and spirited as the first time I'd met him, and it caught me off guard a bit. One of his hands fell at his side while the other was tucked behind his back. "I wanted to talk to you before you left."

"I'm glad you're here," I said—and I meant it. It was nice to be in the same room with him and not feel the awkward tension that had come to be there over the past month. I'd missed my friend. "Come in, make yourself comfortable."

"I've been meaning to ask, will you be back for the holidays?" he said. "They do sleigh rides at Seahorse in December—you don't want to miss it."

"I guess I will be," I said as a smile tugged at my lips. This was my home now, and it wasn't going anywhere.

"Good." He took a seat on the edge of my bed, and I sat beside him, looking at him expectantly.

"So," he said, clearing his throat.

"So…"

"Do you remember the day I found you in the indoor arena lunging Copper?"

I nodded. Ren smiled and continued.

"I asked you about your interest in photography. Do you remember what you said?"

I closed my eyes and sighed. "I said that it was just a hobby."

"And I told you that you should give it a shot because art is subjective, remember?"

"Yes…"

"Have you gotten a chance to look at the stable's new website?" he asked with a clever glint in his eye. "Because I have."

"I skimmed it," I said, trying to be coy but also hoping he would get to the point sooner rather than later.

"I guess you could say Ebony thinks you have a natural talent for photography, wouldn't you agree?" His smile grew wider—it was making me nervous.

"I guess you could say that..." I said as I anxiously twisted the ring on my index finger.

"Well, she's not the only one who thinks so," Ren said, taking his hand out from behind his back. He placed a large manila envelope in my lap, and I immediately recognized the Boston University crest on the top right corner.

"What is this?" I asked, looking from Ren, to the envelope, and then back to him. "What did you do?"

"I may have sent your photos to your school's visual arts college to see what they thought about you joining their photography program."

"No...no, you didn't..." I said, unable to process what he was saying.

"Plus, Ebony wrote you a killer recommendation letter. She even called the program director to put in a good word," Ren said. "She really cares about you, Charlie. We all do."

I stared at him, unsure of what to say. These people mattered so much to me now, and it turned out I mattered to them too.

"Can you just open it already?" Ren said, his eyes bright with anticipation.

I grabbed the envelope and tore it open, carefully pulling out the white pages that held my fate. My eyes fought against my growing excitement as I tried to focus on the top line of the letter.

Dear Charlotte Briarman,

We are pleased to inform you that we have chosen you as the recipient of our Mathewson Photography Scholarship of $20,000 for the remainder of your time here at Boston University, and we are happy to accept you into our program...

Acknowledgments

The first person I'd like to thank is my twin sister, Ginny, who has picked up the phone hundreds of times over the past three years and listened to me talk endlessly about this book. Also, for believing in this book even when it was only a third draft. I hope you love it even more now that it's the real thing.

Thank you to my dad, who has been asking when he will finally get the chance to hold a copy of this book for the past year, and for supporting me through every step of the journey of getting it published.

Thank you to Holly, who read this book a year ago and gave me the final push I needed to get it finished and out there in the world. Without your feedback, this book would probably still be sitting in a folder on my computer.

Thank you to my editor, Katie, who gave me the best advice and pushed me to improve the story to its full potential. I'll never understand how I ended up with the perfect editor for this project, who just happened to be a lifelong equestrian, and I'm so grateful that I found you.

Thank you to Emma, who created such a beautiful cover for this book.

I'm so happy we got to work on this together. Thank you for answering my millions of emails and being the most understanding and hardworking designer out there.

Thank you to my beta readers, Camryn and Arianna, who gave me such great feedback and helped get the book to the final draft, and to Jill for proofreading.

And thank you most of all to Jane Austen. Without her stories, I don't know who I'd be. She inspired me so much during this writing process, and I only hope to touch people's hearts with my stories the way she has with hers.

CPSIA information can be obtained
at www.ICGtesting.com
Printed in the USA
JSHW082046040623
42712JS00003B/4/J

9 798988 300304